Spring

Also by Vina Jackson

Eighty Days Yellow
Eighty Days Blue
Eighty Days Red
Eighty Days Amber
Eighty Days White
Mistress of Night and Dawn

THE PLEASURE QUARTET
Autumn
Winter

Spring
The Pleasure Quartet

VINA JACKSON

OPEN ROAD
INTEGRATED MEDIA
NEW YORK

Cover design by Simon & Schuster UK Art Department

978-1-5040-1686-5

Published in 2016 by Open Road Integrated Media, Inc.
345 Hudson Street
New York, NY 10014
www.openroadmedia.com

Spring

The Beauty and the Knife

It begins in darkness.

A darkness deeper than night.

The silence has the quality of dread.

A thin beam of light cuts a steady glow through the gloom, and grows, an expanding cone beneath which a faint play of shapes and shadows soon becomes recognisable.

One arm emerges. Then another. Blurred movement, like a slowly spreading stain.

Sleeved in dark material, the arms are in motion, somehow connected to a body still hovering on the perimeter of vision.

A wall of bricks.

A man standing tall against it, his face unseen, wearing a shapeless coat wrapped around his elongated body, held together by a length of rough straw-coloured string. Motionless.

Time stretches and I feel an itch in my right thigh as I stand there waiting for the inevitable. But I dare not move. The deliberate lack of speed in the way the scene is unfolding has something of a ceremonial nature that speaks to me deeply. Elongating time.

The peculiar mood transports me back to the sea in New Zealand, just those few months previously when I had attended the Ball together with Iris, and witnessed the beach littered with bodies. There is no comparison of course: this is a strikingly urban setting, and an altogether different example of human passions at play. The brick wall, a faint wisp of fog rising across its height, the pattern of the cobblestones, and not a raging wave in sight. A desolate city at night against the vision of nature unleashed. There could be no bigger contrast. But they are unified in feeling. With me as the onlooker. Voyeur.

A thrill of anticipation runs through me.

A woman appears.

One moment she wasn't there and now she is.

She is small in stature, or maybe it's a case of the man being exceptionally tall. The background is blurred and indistinct and I am unable to decide on their respective heights.

She is dressed in an ankle-length brushed velvet skirt in russet shades, her cinched blouse is white. She is small-waisted. Her hair pours over her shoulders in cascades of auburn curls. Her face is heavily made up, with her lips aggressively rouged. She has green eyes and a calculated appearance of innocence.

She walks across.

Unable to see the man who lurks on her wrong side. He circles her to retain the blind spot, a subtle dance whose movements only observers can discern the pattern of.

The light illuminating the whole scene has imperceptibly grown, chasing the shadows away as the couple continue their progress over the wet cobblestones.

He is following her, his bulk threatening and invisible. His hand moves inside his dark coat. Emerges. Holding a deadly steel blade.

There is a sharp intake of breath.

He holds the blade high.

Like a ritual whose successive steps have long been ordained and are now unavoidable.

He is upon her in a flash.

Her head turns and she catches sight of the knife, her eyes drawn by the way the light flashes on its sharp metal edges. There is no panic, or surprise.

'It's you,' she says calmly.

His face is finally revealed. He is in his mid-forties, is handsome in a rugged sort of way, cheekbones high enough to suggest wildness, the jagged lines of an old scar bisecting his right side from jaw to the folds of his lip. Beyond the danger in his appearance, there is also a note of grief.

'Yes.'

'I knew you would return,' the woman continues, deliberately not seeking to defend herself from the weapon or evade its coming trajectory. He holds his arm steady as he gazes at her.

'I had to find you again . . .'

'And make me pay?'

'Yes. What you did was truly unforgivable.'

'I know.' She sighs.

Her shoulders slump slightly.

The man with the blade hesitates.

The couple are like statues, immobile, frozen in time. The light surrounding them has not ceased to intensify. They are like figures in the centre of a blaze of white.

'I am ready,' the woman says, her body straightening.

'Lulu . . .'

'I will not ask for your forgiveness.'

'Maybe you should?' The tone of his voice is regretful.

'Once, I loved you.'

Hearing her say this, his resolve appears to falter briefly and a shadow races across his eyes, clouding his anger.

She calmly undoes the top button of her white blouse and exposes the pale skin beneath. I immediately wish to see more. The curve of her breasts. Her nipples.

Noting his hesitation, the woman raises her left hand and grips the wrist of the hand holding the knife and lowers it to her throat.

'Do it,' she whispers.

He is frozen to the spot.

'Now,' she orders. Pulls on his wrist.

The serrated edge of the steel blade faintly cuts into her white skin, drawing a thin line of blood.

She gasps.

He screams out loud.

And pulls his weapon-yielding hand above his head before throwing it back at her with rage and violence. This time, the tip of the blade digs deep and wide and the blood flows freely, splashing to the ground, soaking her blouse, its deadly pattern spreading like an alien flower across her front before disappearing into the darkness of her velvet skirt where it takes root.

For just a short moment, the young woman stands, unsteady, her eyes clouding, then stumbles and falls to the ground.

I was expecting something more melodramatic – as if what I had just witnessed hadn't been striking enough – more words, action, but its simplicity hit me in the gut.

Spread across the cobblestones, her body slumped at random angles, a limb quivers in a final involuntary movement. The man, the killer, stands before her, his face a deathly white, tears in his eyes. The light slowly fades, until the couple are captured in a final cauldron of white and the city scene fades back into the darkness where it had been born.

A hesitant clap, then another. The rustle of movement in the audience. Then the applause began in earnest.

The spell was broken.

I took a couple of steps back and pulled aside the heavy curtain through which the spectators would now begin to stream towards the foyer and the busy Covent Garden streets. On the other side of the stalls, another usherette, Agnetha, a plump girl who wore a red ribbon in her dark hair, was doing the same. I stepped aside to allow the crowd past me as she did likewise on her side of the theatre, lines of spectators in a rush to catch a bus or Tube home, filing past in a flurry of hats and coats and gloves and sighs, blank faces pinched in a kind of despair that the magic was over and real life resumed. I imagined that I caught a glimpse into their lives as they went by, the lovers identifiable by the smiles that clung to their cupid lips, the tired and the lonely carrying the ghost of solitude with them as they walked, shoulders hunched, gait a little slower than the others.

It wasn't hard work as it goes, I reasoned, following this initial night in my first London job. But I was unsure how much of the magic of the theatre would sustain itself if I had to watch the play over and over again during the course of its run.

I knew I had been wrapped up in the events on stage, something about the voyeur in me, managing to believe for a short while the events unfolding on the proscenium, forgetting they were actors and banishing the artificiality of the circumstances as the drama gripped all along, while hundreds of spectators munched their sweets and sipped their beers or white wine in plastic cups.

I had always been impressionable, even as a kid, drawn to the dark magic of life in the shadows, real or imagined, that surrounded me. Which was, I reckoned, what had brought me to London. I could lose myself here, in the cobbled streets that wound, labyrinthine, beneath grey skies.

That and Iris, of course. Who would now be waiting for me, in the bedsit we shared by the canal in Hammersmith.

After I had changed back into my jeans and T-shirt, left the now empty theatre, I watched the London night and sights rush by from the top floor of the night bus and thought of Iris – the sea-salt tang of her that I loved to bury myself in, and of the first night that we had properly come together. That first night at the Ball, by the ocean.

I had always been a child of the sea.

It was the one and only thing that I had inherited from my parents who had emigrated from London to New Zealand in the winter of 1947. Although I hadn't yet been born at the time, my mother would later tell me that my love of water came from those six weeks aboard the *Rangitata*, most of it spent on the upper decks navigating the turbulence inside her belly as she endured most of the long journey vomiting across the rails, overcome by rolling waves and morning sickness. My father had fallen overboard drunk and drowned on the way.

We had docked in Auckland and there we had stayed. Having travelled that far, and now husbandless, my mother refused to go any further, and I had been born six months later and, although I didn't have a drop of Maori blood in me, I was named Moana after the ocean and promptly placed into a Catholic boarding school as soon as I was old enough to be enrolled. My mother visited me once a week, but each time we set eyes on each other I saw only the woman who had abandoned me and all my mother saw were the waves that had swept my father away.

I first learned about love through Iris.

We had met, aged seven, at Holy Communion. After opening my mouth and swallowing the dry husk that had been placed there by the robed priest, who had brushed his thumb against my bottom lip too slowly and for too long, I had spied Iris through the curtain of her white veil, trailing her fingers through the Holy Water before an attendant had pulled her away. I had broken from the orderly queue of girls from the boarding school waiting to be escorted back to its cloistered walls and run after the little girl who had dared to touch the untouchable and managed to grab her hand before I too was whisked off by another adult. As we touched, the water had passed between us. I had carefully held my hand out away from myself so as to keep it damp and not wipe the precious droplets away but I could not prevent even Holy Water from drying.

The next week, we had introduced ourselves, and from that day onward I began to look forward to Sundays and led my tutors to hope that this strange girl who had never before demonstrated a pious bone in her body had finally found comfort in God.

I had not found comfort in God, but I had found a friend in Iris. The moments we shared were snatched between hymns or in the cover of darkened alcoves when we were supposed to be engaged in confession.

I even started reading the Bible, but only the Song of Solomon, lying in bed at night in my dormitory and slipping a wettened finger inside myself until the King's smooth words and the rhythm that I played with my fingertip against the silky hardness of my nub created a roaring commotion inside me that rushed through my body like a storm. I thought of this magical sensation as being like a wave. It began with my increasing wetness and gradually gathered pace, waiting for me to catch it at just the right moment, at the crest, and then ride it all the way down again.

One Sunday, I asked Iris about this feeling.

'That's an orgasm,' my friend said knowingly.

I had no idea what she was talking about.

'You're meant to have them during sex. With a man.'

Iris had gleaned this precious information from her very liberal grandmother, Joan, who had once been a circus performer and worked in exotic, faraway places. It was rumoured that she could swallow fire and insert a whole sword inside her cunt. The old woman now lived alone in a shack near the black sands of Piha Beach where every morning she walked the rugged paths through the Waitakere ranges and then played piano so vigorously that the surfers said they could sometimes hear an eerie lullaby of plonking keys audible over the crashing waves.

When I was seventeen years old, I was unofficially adopted by Iris's parents. My own mother had passed away suddenly of a heart attack and left behind neither income nor provision for school fees and I became part of their family.

At the weekends, under the pretext of taking music lessons and keeping an old woman company, Iris and I were driven to visit Joan in Piha by Iris's father in his new Plymouth Valiant with its elaborate chrome trimmed fender and Ray Columbus and The Invaders crackling on the radio for as long as we could pick up reception.

The cream leather upholstery always felt cool against the skin of my thighs as I gripped Iris's hand and tried to concentrate on not being sick. We'd be swung from side to side as the car accelerated around the sharp bends of the tree-lined road that led to the beach with its sand blacker than the night sky and so hot in the sun it was near impossible to walk across without scalding the bare skin of my feet.

Iris's father would spend the afternoons drinking lager with the boys at the surf club as Iris and I plied Joan with questions about her previous life.

We girls would listen in fascination as she recounted tales of lewd events that had occurred in the back of hansom cabs when the twenty-two-year-old Joan had allowed herself to be wooed by the rich men who watched her.

She was still able to lift her leg over her head she informed us one day, before nimbly clambering onto the piano stool and demonstrating this remarkable feat by wrapping one slim wrinkled arm around her left calf and lifting it over her right shoulder as if her hips were hinged and swung open as easily as any front door.

The stories we loved to hear most were those that concerned the Ball, a bizarre celebration that occurred just once a year in different locations across the globe. Joan told us that she had been recruited as a performer for the event by a tall and handsome woman who had waited for her in the shadows outside the Trocadero Music Hall at Piccadilly Circus. She had hair so long it reached all the way to her ankles, Joan said, and it was so flame red that at first glance it appeared she was on fire. The woman had given her an enormous amount of money in advance to secure both her discretion and a lifetime of performances just one night per year and from that evening onwards Joan had travelled with the Ball.

Iris was disbelieving but I listened with rapt attention as the old woman described a party on a riverboat in New Orleans where the walls had been set alight with flames that did not burn and half of the guests were disguised as human torches. She described another held in a mansion on Long Island in New York that from dusk to dawn appeared to be underwater and all of the guests swam from room to room in the guise of mermaids and tropical fish. And another in a vast underground cave beneath a frozen waterfall in Norway where a group of dancers had been dressed from head to toe in diamonds that stuck to their skin and gave them the appearance of glittering snowflakes drifting gracefully from a shimmering ceiling of stalactites.

Joan had never married, but left the employ of the Ball after conceiving a child under a rosebush with a man whom she had met at a garden party. The life of a travelling performer was not well suited to child-rearing, and so, with Iris's mother growing in her belly, Joan chose a new life with the pioneers who were emigrating to the antipodes and she relocated to New Zealand where she gave birth to a child who would inexplicably grow up to be conventional in every way aside from the genetics that had produced her mother and would eventually produce her own daughter, Iris.

She had kept in touch with various other members of the Ball's staff who continued to travel and perform and so it was, shortly before my eighteenth birthday, that Joan learned that the Ball would soon arrive in New Zealand.

'Are the stories true, do you think?' Iris asked me that evening.

'Every single word,' I replied, my eyes no doubt shining with the joy of it all.

When the invitation came, it was on thick white card embossed with gold lettering and sealed with a large glob of candle wax. Joan had asked me to peel it open, complaining that her now arthritic fingers were no match for the heavy envelope although just that morning her digits had flown across the ivories with the dexterity of someone half her age.

I slid my nail along the surface of the paper, peeled off the seal and examined it between my fingertips. It was soft and pliable and smelled of marshmallows.

'Cape Reinga,' I breathed softly as I pulled out the card and read the invitation aloud. I rolled the words in my mouth as if they were a benediction. I had long wanted to visit the point that was often thought to be the Northern-most tip of the North Island, the place that in Maori was called *Te Rerenga Wairua*, the leaping-off place of the spirits. It was said that from the lighthouse that stood watch on the Island's tip the line of separation could be seen between the

Tasman Sea to the west and the Pacific Ocean to the east as the two clashed in a battle of the tides. Along the way was a ninety-mile beach, a stretch of coastline so vast it seemed never ending to the naked eye.

'And what is the theme to be?' asked Joan, her bright eyes glowing with anticipation.

'The Day of the Dead,' I replied, reading further. 'A little morbid, don't you think?'

'Not at all,' replied the old woman, 'and I ought to know, because I have one foot in the grave already.' She lifted a wrinkled hand sternly to wave away our polite protestations. 'Death is just another step on the way of life.'

That night Iris and I lay side by side in the single bed in Iris's bedroom in her parents' ramshackle house on the North Shore. In another life we might have been sisters but in this one we had grown to be something more.

I was in love with Iris. More than in love, I was consumed by her and consumed by the thought of losing her. Now that we had both finished school and Iris had begun working in the office of a local motor dealership there were inevitable suitors. Older men, mostly, rich men, those who could afford to drive, and very occasionally I suspected that their wives too admired Iris. With her thick bush of untamed dark brown ringlets that framed her face, eyes the colour of melted chocolate and wrists as delicate as a child's, who wouldn't?

Iris had a round doll-like face and a look of perpetual inno-cence that attracted people to her like bees to a honey pot. I felt myself to be the opposite. I wasn't fat, but I was stocky, my brown hair dull and straight, my eyebrows a little too thick and my features square and unremarkable. At least, that's how I imagined myself. I rarely looked in mirrors because I found my own appearance ordinary, and I often wished that I had been born a boy so that I did not need to worry about whether or not my hair was combed or my waist was becoming too thick. Most of all, I wished that I had been born a boy so that I could propose marriage to Iris.

As soon as I heard about the Ball, I had wanted to be a part of it, and take Iris with me. There was something mag-ical about the way Joan described it. I felt it in my bones as surely as I felt that perpetual longing to be near the ocean and when I discovered that the Ball was to be held in Cape Reinga, the place where one sea laps over another, I knew that we must go.

We had no way to secure an invitation, or so I believed before another thick white envelope appeared through Joan's letterbox this time addressed to Moana Irving and Iris Lark. I tore it open with shaking hands to find that the old woman had written to the Ball's organisers and recom-mended that both us girls be offered positions in the kitchens. Neither of us could cook particularly well, but that, Joan said when we next saw her, was of little consequence.

All of the food and drink created at the Ball was unlike anything else that we might ever have tasted or would ever taste and consequently the recipes were exotic and heavily guarded. All we would need to do is supply the labour, peeling, cutting, chopping and stirring. It was believed that each dish would be imbued with the particular flavour of the person who prepared it and so the Ball selected only a few trained chefs to supervise the catering. All the other kitchen staff were chosen based on the vibe that they would be likely to pass on to the diners. A combination of personality, enthusiasm for the event and sexual libido. All things which Joan had advised the organisers Iris and I both intuitively possessed in abundance, each in our own way.

With the invitations secured, there was nothing else to do besides find our way there. Joan had declined to attend, stating that she preferred the memories of her youth to whatever inferior adventures her worn-out body might now be capable of.

Iris had convinced her father to loan her the car. She had little experience of the open road but had learned to drive as part and parcel of her employment at the motor dealership and the necessity of opening up and closing down the shop and bringing the vehicles in from display outside to the secure workshop indoors.

We had little idea of what might be required in the way of costumes, but from everything we had heard about the ball I guessed that any of the daringly short, brightly coloured shift dresses that Iris and I usually wore to parties wouldn't do. A brief note that had accompanied the formal invitation advised us that we would be provided with clothing appropriate for our work in the kitchen and would then be expected to change into something more suitable once our duties had been completed and were free to enjoy the rest of the evening's entertainment and would also be expected to attend a ceremony which would occur at dawn.

The drive was long and slow. Iris was cautious behind the wheel and well aware of the eruption there would be at home if she caused any damage to her father's prized Valiant. The vehicle was so roomy and she so petite that she could barely see over the steering wheel and anyone coming the other way might have suspected that the car was somehow driving itself.

At my insistence, we stopped just west of Kaitaia to swim in the sea.

I had never been able to understand the concept of a bathing suit. I always wanted to feel the lapping of salt water all over my body and particularly on the parts of my skin that a bathing suit usually covered. So, as soon as we had traversed the desert-like dunes that led to the ocean, I tugged my blouse straight over my head without even bothering to undo the buttons and slipped my skirt and undergarments down and over my ankles, tossed them aside and ran straight for the waves, not the slightest bit concerned whether my naked form was or was not visible to any bystander. Iris followed soon after me, though she stopped to carefully fold her dress and place it neatly over a bit of driftwood so that it would not crease or be covered in too much sand.

My heart drummed in my chest as I watched my friend walk nude into the water. She had small breasts, her hips jutted out only slightly from her waist, and she had the long slim legs of a wading bird. She was different from the majority of New Zealand pioneering stock who were mostly a hardy and rugged lot, accustomed to physical labour and rude good health. My friend's slightness evoked a protective urge in me as well as a lustful one and when she entered the water and was close enough to touch, I took her hand and pulled her into an embrace and our naked bodies tangled together in the waves. We laughed and splashed and kissed beneath the salty waves until the cold forced us to swim back to the shore.

By the time we reached the Cape it was just beginning to grow dark. There were no buildings besides the lighthouse, and we had expected no formal venue as such. Joan had told us that we would easily find the Ball once we arrived. The venues were always designed or located in such a way that the uninvited might walk right by them, but to anyone who was destined to be a part of it, the Ball would prove unmissable.

I heard the Ball before I saw it. We had left the car parked on a grass verge near the point and as soon as we stepped out of it and my bare feet touched the grass I knew where we were headed. The sound was a strange keening, like whale song. I took the lead, and together we picked our way carefully down the steep embankment to the sea that stretched out on all sides of us.

My mind leapt – it was exactly as I had imagined. Like standing on the end of the world. And there, by the headland where it was said that the dead begin their journey to the afterlife, a hundred or more large white birds flew, their wings beating in unison, diving off the edge of the cliff and then reappearing moments later, twisting, turning, joining with one another in mid-air, frolicking on the strong wind that blew across the Cape. But they were not birds, I realised, and I brought my hand to my mouth in shock. They were people dressed in elaborate feathered costumes. Both men and women and all of them naked besides the luminous paint that covered their bodies and reflected the light of the setting sun in a million coloured shards so that they were almost too bright to look at.

I could have watched these creatures endlessly, knowing that they appeared to be floating free from the burden of any kind of harness or suspension device, but I was aware that Iris and I were expected in the kitchens so we continued onward, still following the whale song down to the shore line.

At first, the beach appeared to be empty. But as my eyes adjusted to the rapidly dimming light I realised that what I had at first thought were rocks were in fact people clad in a skin-tight, silvery grey and glistening fabric and curled up on the sand as still as corpses so that they resembled sleeping seals. As we approached, two of the grey creatures unfurled and stood to greet us. They were women, or at any rate they both had large breasts and erect nipples that were so prominent I found it difficult to meet their eyes as they spoke rather than staring at their chests.

'Welcome,' the women said in unison, before taking both Iris and me by the hand and leading us a hundred yards further down the beach to a screen of ferns which appeared from the outside to be a flat covering over a cliffside. But as we all approached, the canopy of plants parted like a pair of curtains, revealing a high-ceilinged tunnel, as wide as a roadway. The sides of the tunnel were lined with lit candles which stood in hollowed-out skulls set into the rock. Whether human, or animal, or realistic fakes, I wasn't sure, but the effect was more restful than ominous. It made me feel as though we were stepping into another world as we followed the dimly lit pathway.

Music reverberated so loudly through the rock walls that

when I ran my fingertips along the damp stone I could feel vibrations as if I were inside a giant beating heart. I caught only fleeting glimpses of the Ball's guests through openings that we bypassed on our way to the kitchen and the sights that caught my eyes were so bizarre I could not be sure whether I was here at all or if this was all part of some elaborate and mad dream.

Like the two attendants who escorted us and the acrobats who flew over the clifftops outside, the revellers were not properly garbed but seemed to be painted in such a way that their skin appeared almost transparent, as if they were ghosts, travellers who had already been to the afterlife and returned. They were unashamedly naked and some of them were joined in passionate embrace, a tangle of arms and legs and a corresponding cacophony of moans that were sometimes an utterly human expression of pleasure and at other times like the otherworldly cries of angels or demons.

Iris caught my hand and pulled me into an embrace, kissing me briefly on the lips. 'It's incredible,' she whispered. 'I'm so glad we came.'

We were ushered into the kitchens and were unceremoniously undressed before being ordered to bathe – not just our hands were to be washed but our entire bodies – and we did so in a shower area that resembled an underground waterfall set into the rock wall. Then we were provided with filmy dresses that served as aprons and were shown to our work stations.

I was given the task of assembling brightly coloured sugar flowers. I was assigned a mountain of pre-made petals in every hue of the rainbow and shades unknown and required to turn them into sprays of blossoms. The recipe card that served as an instruction manual did not contain the necessary steps to accomplish such a feat but rather advised me that I should concentrate on evoking a mood of longing in order to fill the dessert and all who ate it with desire. With Iris squeezing cut mango, strawberries and banana between her bare hands on a bench in front of me and the curve of her buttocks and small of her back visible beneath the sheer smock that she wore this was no difficult task.

The hours passed quickly and hypnotically, leaving me with no idea as to how many blooms I had actually created because as soon as I had finished a bunch a white-gloved attendant would appear and whip my handiwork away on a silver tray to be consumed by the hungry guests. Eventually we were relieved of our duties and instructed to bathe and change again in preparation for the ceremony. We had been working all night and it was now nearly dawn. Before bathing we were given a plate of food. There were perfumed jellies in the shape of skeletons and flavoured with coconut, jam-filled pastries so light that they crumbled to pieces if I squeezed them too hard between my thumb and forefinger, a thin and bright purple soup that was supposedly carrot but tasted of blueberry, and for each of us a bunch of the crimson flowers that bloomed on the Pohutukawa tree which I had fashioned with my own hands and a glass of the juice that Iris had squeezed.

The strange supper fed the hunger pangs that had arisen in our stomachs but left us with a new type of hunger, a longing for each other that raged so fiercely we barely made it back beneath the water spout of the shower before we set upon each other. I carried Iris to the bathing area and in front of half a dozen other kitchen attendants I lifted my friend's skirts up to her waist, fell down to my knees on the wet floor and buried my face between her legs, lapping at her now engorged lips as reverently as if the juices that flowed there were a nectar fit for gods.

The sound of Iris's moans were not dulled by the heavy trickle of the water that surrounded us and served only to urge me on. My arms began to ache from the effort that it took to hold them and Iris's dress up around her hips and my knees were now hurting on the rock floor but I ignored every discomfort. It was nothing in comparison to the joy that I took from orchestrating my friend's pleasure, running my tongue over Iris's sensitive flesh, flicking the tip over her nub, worshipping each crevice and fold as if she were a chalice that held the sweetest wine.

I could barely breathe as Iris wound her fingers through

my hair and held me firmly against her, pushing my nose into her entrance and riding my face until she shuddered in orgasm and collapsed into my arms.

Immediately we were both lifted and carried by a dozen hands who took us to one side, dried us with fluffy towels and with deft strokes painted every inch of our bodies in glittering silver so that we each resembled slivers of moonbeam or spirits.

Iris was smiling and laughing as gleefully as a child and I felt as though I was drunk, intoxicated on the fluids that I had just licked from her entrance.

'Dawn is coming ... the ceremony ...' whispered voices who urged us on and we blended into a flow of shining bodies exiting from the underground caverns and moving through the tunnels towards the beach and the growing light of day.

The sand was cool and soft beneath my feet and I nearly stumbled, thrown off balance by the change of texture underfoot. We had emerged from the curtain of ferns and joined the congregation of revellers who gathered by the shoreline, all of them naked and all of them shining like a school of fish that had inadvertently slipped out of the sea and onto dry land.

They were staring in the same direction and some were cheering and crying out, 'Mistress, Mistress ...' and I turned my head and gasped when I saw the carriage moving towards us. A woman was sitting upright on a chair that had been made from the bones of a whale and was being carried on the shoulders of six men who were a head taller and twice as muscular as any man I had ever seen before. They were practically giants, and each of them was nude and possessed a cock that looked a foot long and slapped against his thighs as they ran up the beach with their precious cargo.

She was painted, but pure white rather than silver and in such a way that every bone beneath her skin was highlighted so that she appeared half angel and half flesh. Besides the paint, she wore an elaborate costume of feathered wings that moved in and out from the centre of her spine as if it were not a costume at all but a part of her.

The crowd stepped back, formed a circle, and the woman was laid down in their centre. She spread her arms and legs like a crucifixion and for a moment I felt I might laugh as the pose reminded my of afternoons spent on the beach as a child laying on my back and moving my limbs up and down to create the impression of a flying creature in the sand. An eerie silence fell over the congregation and the only sound was the steady lapping and crashing of the waves behind us.

A man stepped from the audience. His hair was jet black and his body fit. Between his legs his cock stood erect, proud, aloft, like a compass pointing North.

Just as the sun began to rise over the sea the man fell to his knees in front of the woman and she rose again and pushed him onto his back and then lowered herself onto his hardened flesh. As they were joined her wings began to beat and the crowd began to cheer.

I cried out in astonishment as something moved over the woman's body. Her flesh was no longer pale but now covered with images that flashed as brightly as the sun's rays roving over the sea. A landscape of spirals, hieroglyphs, creatures winged and land bound, fishes and reptiles etched across her flesh and all of them joined by a pulsing vine that wound around her entire body like a thin net crowding them all together.

'The inking,' said voices alongside her reverently. 'It is done.'

Dawn broke that morning in the same way that it did every other day, but I knew nothing would ever be the same again.

The shore resembled a scene after battle. Bodies were scattered haphazardly across the sand, nude, lithe, breathing in unison as if the scene which we had all witnessed had unified the crowd in some unearthly way.

I turned to look at Iris. She was laughing, as if the events of the previous night had filled her with giddy amazement. The wind pressed a long lock of her brown hair against her lips and into her mouth and she did not bother to push it away.

She turned, and kissed me.

I kissed her back, aware all the time that the taste of her still lingered on my lips. Kissing Iris was like biting into a fig. She was at once both firm and soft and the shape of her mouth caused inevitable associations to rise up in my mind. I wanted to spread open her thighs again and drink from her well. I would have died for one more moment of her lips pressed against mine.

'I love you,' I told her, but she just laughed again and pushed herself to her feet and took my hand. Her fingers were slim and slipped through mine like silk. It was like being in love with a china doll, caught between wanting to embrace her savagely and fear that I might break something.

She pulled me up.

'Come on,' she said. 'Or we'll get caught in a long line of cars behind everyone else getting back.'

It occurred to me then that all of the things that we had seen had been a performance. Already, the beach was littered with bits of costume, a solitary wing that had come off an angel's back poking up out of the sand, a set of false eyelashes that had peeled away sitting on a piece of driftwood, spider-like, still with the glue attached. A clean-up crew was moving slowly towards us packing the debris of the previous night away into rubbish bags.

Had our lovemaking been a performance? I wondered.

27

The thought cut a valley through my heart. It had not been that, to me. If I had been drunk on anything, I had been drunk on Iris, her private river seeping over my tongue, leaving an indelible mark on the inner landscape of my flesh.

It took us nearly a whole day to drive back to Auckland. There was a slip on the road and we'd had to wait as the workers cleared it. Iris had been given a short summer dress by one of the Ball staff, since her own garments had evidently been picked up by someone else or lost. It was shorter than the length that she normally favoured and bunched up almost all of the way to the top of her legs. The pale expanse of her thighs was a vision that engrossed me for the full hour that we sat stationary. It was unusually hot and the tar seal was tacky, visibly slowing the steps of the road worker who eventually waved us through. I watched Iris watching him, her gaze transfixed on the pattern of muscles rippling on his chest, shirtless beneath his bright orange hi-vis vest. He was young like us, maybe eighteen or twenty, tanned and hairless. I imagined him navigating the waves that we drove alongside, cutting through the sea like a snapper. I wondered how big his cock was.

The puzzle of my love for Iris caught me momentarily, like a prison of mirrors, each door supposedly leading to an exit but only reflecting another trap back. I could not ban from my mind the vision of her making love to another, being made love to. I could not decide whether the reality of such a thing was something that I wanted or not.

Finally the man in orange turned his sign from red to green and we continued, stopping only once more, at a chip shop on the outskirts of Whangarei for our supper. We ate in the car, from the newspaper that our dinner came wrapped in. Iris ordered a battered sausage and tore into it lustily. It was our first meal since the strange buffet at the Ball the night before. I watched her lick the salt from her fingertips.

When we arrived back, we learned that Joan had died, the night of the Ball. Somehow, I wasn't surprised.

Iris and I shared her single bed that night, like we had when we were children, and I held her head to my breast and stroked her hair as she cried. We found a mutual comfort in each other's nudity. There was a closeness in the touching of our skin, unbroken by the barrier of clothing. She was open against me, like a flower blooming. I woke to find Iris's lips around my breast, her tongue flicking my nipple. Her fingers delved inside me, spreading my folds gently as though she was searching for the right path on a map she hadn't seen before.

'I love you,' she said softly, and slid up my body, making a sandwich of our flesh and pressing her lips to mine.

It was a revelation.

I still did not always believe her. I guessed that by making love with me she was exorcising her grief. Or was she? Iris was the flitting bird that I could never keep in the palm of my hand. I must watch her fly.

If Joan had a vast fortune buried away somewhere as was rumoured, then it was either lost, or forgotten. Her will was sparse. She left Iris and me no money – not that either of us had even thought of it – but an envelope that contained two one-way tickets and a note of white paper, folded twice, that contained one line of writing in black ink: **Go to London, and find the ghost of me there.**

And so we went.

Iris's parents were sad to see us off but did not fight the move. Our entire country was made up of immigrants. The urge to roam was strong in our genes and a desire to travel overseas, therefore, unremarkable. We promised to write, but knew that we probably wouldn't do so often enough.

When we arrived in London the city seemed to me a thrumming, caterwauling mess, a hotchpotch of traffic roaring and grime that clung to walls like cement and people who stared right through you as though you weren't there at all. I fell in love with her immediately. Living in London was like living at the centre of a beating heart. I thought of her as a woman, alive and full of contradictions, of light and dark corners waiting to be explored, straight rows of red-bricked houses standing in perfect uniformity alongside crumbling squats and derelict warehouses, parks filled with neat hedgerows and populated by swans or with murky shadows and things unknown lurking in them and best left alone, depending on your postcode.

We had saved enough money between us to put down a bond and the first six week's rent to secure a ground-floor, semi-furnished bedsit. One room that contained a small double bed we planned to share, a kitchenette and bathroom. An old sofa that might have once been white ran along one wall. A too-small window above the sink, with a sill that wouldn't come clean no matter what we scrubbed it with, overlooking a lemon tree. We pooled the last of our cash to buy a dining table, a stamp-sized, square of a thing that was barely large enough for us both to sit and eat at, a green glass jug to fill with flowers, a set of new sheets and a bed cover, all in white.

At night we made love. Even though I knew that we were alone and the door was locked, I always waited until we were under the cover of darkness before I reached beneath the sheet and curved my palm over the silk of Iris's ankle, or cupped the slight hillock of her breasts. Her nipples jutted out, but I never pinched them, only brushed them lightly with the very tips of my fingers, or blew on them softly until she shuddered and they turned even harder. Almost invariably, I took the lead role, beginning by her side and arranging her limbs as the mood took me, letting her chorus of soft sighs and moans be my guide. Sometimes I rode her, grinding my mound against hers and even, once, pressing the C-shape of my thumb and forefinger against her throat until she gasped.

Yet, I was possessed by the idea that something would go wrong, that by living with Iris I was trying to keep a handful of quicksilver from vanishing between my fingers.

She found a job quickly, temping as a secretary in a law firm in the West End. I knocked on the doors of every theatre that I passed and was rejected from most until finally the Princess Empire Theatre offered me a week's trial as an usher, leaving me under no uncertainty that if I was clumsy, slow or loud I would be out of the door as quick as I'd come through it.

The bus pulled into my stop and I leapt off my seat and down the stairs in the nick of time, thankful that another passenger had pulled the cord. There was still a ten-minute walk to the bedsit, along dimly lit streets, and I huddled into my jacket, seeking protection from the dark as well as the cold. It had rained earlier and my shoes slid along the slippery street. I concentrated on navigating my way around the puddles that filled the uneven footpath, trying not to notice the similarities between the scene around me and the one that I had witnessed earlier that night unfolding on the stage. A cloud had covered the moon and what remained of the light filtered over trees and buildings in eerie long fingers of blue and grey, cold and ominous.

When I turned onto our street the light from the kitchen window over the lemon tree shone like a beacon and I hurried towards it.

I turned my key in the lock and heard voices.

A man's voice, and Iris's, but hers was full of high notes, tinkling like water running over broken glass. I hadn't heard her sound so excited since the night of the Ball and the morning afterwards, when we'd still been drunk on each other.

I pushed open the door.

Iris was wearing my favourite dress, a canary yellow shift adorned with rivers of gold braid that swam and danced over her body as she moved. She wore white high heels on her feet, the only party shoes she owned, and her left hand was encased in a short ivory glove that closed with a button at her wrist. Her hair was pulled up into a bun at the back and a pink feather perched gaily behind her hair. It looked suspiciously as though it had recently adorned a feather duster. In her right hand she held a champagne flute, half full of bubbling amber liquid. She threw back her head, exposing her long, bare throat, and took a sip. Then she saw me.

'Moana!' she cried, as though she hadn't just seen me as recently as that same morning. 'You must meet Thomas.

His father works at my law firm,' she added, by way of explanation, and perhaps to mitigate the fact that a man whom I had never met was draped over the double bed that we shared together. 'And it's his birthday tomorrow. He'll be twenty-two. Twenty-two, can you imagine!'

Since we were both now nineteen, I could easily imagine, but I refrained from pointing out that he was not so much older than we were.

I nodded politely towards Thomas, put my bag down, and walked in the direction of the stove top to turn the kettle on.

'Oh no,' Iris cried, grabbing my hand with her gloved one. 'You must have a drink with us, mustn't she, Thomas?'

'Oh yes, of course,' he said with exaggerated politeness. 'Do forgive me.' His voice was all plums and honey, as smooth and silky as a hot chocolate with a rich lilt that sounded like someone from the television. When he sat up I noticed that his clothing was as bright as the dress that Iris had borrowed from me, a look that I wasn't used to seeing on a man, although I knew that I was still adjusting to the different fashions here. New Zealanders typically wore sombre tones, black and grey and navy and olive green, colours that would meld into the native bush that covered the country as easily as a sparrow's wing disappearing on the backdrop of a tree branch. His trousers were tight and the vivid red of a post box and his collared shirt was the watery,

34

lake-like blue of a cloudless sky. His top two buttons were opened and revealed just enough of his bare chest to indicate informality. He reached towards the bedside table and picked up a tan corduroy flat cap, tossing it over the bed to reveal the champagne bottle in a bucket of ice beneath. A flash of gold lining revealed itself as the cap streaked through the air. On the ice bucket was Iris's other glove, hanging limply over the side. I imagined Thomas pulling it from her hand, bringing her bare fingertips to his lips.

'Do you have another glass?' he asked.

'No,' I replied curtly.

'Oh, we can share, darling,' Iris piped in. She never called me that. 'So how was the play?' she asked me as an afterthought.

''Twas Jack the Ripper that did it.'

I tried to mimic an East End accent but knew I was making a poor job of it. Thomas was too polite to mention the fact, and Iris too tipsy.

'Wow!' she exclaimed. It was the first time that either of us had ever been to the theatre, and I realised then how much I had been looking forward to coming home and telling her about it. All of the exciting things that happened to us always seemed to begin with Iris. It was rare that I had a note of glamour to add and Thomas's unexpected presence had cast a shadow of dullness around my night's adventures.

I tried not to show it, but could feel my lips pinching together into a frown.

Iris threw her arm around my shoulders and pulled me against her side. She pressed her glass to my mouth and I took a sip, coughing as the bubbles tickled my throat.

'Thomas is having a dinner party,' she said, 'and we've been invited.'

'Yes, you must come,' he said. 'Both of you.' He looked at me as he said it. His eyes were blue and his hair dark only just brown, as though he'd been blond as a child but grown out of it. Long locks hung over his forehead and he occasionally scooped them back. He was slim, in an elegant, nonchalant sort of a way. His smile was wide and his lips so full and red they almost looked unnatural. He had an easy-going air of sensuality, and was utterly aware of it.

I wasn't sure whether I liked him or not.

Thomas left shortly after issuing the invitation, offering a need to study for his upcoming university exams as an excuse, but in truth, he looked faintly embarrassed at having been interrupted.

At the door, he handed me Iris's glove, as though he'd picked it up without thinking.

'I could easily fall in love with your friend, you know,' he said jokingly.

'I am already, Tom,' I replied.

'Never Tom,' he said, 'or Tommy. Just Thomas. Please ...'

He put on his hat, tucked his jacket under his arm, turned and walked into the night.

2

The Watcher and the Watched

I heard the downstairs front door slam shut, and turned towards Iris.

'What was that all about?'

'What do you mean?'

'This guy, Thomas . . .'

Iris's cheeks were as pink as the feather that remained in her hair, now at a lopsided rather than jaunty angle that lent a touch of madness to her expression. She was uneasy on her feet. Her smile was forced.

'He's the son of one of the partners. Came to the office, we chatted and he invited me out for a drink. I thought he was amusing . . .'

I interrupted her.

'But you thought enough of him to pop home first and put on my favourite dress.'

'I didn't think you would mind. We always borrow each other's clothes. And I slipped into this afterwards, anyway, just for fun. I've barely had it on for two hours . . .'

I swallowed. I couldn't help thinking of Iris shedding her plain office attire in front of him and walking around the flat in the chemise she always wore under her blouse as she searched for a party frock to put on. Jealous as I was, I knew she wouldn't have been that bold. She'd have taken the outfit into our box of a bathroom, and left Thomas to lie on the bed and listen to the rustle of her skirt's modesty lining sliding over her skin, the almost inaudible pop of buttons as she removed her shirt. Sounds that I knew from experience might go unnoticed by any ordinary casual observer, but to the desirous were like a choir of temptation.

The zip on that yellow dress was impossible to pull right to the top unaided. She would have asked for his help to cover the last few inches and close the hook and eye at the neckline. His fingertips trailing over the gossamer velvet of her shoulder blades, hesitating at the nape of her neck. Drawing the clasp closed, standing with his chest nearer to her back than was necessary. The gentle wind of his breath caressing her earlobe. The awkward pause when he'd finished and one of them broke away. Iris of course, she'd have thanked him and laughed gaily, stepped to the side and spun around like a wind-up toy on a child's music box.

Was it possible, I wondered, to hate someone and love them at the same time?

'And those?' I pointed to her gloved hand and the matching glove Thomas had handed over to me as he left. I knew the pair had not travelled with her all the way from New Zealand. I knew every single item of clothing that belonged to her.

'Ah, those . . .'

'Yes, those.'

'Thomas gave them to me,' she said

'You just meet the guy today and already he's giving you things?'

'It just happened,' she explained. 'He was holding this cute little Liberty bag and I asked him what was inside, and he'd bought the gloves for his mother but then suggested I try them on and they happened to fit me perfectly. So he said I could keep them . . .'

'Just like that?'

'Oh come on, Moana, he's just a friend, that's all. We need to make friends, you know, we can't stay in this tiny room together every night of the week.'

I could feel myself turning into a rather unpleasant sort of person. And I wasn't enjoying it.

She was on a roll, and continued to make her point as I stood sullen, with my arms crossed, and listened.

'He's a guy, Moana.'

'So?'

'So, what I mean is that even if you and I play around, it's not all there is to life, to sex. It's nice, I have very tender feelings for you, but I know there must be more. Us, it shouldn't be exclusive, you understand. So far, he's just a nice and funny guy. But one day I want to know what it feels like with a man, you know. Him, someone else, I just want to know.'

As Iris said this, she also lowered her gaze as if she didn't want to look me squarely in the eyes. My heart dropped.

'I don't.'

Was I being jealous, petulant, spoiled? Somehow the way Iris was explaining things, more articulate than ever before on the subject now that alcohol was flowing through her veins, sounded unchallenging, normal. She had never been very vocal. Passive, even. We had gravitated towards each other because of our closeness, situations, but we had never actually discussed it. It had just happened. In fact, it struck me, we never did talk much together, did we?

I decided to drop the subject. For now.

She chose to ignore my reaction to the situation.

My stomach rumbled.

'Have you eaten?' I asked her, deliberately not mentioning the possibility that Thomas might have bought her dinner.

She shook her head. 'I haven't had time to do any shopping.'

'It's okay. I'm sure we can find scraps in the kitchen. Actually, bread and peanut butter would suit me.'

'We can fry some eggs; there's some slices of bacon left too, if you want.'

'Not sure I'm up to bacon. The play was a touch violent, not the sort of thing to trigger much of an appetite . . .'

'Tell me all,' Iris demanded.

We trooped over to the kitchen. Reunited for now.

Thomas was never mentioned for the rest of the evening. We fed on leftovers, not that either of us was very hungry. Then settled down on the narrow couch and watched the telly. Usually, Iris cuddled against my side, or lay down with her head on my lap, but tonight she sat cross-legged next to me, as if an invisible wall had appeared between us despite our earlier apparent reconciliation. The distance made me glum.

'Shall we go to bed?' I suggested, hoping that there we would find the intimacy that words had not yet been able to restore. The flat was so cramped that the bed was barely a foot away from the sofa, and yet we persisted in making the most of the little space that we occupied by eating most of our meals at the dining table and using the couch as if it were a living room, saving the bed for sleep and sex.

Iris readily agreed.

I was working a matinée and an evening show the next

day at the theatre but she had the weekend off as a reward for the monotony of her 9-to-5 job. So neither of us had to get up early, which suited me fine.

I'd just stripped and slipped my pyjama top on and moved to our bed. Iris was in the shower. The water had been running for an age, and I imagined her standing under it still in a champagne daze. She'd never had much of a resistance to drink, even back home. I was sitting up in bed, two sets of cushions behind my back shielding me from the some-times damp dirty beige wall we had to endure to justify the low rent we paid. I was leafing through a programme I'd brought home for the play I'd watched earlier. I'd actually counted how many I'd managed to sell before the perfor-mance began and at the interval: a round thirty. Which was a bit of a surprise: like all theatre programmes, it was slim and unsubstantial and damn expensive. The biographies of the actors consisted of lines of credits for other plays, TV shows or movies I'd never heard of.

Iris tiptoed out of the bathroom. She was naked.

Somehow the light shone on her sideways, a combina-tion of the bare bulb on the bedside table and the flickering neon of the fish-and-chip shop across the road bouncing across our windowpane, and her body was momentarily captured in a stage-like well of brightness that gave her a 3-D quality that I found entrancing.

Her hair was still damp.

'Can you pass me my nightie?' she asked.

I dug my fingers under the pillow on her right-hand side of the bed. The garment she'd requested wasn't there. I explored deeper, checking under the sheets in case it had slipped down the bed.

'Not there.'

Her lips twisted.

'Damn,' she said. 'I remember now: I put it in the washing this morning. It needed to be cleaned ... And my other nightie, the black silk one, is also in there; we're overdue for the launderette.' She sighed.

I smiled.

'Just come as you are,' I suggested. 'I'll keep you warm.'

Iris hesitated. She always made it a habit of wearing something in bed. Normally, I preferred to sleep at least half naked.

She turned and stepped towards the dresser.

'I'll find a T-shirt instead,' she said.

'No ... Please ... Don't ...' I pleaded.

I wanted her nude.

Close to me.

Skin to skin. Where I could smell the receding echo of the soap she had washed with, the tinge of the toothpaste she had just used.

She still appeared unsure. It was a cool English summer

and arriving in the bedroom, with its open window, was a comedown from the steamy heat of the shower.

'Promise I'll keep you warm,' I said.

She shrugged and joined me, quickly pulling the top sheet all the way to her throat as she positioned herself between the covers and snuggled up against my side.

'Friends again?' I asked.

'Yes,' Iris replied, her voice just a trickle of sound, as if she were a touch unsure.

I switched the bedside lamp off.

'You're not reading?' she asked.

I usually did before sleeping.

'No, not tonight.'

She turned, her bare back to me. My hand was caught between our two bodies, fingers grazing her buttock. Her skin was soft and silky. God, I thought, no man could ever be so smooth, surely. I was harder, more athletic, in spite of the fact that I seldom exercised and was never much of a participant in sports back at school.

Silence fell, punctuated by the slow, almost imperceptible in and out of her breath and the occasional confused mess of pop music from open-windowed cars racing by on the road outside the building.

Iris broke the tension.

'Sorry,' she said.

'What for?'

'About earlier.'

'No need to be sorry ... Kiss me.'

She rolled over, moved her lips towards mine until we were in alignment.

My heart lightened.

The peppermint freshness washing across her tongue was tempered by the now remote sweetness of alcohol and triggered a mighty flow of emotions inside me and I closed my eyes. I wanted to float in darkness as my taste for her rose and we embraced, our bodies fitting together as naturally as a pattern of stars aligning in the night sky.

My Iris.

My sweet, delicate doll.

Her hands shifted under the covers and moved over my waist, holding onto the jutting ridge of my hipbones. Her grip was tight, as if she was trying to pull me open. Our breasts touched. My tips hardened. So did hers. I wrapped a leg around hers and Iris gripped my thigh and pulled me against her tighter, her fingertips nearing my opening, teasing me but not venturing closer yet. We both knew we had time for this. Savouring the gentle lull before the fever pitch. A silent ballet morphing into a jigsaw of limbs, the pieces fitting together neatly as our lust awakened with all the ease of familiarity, a sequence of movements that we had perfected over months of sharing a bed. I loved this part of it, the prelude. Like feeling the steady suck of the pulling tide before being knocked by the roaring crash of a wave.

I knew I still had to learn a lot about sex. Real-life sex, not the sex I'd read about in snatched glances at the pages of women's glossy magazines that hinted but never revealed enough or heard about in the playground from other girls who had been as ignorant as me, and inevitably, all of my unreliable sources spoke only of the love between a man and a woman. Even Joan, Iris's liberal grandmother, in all of her blunt stories had never recounted wooing or being wooed by another woman, although I often wondered whether something more than Joan ever admitted had occurred between her and the beautiful flame-haired woman who had discovered her outside the Trocadero.

The light breeze outside picked up and the window pane rattled, as if even the elements were following the course of our lust. A gentle gust blew into the room and I felt the cool kiss of night air against my slit, a damp breath of air caressing my open thighs. I was lying on my side, one leg straight, the other linked over Iris, my knee at a right angle bent up to her waist and her arm around me, her hand stroking over my flank and down my waist and around the curve of my arse. I twisted on my hip, tightening my grip on Iris's body and widening the gap between my legs, letting my cunt spread open.

Iris's fingertips journeyed between the valley of my

buttocks, feather light. Her touch was tentative, a promise that one day she would venture inside me there, fill my hole with the velvet of her flesh. Each time she glossed over my pucker I arched my spine like a cat's, ever so slightly encouraging her to push harder, to press her finger inside me now. I stopped short of asking her for what I wanted though. The words formed in my mouth like sawdust and floated away, unspoken.

The pace of her sweeping hand quickened. Her fingers clenched in small, juddering bursts – in out, in out, open and close – and I knew this meant she was climbing higher, nearing the crest of her appetite. She craved for more.

Iris's desire fuelled me. Her need was like the current in my ocean. Hearing her soft cries, the in-breaths that caught in her throat and came out in a whisper of sound like chiffon falling through the air, made my heart thrill and my quim slick. I thrummed, pulsing with a swell of barely contained need that spilled from me in wet kisses and juice dripping down my thighs and fingers that held onto her too tight. I was an overripe fruit, breaking through the skin, seeping want.

My fingers travelled over the curve of her mound until I found her entrance and circled her nub. Her clit was hard, already erect, and felt even hotter than the fiery surroundings in the heart of which it dwelled. I drew closer to her centre and Iris's whole body stiffened and exhaled.

'Oh,' she sighed.

I stalled for an instant. I was too fast, too eager. I allowed my mind to wander for a moment, finding a place of calm to pause within. Always, when we made love, there were brief epiphanies, stretches when it felt as though we were melded in one, both of us connected like strands of the same coil.

Between those flashes of connection were spells like this when I retreated from my body to my thoughts. All kinds of things danced through my head during these intervals – the lewd and the banal, dreams and memories. Tonight I imagined the pair of us on a stage, through the eyes of a watchful audience. The velvet milk of our skin, unbroken by the restriction of costume. Naked. A beam of light bouncing across the dew of our sweat. Limbs entwined. A silent theatre, a hundred anonymous voyeurs, ears bent on catching the muted choir of our yearning. I painted the picture of us fucking from the stalls and the wings, from up above. The view that God would have if he were watching, wicked thought. I didn't care, I would be wicked.

Time spread out like a string of pearls and we floated along the beads.

'Go on … please …' Her voice was a murmur of wind, barely audible.

I held my middle fingers together and slid deep into Iris, searching back and up until I found it, that ridged coin of flesh inside her that made her whole body convulse when I pressed against it. She shook with tremors, feverish. Her mouth parted and she buried her chin in the hollow of my neck, her hair brushing against my cheek.

I shifted slightly, my teeth nibbling her ear lobe, my tongue flitting inside her ear's hollow.

'More?' I whispered.

'Yes, yes.'

I drew my face away from hers, distanced my hand from her sex and moved down between the crumpled covers, plunging deep through the moist heat that our bodies were generating in their closeness until my lips reached the coarseness of her pubic bush. I got up on my knees, my rump tenting the bedcovers and, extending my hands held her cunt open and lapped the length of her opening from bottom to top, then delved between her inner lips and finally plunged my tongue deep into the simmering heat of her.

Iris tensed her feet and lifted her butt up in immediate response. But the weight of my own body pressing down on her kept her pinned to the bed.

There was nothing that I could compare the taste of her to. The particular tang that was Iris, warm, sweet, sharp, salty, sometimes sour, but never bitter. Joan had once told us about a fleeting love affair she'd had with an Asian man who had introduced a fifth taste to her palate, umami, that was somewhere between indescribable and all four other tastes combined, in perfect balance. I wondered if that was how Iris tasted. Knowing those secretions were the very essence of Iris was a feeling like no other, it gave me a sense of awe, of almost religious adoration and I had no need to analyse it. I just wanted to experience it, wallow in its oh so shocking intimacy, the way it connected us for ever. Her juices marking me as hers and my consuming her was a communion far greater than any I had ever undertaken in church.

My tongue dived deep inside her, until it could venture no further, embedded, my taste buds mapping the texture of her pink inner walls, my lips on heat brushing against the hardness of her jutting clit, her white thighs clamping me in place, tense, vibrant, her whole body under my control, open, effervescent, singing to the tune of my tongue.

Iris dug her fingers in my hair, pushing me hard against her midriff, holding me down.

'That feels good,' she moaned, her words reaching me through a cloud of sheets.

I briefly came up for air and then went down on her again with renewed energy and lust.

I was floating in space when I heard her 'Do you want me to ... do the same?'

I shook my head. I wanted to stay like this forever. Abolish time and space. Me, Iris, London, this bedroom, this bed, connected in greed and desire with her. Nothing else mattered. No one else. This was pleasure enough.

With every flick of my tongue, Iris shivered.

With every passage of my lips across the beautiful ravaged rawness between her wide open thighs, Iris moaned, squirmed, swam against me.

Again, intent on pleasuring her until I dropped with exhaustion or cramp, I realised I was holding my breath and inhaled deeply. The heat floating upwards from her cunt warmed my whole face. Her aroma washed over me. Stronger and stronger as I orchestrated her senses towards further delirium.

Buried in the welcoming delta of her legs, I failed to hear the words she muttered.

'M . . . Moana . . . love . . . I . . . want . . .'

I surface from the sheets to understand her better.

'Inside me . . .' Iris gasped.

I froze. 'Are you sure?'

'Yes.'

'Really?'

'Absolutely.' I knew what she meant. It was something that until now we had shied away from. Like a border post for which we didn't carry a valid passport.

I returned to the moist darkness that lay between the bedcovers and the sweet embrace of her thighs.

My fingers journeyed towards her opening and its humid warmth.

I inserted one and then another, and finally a third until it felt as if I was filling her.

Iris responded silently, a vibration rushing across her stomach as she pulled the badly crumpled sheet away from the top of her body and uncovered her slight, delicate breasts. My fingers delved inside her, wading through heat and juices. Her plaints grew in intensity. I attempted as best I could to synchronise my fleeting movements within her soft walls with the inhale-shudder-exhale-grow limp rhythm of her mounting orgasm, slowing, accelerating, forever delaying the moment. Stimulating her knowingly, timidly, fiercely in turn.

We had played with each other in this way before, but I had never delved so far inside her and so fully, somehow, it felt as if she was opening further and further to my exploration.

A thought rudely intruded in my mind. Would this be how a man's penis would similarly enter her, a woman, any woman, me? I closed my eyes to banish the image, but it persisted.

As if telepathically connected to me, Iris opened her lips. 'More ... please ...'

'I can't,' I pleaded.

'You can,' she said.

I wasn't a man. Never would be. Whenever Iris was making love to me, I was content with her tongue, the feel of her breath against my skin, the knowledge electric of her affection. Had no need for actual penetration. But again I couldn't banish the image of the hard cocks we had witnessed by the sea at the Ball, and how the recipients of their favours and thrusts had so often ecstatically responded. I wanted to know how it would feel.

'It will hurt,' I said.

'I know,' Iris replied. 'That's what I want. No pleasure without pain,' she added, her voice a thin trickle of sound, reaching me in a strangled tone from its point of origin in the heart of her throat.

I swallowed hard. Reached as discreetly as I could manage for the small tub of Vaseline that I kept on my side, below the bed, in case we ever needed it. Flexed my fingers at the breach of her lower lips, bunched my hand into a fist as compact as I could manage it, and slowly began to push against her opening. We both had small hands but I still couldn't believe I could insert mine inside her, without breaking her, tearing her badly, even with the additional lubricant. There was resistance at first, and I began to hold back, but Iris sensing my hesitation forced her pelvis forward to meet my hand's assault.

Micro inch by micro inch, my hand buried itself past her labia, seeking out her heat, the folds of her outer skin merging with the pink irregular waves of her inner walls as I slowly slid in. Any moment now I was expecting Iris to scream out with pain, but she remained silent, apart that is from the rising rhythm of her moans.

'Tell me when to stop,' I asked.

Iris remained silent. Lost in her private nirvana. I felt the outer reaches of her opening almost click. My hand was swallowed whole.

It felt as if I had lowered a part of me into a raging fire.

I was inside her up to my wrist.

What did I do now?

'Move a little,' a breathless Iris begged me, aware of my uncertainty.

I thought I had been in charge of the situation, but now Iris was taking over.

I obeyed.

Turned my buried hand one way and then the other. It fitted her like a glove.

Her whole body shuddered in an instant and she came with a terrible cry of joy and relief, and my captive hand felt as if it was washed over by a tide of wet fire while held in the iron vice of her cunt.

Shattered, I collapsed onto Iris's delicate body.

We remained in silence for what seemed like an eternity.

Finally, Iris moved and I gently withdrew my hand, wiped it against the sheet and she took me into her arms.

We kissed.

'Friends again?'

'Hmm hmm . . .'

But I knew from the look in her eyes how intense the experience had been, and with an ebb of sadness now taking a hold of my senses had become painfully aware that she would never lose that urge to be filled, invested, and the fact that others would also be able to do so to her. That I was no longer indispensable. Perhaps I had never been.

As we fell asleep, I resolved to fight them, whoever they were. Keep Iris mine.

On the one hand I was blissfully happy to be living independently under the same roof with Iris, away from all the restrictions that life in New Zealand had imposed on us and I found London enchanting. On the other, I was painfully aware of dark clouds on the horizon, doubts, questions about where our relationship could go and whether it could survive the thousand obstacles and potential new encounters the city now scattered in our path. So I lived day by day, holding on to hope, never quite knowing whether I was fooling myself or not.

London was not just a city, but a curious warren of villages and we spent our week-ends exploring. Sometimes we would make plans, while at other times we improvised, walked onto the Tube or caught a random bus with no destination in mind and progressed thanks to the occasional flip of a coin or deciding whether to turn left or right depending on whether the name of the first pub we passed appealed or not.

Everyone told us the weather wouldn't last and to wait until we had survived a London autumn followed by winter before we made up our mind for good about the tentacular city, but we brushed their negativity away. Few people realised how much rain and what capricious, unwelcoming conditions there had been in Auckland, and the old weatherboard house that I had shared with Iris's family had provided no great barrier against the cold wind and frosty mornings.

We enjoyed picnics in a variety of public parks, known and hitherto unknown, concealed behind rows of houses, oases of greenery and shrubs, secret refuges we hardily explored; we roamed from area to area, from Epping Forest and its forlorn ponds to Golders Hill Park and its children's animal enclosure with pretentions to being a zoo and so far off the mark, frisbees in the breeze flying up the hill as we gallivanted without a care in the world. The Princess Empire suffered from a rapid turnover of staff so I never managed to make many friends there, but Iris, who was anyway much more of an introvert than me, despite her often passive attitudes in private, found it easy to strike up friendships with her colleagues at the law firm where she worked and quickly had a thriving network of acquaintances ranging from young to old, from legal backroom staff to court and chambers personnel. I happily tagged on.

Summer passed all too rapidly.

Autumn came.

By now I was almost a veteran at the theatre. Maybe it was because, unlike the others who had come and gone, I actually had no major ambition or wishes for a career in the arts, or for that matter anywhere else. I was just happy to be, to live in London and be with Iris.

I was enjoying a few days off from work. Iris was at her office job and I was sitting at home sewing, catching up on some ironing and repair work on some of Iris's and my clothes and stockings. The phone rang. It was Gerry, the theatre's Assistant Manager. Two of the small backstage team had the flu and he was short of staff and was wondering whether I was willing to come in and help out despite the fact that I was on a break, but he was aware I was still in London and had not gone away. He was offering double my normal pay, and the money would certainly come in useful. I agreed. And I was about to hang up the receiver when he cleared his throat, and added: 'The new Art Director has requested you specifically.' His tone indicated that he had some misgivings about this fact. I didn't pay much attention to the goings-on among the other staff, particularly those in the higher echelons, since I had no ambitions towards promotion, but I was aware that the Princess Empire had called in a freelance Art Director to assist with their latest productions, since the last permanent person in the post had retired some weeks ago and a long-term replacement had not yet been found.

Such an event would not usually have roused any feathers, were it not for the fact that the freelancer was a woman, and a relatively young one to boot. Her appointment had been announced at a rare staff meeting, and I had heard the whispers afterwards – that she had studied fine art, and not theatre, that her father must have connections, that her recent success elsewhere was a fluke, that she would inevitably fail. Adam, another usher with pockmarked skin and hands that shook when he worked, had hissed '*lezzie*' under his breath, and I had walked away from him, feeling as though someone had punched me in the chest. I sought out the Art Director's photograph in the next batch of programmes, but it was hard to assume much from the small black-and-white thumbnail. Her face was thin and her chin pointed. Her dark hair was either cropped short, or pulled fiercely back from her face. She had thick brows and a sharp look about her. Her name was Clarissa. Clarissa Beauchamp.

Weeks passed, the new show was well reviewed. Nothing had apparently changed, besides Gerry being in a slight huff since he had apparently had his sights on the job and been passed over.

And now this. I wasn't even sure how Clarissa

Beauchamp knew who I was, but I supposed she might have picked my name from a list of available ushers, based on the fact that I was by now one of the longest serving. That must be it.

Still, as I hurriedly dressed and ran for the bus, I couldn't help but invent scenarios that might have attracted her to me, and picture the parts of her that the photo had not revealed. From her sharp features, I guessed she must be slim. Would she be tall, or short? Large breasted or small? An image popped into my mind, Clarissa naked, her thick pubic hair a dense, gleaming triangle practically glowing between her thighs, her breasts small, pointed triangles, her nipples large and pink and hard. By the time I arrived at work, I was nervous and flustered and assaulted by pinpricks of guilt that I was thinking of someone besides Iris in that way.

But all of my worry was in vain, as Clarissa didn't even come out to meet me when I arrived, sending instead another assistant to instruct me in her place. I felt simultaneously relieved and deflated.

The first job I was given was to travel to the Petticoat Lane area to pick up some costumes and fabric from the workshop of a designer who was working on the company's next production. It was urgent enough – the lead actress they were for was only available for fittings that afternoon – that I was given the money to take a cab there and back, a luxury that I was still unfamiliar with in a place like London.

The building was an old East End warehouse which had once been a shoe factory and had recently been converted.

There was a strong smell of curry in the air, as the building was flanked by two almost identical Indian restaurants. It made my mouth water in a trice as I alighted from the black cab and studiously asked for a receipt.

The designer I had been expedited to visit had her studio on the top floor and a rickety goods lift was the only way of reaching it. I called up and she explained how I should operate it. Her voice had a friendly, musical tone.

'Welcome, welcome.' She pulled the sliding latticed fence-like door open as the industrial and unsteady lift clicked to a halt and into place.

She was striking.

Her eyes were dark ebony pits that shone like coal against her olive-toned skin. She was almost bald, her perfect oval of a head covered with just a millimetre of grey hair. Long chandelier earrings dangled from her earlobes.

I was so taken by her features that I forgot my errand and my manners, and just stood frozen and silent on the spot as though I had been struck dumb.

'Come on in.' She offered me her hand, and led the way into the large open space she used as a studio. Daylight streamed in through the wide open windows and the glass roof divided into even square panes, stained slightly green by the past onslaught of the wet London weather.

The surroundings of her studio did nothing to make me feel more at home.

Her imperiousness. The sheer size of the space in which she worked, which must have been four times the size of our bedsit. The fragrant, aggressive, almost animalistic notes of the perfume she was wearing – banishing the earlier smell of curry away by a technical knock-out.

'So you're Clarabelle's new girl?'

I nodded, confused by the nickname but presuming she was referring to Clarissa.

'You can call me Patch.' She said it as though she was bestowing a gift.

'I'm Moana,' I told her.

She smiled, revealing a wide mouth and a set of perfectly straight teeth. A dimple puckered just below her right cheek. She didn't have one on the left to match, which gave her grin a lopsided look that was at once endearing and mischievous.

'I can see why Clara chose you,' she replied. 'You can come closer, I won't bite.'

I stepped forward. The original wooden floor of the cavernous room had been waxed and shone like a skating rink.

'Very pretty,' she said, her gaze still locked on me. She

cast her eyes over me from the tip of my head to my toes. 'Maybe a bit butch, but there's no harm to that, is there?' she added. 'You could dress better, but we could fix that and happily turn you into a butterfly, couldn't we? First, though, we need to work out what sort of butterfly you want to be.'

Her words broke through the spell that she had cast over me like a tennis ball shattering a window. Who did I want to be? I wasn't sure. I hadn't even worked out who I was, never mind who I wanted to be. Looking around at the racks of clothes that lined the walls of her studio and the mountains of fabric that covered two trestle tables set up alongside a large, industrial-looking sewing machine, it occurred to me that my identity didn't need to be fixed. I could change the way others saw me, maybe even change myself, with just a new outer layer. I briefly took hold of a heavy pair of satin, tuxedo-style trousers hanging on a rack near me, my mind overflowing with possibilities. A thick white tag dangled from the bottom of one leg. 'Patricia McLaughlin designs,' it read, without a corresponding price tag. I set the garment back on the rack as I realised I would never be able to afford such an item. I probably couldn't even afford a length of the cotton that stitched them together. I put my hands behind my back and twisted my fingers together, suddenly worried that Patricia – Patch – would think me impertinent.

'You would look wonderful in those. Try them on if you like,' she said.

'Oh no, I shouldn't have. Sorry,' I muttered, feeling a flush of red rush up my cheeks in embarrassment.

'Yes, you should. It won't take long,' she said. 'You'll still be back in plenty of time, and you can tell the theatre that I kept you waiting. Anyway, Clarissa will be arriving soon.'

'She's coming here?'

'Yes – she didn't mention it? She's very particular, you know, wants the final say over every last detail. Oh, she won't be giving you or me carte blanche over the costumes any time soon, believe me ...'

I swallowed, my mind turning back into a tangle, thoughts darting here and there like a flock of birds disturbed and rising into the air en masse.

She walked quickly towards me and stretched out a long, slim arm to the rack of clothes, so close to me that her wrist nearly brushed across my breasts. I felt my nipples harden and hoped that they weren't visible through the regulation white blouse that formed the top half of my uniform. Her forearm was stacked with silver bracelets that clattered as she held the hanger out to me. I took it, careful to not allow the material to touch the floor and collect any dust that might linger there, and looked around for a changing room, but there was evidently nowhere set aside for that purpose, not even a screen.

'Not shy, are you?' she said.

I shook my head to indicate that I wasn't, although it was a lie. I felt lumbering and awkward, like I was swimming, the support of water turning my limbs lithe and supple. On dry land, my body just 'was'. A vehicle for my thoughts and dreams and passions, nothing more. I thought of the bodies of others as something enticing to look at, but I thought of my own as merely functional. Being nude in front of Iris was different. We had known each other's bodies for so long, it became second nature to be unclothed in her gaze. But I never felt as though she looked at me the same way that I stared at her. Lustfully.

I fiddled with the clasp and zip at the back of my thick, plain black pencil skirt. My nerves had made me clumsy and turned my fingers into sausages.

'Allow me,' Patricia said, softly. The tone of her voice changed as she drew nearer to me. She spoke in a hushed whisper, as if we were sharing a secret.

Her knuckles grazed my spine as she searched for the zipper. Undone, the skirt slipped down to my hips where it stopped, prohibited by the rounded flesh of my buttocks. Patricia gave the fabric on either side a sharp tug until the garment dropped to the floor. I expected her to move then, but she didn't, and I stood frozen to the spot in front of her, half unclothed, my usherette uniform pooled at my feet.

Goosebumps rose on my flesh, and not in response to the

temperature. The silence between us became a palpable thing, and the longer it lasted, the more any words that I might speak seemed unnecessary and hollow.

At that moment, the door burst open with a bang so loud in contrast with the tomb-like quiet that we had been standing in that I cried out 'Oh!' and jumped into the air.

'All those murder mysteries affecting your nerves, girl?'

'No, no . . .' I shook my head. 'I'm fine.'

Clarissa. I recognised her immediately. Her hair was indeed short, and had not just been pulled back from her face in the picture. She wore it styled in a pixie cut that only served to elongate the pointed edge of her chin and nose even further. She had the look of someone who would slice through the air instead of move through it, her body a collection of angular points carving its way from one perfectly aligned geometric position to another.

Her arms were draped with long bolts of fabric, one grass green and the other ocean blue and both evidently so heavy that they slowed her progress towards us. The colours of the swathes of material weighing her down were all the more vivid as she was dressed all in white in a flowing jump suit with a drawstring tie that sat at her hips. I moved forward to help her, forgetting in my haste that besides my underwear I was naked from the waist down, and my skirt was wrapped around my ankles.

'Oh, don't let me interrupt you,' she said, and strode

towards the nearest trestle table and carefully laid the lengths of silk down. Her high gold heels clip-clopped against the wooden floor as she walked.

Every word that came out of her mouth sounded as though it meant something else. I didn't know how to respond.

She bustled over to us before I could think of a word to say and placed two fingers under my chin, lifting my mouth closed.

'You have a very pretty pair of lips, Missy, but there's no need to stand there with them hanging open like that. Remind me of your name again?'

'Moana.'

'Ah yes, I remember now. A unique name to suit a unique girl. Mo-ah-na,' she enunciated, copying me breathily, lengthening the A as it should be. I hated when people called me Mo-anna. 'And why are you standing there half dressed, Moana?'

'We were trying on a change of style. These trousers would be darling on her, don't you agree?'

Patch held up the hanger. I wished that the ground would open and swallow me. No doubt, just as I had begun to get excited about the idea of some extra responsibilities at the theatre, the job would be taken away from me since I couldn't even run a simple errand without getting distracted.

'Oh, how rude of me, Patch, lovely to see you of course.'

Clarissa leaned forward and kissed Patricia on each cheek, awkwardly sandwiching me between them as she did so. I smelled their perfumes mingling, or maybe it was just the scent of their skin. Clarissa's was somehow dark, and musky, like the earth in a rose garden after a hot storm, part dank and dirt and part floral, humming with life. Patch's was light and citrus, lemon sugar. I imagined being wrapped between them in bed and how it would feel to have a wet pussy pressing against my ass and another against my cunt. Two pairs of hands caressing my body.

My breathing quickened, and I felt certain that my thoughts were printed all over the portrait of my stiff limbs.

Greeting complete, Clarissa picked up the trousers.

'You're right of course, Patch, they're just the thing.' She pulled them off the hanger and dropped down to her haunches in front of me, her face passing just a few inches away from my opening. I could feel myself becoming damp, there. Perhaps visibly so, and I was thankful that my knickers were cheap, thick cotton and not a thin, expensive ribbon of silk that might have looked obviously wet. I wondered if Clarissa could smell me, if she liked that smell in the same way that I loved the smell of Iris, and her taste.

She held the trousers open as if I were a child and I stepped in, one foot at a time, and placed my hands lightly on her shoulders for balance as she dragged them up over my calves, thighs and hips. She ducked her head to my waist to fasten them and I felt the warmth of her breath travel over my belly. I sighed.

Clarissa stepped back and looked me up and down, reviewing her handiwork. Patch joined her. Both of them, appraising me.

'Good, I think,' Patch said. 'She just needs some heels.'

'Yes, heels, definitely,' Clarissa added, 'and also, I think, something else with her hair . . .'

She stepped forward and ran her hands through my limp locks, first pulling my hair up and back and then over to the side, each time leaning away to view the result.

'Wonderful,' she breathed, but didn't say which look she preferred. 'We'll take them. The trousers.'

'What?' I cried, flustered and embarrassed. 'Oh no, I could never afford anything like these,' I said. I didn't even know what they cost, but since I couldn't even afford ordinary clothes I knew that something designer would be laughably out of my budget.

'Nonsense,' Clarissa said, 'they're perfect for you. Patch will add them to my tab, and I'll think of a way that you can earn them back. An end-of-year bonus, perhaps.' She winked at me, kissed me lightly on one cheek and then took hold of my waist again, unbuttoning the clasp and pulling the slacks down to my feet, where I obediently stepped out of them, trying hard to maintain my balance and finding myself half-naked once more.

She handed Patricia the silky black bundle.

'Would you wrap this in tissue, darling, and add it to my bill, while we gather up all the samples?'

'Yes, of course.' Patch nodded smoothly.

I touched my hand to my face. My cheek was still burning where Clarissa's lips had landed.

The rest of the afternoon passed without incident. I carried bundles and bundles of dresses and basques and men's thick jackets from Patricia's studio into a waiting taxi and then down the theatre's long corridors and creaking stairs to the dressing rooms where they were carefully hung again on the garment racks. Clarissa showed me how to use the steamer to press out creases and the location of the sewing kits and explained how everything must be kept precisely in place so that if a button or hem needed stitching between scenes the right tools could be located in moments to avoid any delays and avert disaster.

By the time I reached home I was exhausted. My arms ached. It was the most satisfying work that I been involved in for a long time though. Something about the combination of physical labour and the cerebral strain from learning so many new things had made me excited to do more and nourished my soul. It wasn't until I pushed open the front door and saw Iris waiting that I remembered the trousers

Clarissa had bought for me, wrapped in violet tissue paper and stored safely in a cranny within the dressing room that I used as a makeshift locker. Guilt swept over me.

'Hi,' I said.

'Hello,' she replied. 'You were longer than I expected.'

'Sorry,' I said to her. 'It was busy. Gerry needed me.'

'Oh,' she said.

I thought of telling her about Clarissa and Patch but I couldn't. My tongue froze solid in my mouth. Instinctively I felt that Iris would not understand. The thought threw me. She was my best friend, and I had lied to her, if only by omission. A seed had been planted.

She cleared her throat. I gazed at her, and noticed the awkwardly formal way that she was sitting, perched on the end of the bed with her feet on the floor, her back straight as a board and just the edge of her buttocks on the mattress, as though she was about to get up. She was wearing her cream blouse, neatly pressed, a plain navy skirt with her matching kitten heels, and on her hands, the gloves that Thomas had given her. Her hair was loose around her shoulders and shining as though she has just brushed it.

'Going out somewhere?' I asked her. I felt a stab of jealousy. It would surely be with Thomas. She had been seeing more and more of him lately. A movie here, a dinner there. And more than that, I was sure, at her office. Occasionally she mentioned that he had popped in and they had eaten together, or I smelled or tasted a sour note of white wine on her breath.

'Actually,' she said, 'yes. But I want you to come. I need you, Moana.'

Her shoulders were tight and her smile pinched, her face twisted into an expression of fear and worry.

I dropped my bag and rushed to her. I had been standing in the door clutching my purse all that time, like a visitor in my own home. What was happening to us?

'Of course!' I said. In truth, I was tired, and looking forward to an evening in, but I would not abandon Iris in an hour of need.

'What is it? What's wrong?' I put my arm around her shoulders.

She pressed the tips of her gloved fingers together, gathering courage.

'The thing is,' she said, 'I want to be with Thomas. I want to ... I want to fuck him. And I want you to be there too.'

She slumped forward, relieved, as though she had expelled all of the air in her lungs along with the words she had spoken.

I was stunned. She went on.

'I'm seeing him tonight. I wondered if you would come. I just have to know what it feels like with a man; surely you understand? I need you to be there ... It's confusing ... to have your blessing, so to speak. That way I won't feel as if I'm betraying you ...'

She turned to face me. Her eyes were deep oceans of blue, full of hope and questions.

I couldn't turn her down.

It began with me seated on an ottoman, clutching a flute of sweet white wine that I had barely taken a sip of.

Iris had telephoned Thomas from our flat to confirm my agreement and he had sent a car to collect us and deliver us to his flat in Maida Vale. The vehicle arrived so quickly I presumed he must have had the driver on standby and I wondered how long they had been planning this and what they would have done if I'd said no. Was it really Iris's idea? Or was this Thomas's way of pushing the two of us into an *ménage à trois*?

Iris buzzed the intercom and we walked through an imposing set of wooden double doors that acted as the gateway to the main building, past a uniformed doorman who did not even look up and then down a marbled corridor to the elevator at the end. Iris walked confidently and I trailed behind her. She had clearly been here before.

Thomas's apartment was unsurprisingly on the top floor, but inside, it wasn't what I had expected. Smaller, for a start, though despite that even his bedroom totally eclipsed the size of our entire flat.

He pulled the door open before we knocked.

'Hello, come in,' he said, and ushered us inside where we stood together in the entry area, cramped and awkward, until he offered to take our coats and hung them on hooks that decorated one wall.

Below, his shoes were neatly laid out along a shoe rack. He had more shapes and styles than I had ever thought a man might own in a variety of gregarious patterns. Plain tan leather, sharply pointed at the end. Shinily polished brogues. Deep purple ankle boots with an embossed crocodile print. Another pair, knee high, gleaming black and with a somewhat malevolent air to them, the sort of footwear that I imagined Jack the Ripper wore when striding down dark alleyways in search of hapless victims. Perhaps I'd just been watching too many Victorian thrillers at the Princess Empire.

Iris had turned pale and still, as was her habit when she was nervous.

Thomas was flushed. His eyes glittered and his voice was unnaturally loud, as though he was covering an inner shyness with overconfidence.

He wore an aqua blue collared shirt and dark blue, tight jeans that highlighted the thickness and strength of his thighs and calves. A single, stray thick curl kept falling down over his forehead and he flicked it back.

He took hold of Iris by the elbow and propelled her through the open-plan kitchen and sitting area, towards his bedroom. I followed slowly, taking in the surroundings as I went. A large bookcase against one wall, stacked mostly with records and magazines rather than books. A couple of squat statues of Buddha alongside a bowl filled with foreign coins. A sketched drawing in a frame depicted the lines of a nude woman, lying with her back to the artist. The lights of the city glittered like stars through the big bay window that spanned half of the wall, behind his cream-coloured sofa. There was no glow of broken fish-and-chip shop neon strip lighting upsetting the view here.

'I've poured us some wine already,' Thomas called, half apologetically, 'and it's more comfortable in here.' I hurried after them and he pulled the door shut behind me. It closed silently, without a creak or a click.

Iris was sitting in exactly the same way as she had been when I had walked in the door at our place, and found her waiting for me. Perched on the end of Thomas's bed, her gloved fingers entwined, back straight, eyes downcast at the floor. She looked like a schoolgirl waiting to be reprimanded. Had we been alone, I would have gone to comfort her, but here, I demurred to Thomas.

'Please sit,' he said to me, pointing out the ottoman, a thick, red-and-gold batik-patterned stool at the end of the bed. The whole room was decorated in a similar fashion. All of the furniture was carved from dark, heavy wood. The carpets were thick and the bedspread a deep crimson shade, like the inside of a damson plum. There was no window and the air was still and perfumed with the lingering odour of Thomas's cologne, a rich, musky scent with a note of cinnamon that I found cloying. The lights were turned out and he had lit candles all around the room, precariously set on small saucers that immediately made me fear for the health of the surrounding drapery, and our lives, if all were to go up in smoke.

The cushioned seat was low, and atop it, the line of my gaze was only a few inches above the bed. I could not make eye contact with Iris without craning my head back but I had a vision of her stockinged calves and the onset of her knees peeping out from her skirt. Shadows from the flickering candle flames crept up the walls around us, like a ghost's long fingers on the verge of coming to life.

Thomas handed me a glass filled with pale liquid, and then the same to Iris. His hands were unsteady.

'Take off your shoes,' he said to Iris. The instruction was whispered, but loud enough for me to hear.

She gripped her glass to avoid tipping it and prised the heel of one shoe off with the toe of the other, then kicked off the second shoe. The carpet was so thick that the sound her Mary Janes made when they dropped to the floor was barely audible.

'And your stockings,' he said.

I was both shocked and aroused by the dominance he

76

was displaying, and Iris's almost meek obedience to his diktats.

She lifted her skirt and still clutching her glass, struggled with her garter one-handed. Then set the wine down and unclipped the fastenings that held the sheer fabric tight against her thighs and peeled away one stocking, and then the other.

Neither Thomas nor I made a move to help her. There was something terribly erotic about watching Iris's movements, each one of them stilted and unnaturally slowed, like a film playing at half speed. The bare skin of her legs had an unearthly shine to it and I wondered if she had oiled them.

Thomas sat down next to her. His presence affected her posture; the slant of her shoulders immediately relaxed, as though up until now she had been holding her breath.

His hands travelled to her face and caressed the line of her jaw. She lengthened her neck, swan-like, to encourage him, almost in imitation of a cat being petted. His fingers moved lower, down to her clavicle and then to the top button of her blouse. His progress was glacial, infinitesimally slow. I was straining so hard to pay attention to each small detail that I fancied I could hear the touch of his skin on hers, a faint rasping, like silk on silk.

The candlelight cast them both in an eerie glow, like puppet figures on a makeshift stage. I focused my gaze on Thomas. He was beginning to sweat. His full lips looked fuller, overripe berries ready to split. He had an erection, I knew, by the bulge pressing through his jeans. I found it easier to watch him than Iris. I could imagine myself in his place. I was at once terribly curious – knowing that I would soon witness a man's cock for the first time since the fascinating if confusing flashes of carnal activity at the Ball – and also terribly jealous. How I wanted to be the one inside her.

He unbuttoned her blouse, so neatly the clasps seemed to fold through the holes, a gesture he had no doubt practised many times and perfected. The faint hills of her breasts appeared, the mid-line of her brassiere and a window of her torso, the white fabric on either side like drapes hiding the view behind. He pulled the blouse apart further, slipping it over her shoulders and revealing the top half of her body.

I had seen Iris naked many times before. Every day, now that we lived together. But never like this, unpeeled slowly like a piece of fruit in front of my eyes. Thomas was deliberately unveiling her for me, giving me a show, I was sure of that. I felt a sudden kinship with him despite my jealousy. As though we were collaborating in Iris's deflowering.

Her bra came off next, unhooked and dropped onto the floor on top of her shoes with little ceremony. Her small breasts stood pert, nipples erect. He lowered his head to her chest and kissed them, keeping his profile to the side so that I could see. My own nipples were hardening in response. I dared not make a sound, not a single sigh of pleasure, for fear of startling Iris and causing a scene. I sat silently, pressing my thighs together hard as I felt my desire quickening inside inexplicably fanned by my status as an intruder, a voyeur.

She lifted her buttocks slightly from the coverlet, allowing him space to peel away her skirt. He left her knickers on. A lacy lavender-coloured pair that I hadn't seen before. Another gift, I guessed, and a presumptuous one at that. A piercing stab to my heart, a burning knife twist, knowing that Iris had hidden them from me.

Thomas stood and undressed. Removing his own clothes, he was hurried and clumsy and I took a small delight in watching him struggle to wriggle his tight jeans down his calves, totally failing to maintain any dignity at all. Iris stared as he slipped his grey cotton jocks down to his feet and his cock immediately sprang out. She looked away quickly, shocked, embarrassed perhaps. A flush crept up her cheeks.

'Touch it,' he said, and she turned back and reached out a hand, hesitated, and removed one glove. Her bare fingers crept closer until she grazed the head, and then trailed down his shaft and finally took his balls into her hand and cupped them gently. Thomas's eyes fluttered closed. He moaned softly. She gazed up at him with an expression of wonderment plain to see on her face. I resisted the urge to throw my glass of wine over both of them and rush from the room.

His eyelids flickered open again and he stepped closer towards the bed and laid his palms over her breasts. For a moment, my view of Iris was obscured, bar one of her feet and a hint of her ankle. Instead I was faced with Thomas from the back. His buttocks were hard with one dimple indenting the base of each cheek. Thick thighs. His legs were long and covered with a light coat of downy hair that extended only to the onset of his arse. His back was totally smooth and hairless. He was lean, almost but not quite thin.

Perhaps sensing that he was blocking my vision, Thomas lifted Iris up and scooted her body along the bed at an angle, so I could see the full length of her. He raised himself up onto his knees, leaning over her, and pulled down her knickers, exposing her bush.

Somehow I hadn't expected that he would go down on her, but he did. He slid down the length of her body and inserted himself, kneeling, between her legs, then lowered his face to her pussy, pulled her lips apart and began to lick.

Iris groaned, and her whole body sank as she relaxed on the coverlet, melting into his touch. She tangled her fingers in his hair and held his head, pushing his face into her slit.

Unbidden, the taste and smell of her arose from memory in my mouth. My tongue moved between my lips and I closed my eyes and imagined that I was pleasuring her. Wetness seeped between my legs. I hitched up my skirt, as quietly as I could manage and began to rub my fingers against my clit. Wondering if Iris would notice.

I opened my eyes, they were both oblivious to me.

Thomas was totally engaged in his task, ignoring any discomfort that might have arisen in his knees or his hunched-over back as he continued to lap her, his arse pointing into the air. I admired him, begrudgingly, for attending to her pleasure. Somehow, I hadn't thought that he would.

Her lips had parted and her eyes were closed. I could tell that she was close to orgasm. Her arms moving over the bed, octopus-like, grabbing and pulling at the blanket, then embedding her nails in a pillow and then pushing it aside in frustration and returning her grip to his hair. Thomas did not falter, despite the fierce grip that she had on his locks, or the violent squeeze of her thighs against her head. I knew from experience that Iris was ferocious when she was about to come. Licking her until she exploded was akin to riding a wild horse as it bucked. Sometimes it was all I could do to keep my tongue fixed to her clitoris and continue the evidently effective pattern of my strokes over her bud as she wiggled and squirmed beneath me.

I followed Iris's rise into the peak of arousal in my mind, trying to catch up with my body. I concentrated on the rise and fall of her breath, the flush of her skin, the faint sheen of sweat that appeared on her forehead and her upper arms. My cunt began to twitch in sympathy with hers and I rubbed faster, stretching my legs out in front of me and leaning back as far as I could without tumbling off the ottoman. I usually masturbated with my eyes closed. Doing so with them open felt daring. I watched Iris's breasts sway as she moved up and down on the bed, pushing herself against Thomas's mouth.

She came, and I shortly after. The sound of my climax was lost in the aftermath of hers. Neither of them turned to look at me. Iris lost in her lust and Thomas lost in her. He did not lift his face from her opening until her shuddering had subsided and she had begun to grind against him again, signalling that the hypersensitivity of her orgasm had passed. I pulled my skirt down, now somewhat satisfied in my body, if not my mind. I had been arrogant enough to think that only I could induce raptures like this in Iris, now I knew I was wrong.

I picked up my wine and took a sip, and then another. The sweet liquid did little to soothe my troubles, but it did make me thirst for a glass of water. I could hardly get up now, though.

Thomas had flipped Iris over onto her stomach, her head facing me on a diagonal so that I could see them both in profile. She struggled to lift herself up, supporting her body on her elbows. He pushed one of her knees forward into a right angle, exposing the cleft of her arse. Briefly I saw a flash of his cock jutting out, straight and hard, resting in the valley of her cheeks. His face creased in concentration and hers tensed in premonition of what would follow. He pulled his body over hers, holding himself upright with one arm as his other hand directed his head into her hole.

I braced myself, expecting Iris to cry out or shudder in pain, but she did not. The moment that he broke through her passage, barely a flicker of discomfort passed over her face. She winced momentarily and then relaxed again, like a rag doll. Thomas, initially tense that the moment had arrived looked at first relieved as he entered her at last, and then elated as he began to thrust, slowly at first, waiting for her to adjust to the sensation and then quicker as she pushed back against him, encouraging him on.

The actual fucking lasted a few minutes. Just at the point when Iris looked overwhelmed by pleasure – eyes closed, cupid lips parted, her breasts swaying as Thomas pumped into her, nipples hard – he came, and collapsed on top of her. I felt a stab of bittersweet joy at the flash of disappointment evident on Iris's features, before she turned to curl up in his arms. You might have a cock, I thought vengefully, but if I were to wear a fake one and plough her, at least it wouldn't be over too soon. I would fill Iris until she was satisfied, even if it left me exhausted.

Thomas lay on his back with his arm beneath Iris's neck, pulling her against his side. I wondered what he was thinking, if he was worried that it hadn't been enough. I hoped so, I thought, bitterly.

Iris turned herself awkwardly onto her stomach and

craned her head up to look at me. Our eyes met. She reached out her hand. Even now, I could not bear to refuse her. I stretched out my arm and grazed my fingertips against hers. A gesture of affection, understanding, forgiveness, perhaps.

Or maybe just love.

3

Letter to a Lost Lover

Nothing changed overtly following the uncalculated tryst: life continued, a quiet routine, but there was an uneasiness in the air. It just floated there like a cloud whenever Iris and I were together and the silence became too heavy. The unseen curse of the days after.

Unfortunately, we were spending less and less time with each other. She had a 9-to-5 job, and then would often spend the time with workmates (and Thomas?) having drinks together when their stint at the office ended, by which time I had already left for my work at the theatre. By when I would get home, she was all too often asleep and even though she still instinctively cuddled up to me in bed when I slipped between the covers, it was more of a heat-seeking reaction, a habit rather than an overture to sex. When sex between us did occur, it was tepid and, on her side, unenthusiastic, as if she was discharging an obligation or merely being kind to me and her heart was no longer in it. Under me, over me, in embrace, Iris grew ever more passive and quieter. While I kept on being held hostage by tendrils of want.

Our weekend opportunities together were also limited to snatched hours as the Princess Empire was currently featuring matinée performances on each day due to a strong demand for the show, curtailing my free time with Iris.

I invariably awoke to an empty bedsit, my sleep barely disturbed by her movements rising and dressing earlier, while she ventured as discreetly as she could to the kitchen area so that I wouldn't be disturbed by her breakfasting sounds or the swish of the front door closing as she left for work. All this faintly registered with me in the periphery of my dreams as I sleepwalked towards day.

Knowing I was alone and there was no reason to actually get up, I unconsciously prolonged my time in bed, basking in the heat retained between the bedcovers, stretching endlessly in a vain bid to settle the turmoil dominating my body and thoughts, tossing and turning until the light seeping through the washed-out grey net curtains won its battle against my laziness. Which left me with too many free hours until I had to present myself at the theatre again.

Increasingly unsettled in our tiny rental when I was alone and a dangerous prey to my unexpressed fears, to fill the time I would often take public transport at random, catch a bus on a whim and just explore new parts of London, wandering aimlessly through the city's immensities and quirky corners, uncovering secret parts, hidden parks, miraculous waterways and low-slung bridges, empty estates and industrial zones. And when autumn began in earnest and the weather started to limit my urban travels, I would sit idly at the kitchen table trying to make my coffee and toast last longer, or attempt to read a book and wake up from an aimless reverie an hour or so later still focused on the same page and with no memory of anything that had occurred earlier in the story in question.

That morning saw me again prey to inactivity.

The phone rang.

'Moana Irving?'

'Yes, speaking.'

'Wonderful. It's taken me ages to trace you . . .'

'I'm sorry?'

A man with a youthful voice and a pronounced self-satisfied Oxbridge tone. Somehow the wrong sort of voice for a nuisance or unwanted sales call.

My mental cobwebs still lingered.

'And you are?' I ventured.

'Your cousin.'

'You must have called the wrong number. I don't have any cousins . . .'

'Oh yes you do ... I'm Gwillam.'

'Who?'

'Gwillam Irving. I realise it's a bit of an uncommon first name, but it's the one I was given at birth. Never had much of a choice in the matter, I fear.'

I felt inclined to like him after that. People were forever getting my name wrong too.

I took another sip of coffee from the mug. It was cold and useless.

'So how exactly are we related?' I asked him.

'Ah, it's a long story,' he replied.

'I'm all ears.' I still found the whole thing dubious.

'Not actually a first cousin. The connection is more remote. Your dad had a step-brother. He married my mother.'

It was the first time in ages I'd had to even think of the father I had never known. I felt a pang of anger.

'I think something happened and they all became estranged. I've never found out what exactly happened,' he continued.

'My father died before I was born,' I told him. 'On our way to New Zealand.' There was no need to explain the actual circumstances.

'Oh ... I wasn't aware of that ... I'm so sorry. That's very sad. I feared something of that nature as there were no traces of him in any of the documentation or searches I made.'

Spring

'So how did you come across me?' I asked my new-found distant cousin.

'A death notice in a newspaper, for your mum. I located it on a micro-fiche ...'

I recalled how, after my mother had passed away, Iris's parents had insisted on placing the formal announcement in an Auckland publication. 'No one should depart this realm in total silence,' Iris's father had said. He was always a very dignified person, a man with compassion and consideration.

'Why were you looking?'

'Genealogy is a hobby of mine. I'm studying for the bar,' he said. 'So it's the sort of research that can always prove useful,' he added. 'And I was curious about our family tree.'

It felt odd, but I was intrigued. In a strange way, it meant I wasn't totally alone, in the blood. Gwillam was such an uncommon name, though. And he sounded so terribly posh and worldly!

He beat me to it.

'We should meet,' he suggested.

'Absolutely,' I agreed.

I had to explain my lack of availability in evenings. He sounded genuinely excited by the fact that I worked in the theatre, before I had a chance to reveal how menial my position at the Princess Empire was. He confessed to me that life as a legal student was mostly dull and he was envious of me moving in such by comparison decadent circles. I was about to correct him, but then thought why the hell should I?

I, dull and repressed Moana, could become his highly exotic cousin!

It then occurred to me that maybe this was some sort of prank being played on me by Thomas, or even by Iris. After all, she was employed at a lawyer's, and Gwillam had similar connections. Was it just a coincidence?

I asked Gwillam where he worked and he mentioned a chambers in the Inns of Court that didn't sound familiar to me. Iris was with a large firm of solicitors based in Chancery Lane. Which didn't mean that there was no collusion between them all, but still made me less suspicious. We settled for lunch a couple of days later. Gwillam suggested the Tavern Bar on the corner of Bleeding Heart Yard, off Greville Street. It was a part of London I was unfamiliar with but within walking distance of his office.

He was standing to the right of the bar counter when I arrived and was nothing like I expected. Medium height, wearing plain NHS-issue brown-framed glasses, a blue cotton button-down shirt, black jeans and brown leather moccasins.

His hair was lustrous and fell to his shoulders, which made him the least lawyerly lawyer I could have imagined. It was pale brown and combed back, highlighting a vast, smooth forehead beneath which his eyes twinkled incessantly, combining with a permanent half-formed smile to give the impression that everything amused him. To me, he looked like something of a hippie, were it not for his more traditional clothing. Had he come from his workplace dressed like that? Back in New Zealand, I knew that a lawyer, even an apprentice, would have been clad in solid black from head to toe, and a plain white shirt with an anonymous necktie. I remembered the gloomy office Iris and I had been summoned to, where we had been passed Joan's note and the open tickets for the journey to Britain.

Were it not for our respective expressions, and if we had switched hair length, I felt we could have been brother and sister, with me the introvert one and he the extrovert. I warmed to him immediately.

'Hello, cousin,' he said, his smile creasing further into welcoming realms of irony. 'So, what's your poison?'

He was drinking Guinness. I asked for the same, but in a half-pint glass to his larger one.

We found a seat in a corner of the darkened bar and made ourselves comfortable.

I was bursting with questions and the first hour we spent together rushed by as we compared stories about our parents, families, and connected all the necessary dots. Apart from actually learning their names and personal idiosyncrasies, there were no major revelations, but I found it warming to learn of his side of my family and get an idea of what my parents had left behind when they decided to emigrate.

We were already well into our second round of drinks, and the bar was almost empty with just a handful of pin-striped City types lingering in the gloom, when the conversation turned to me and my growing up in New Zealand. I tried to make a dull subject interesting. By the time I reached the point in my story when my mother died and I had kindly been taken in by Iris's parents, I found it difficult not to reveal the fact of my almost puppy-like attraction to Iris. Whether Gwillam could read between my halting lines and guess the feral nature of my feelings was hard to say, but he refrained from bombarding me with questions in response to my awkward reticence when it came to Iris.

A mad, stray thought rushed across my overworked brain when Gwillam left me on my own for a few minutes to visit the toilet, that he was just perfect; if Iris truly needed a man in addition to me, he would make an ideal candidate that I could more than tolerate.

I would quickly learn how absurd that concept was.

'So what prompted you two to come to England?' he asked when he returned.

I explained Joan's bequest and described some of her stories to him. Although I held back on the episode of the Ball. It was a shared memory that belonged to just Iris and me, and I didn't feel comfortable revealing all its details, even to Gwillam, apart from the fact that so much of it would sound absurd to an outsider.

'She sounds like she was the life and soul of the party, Grandma Joan.' Gwillam smiled. 'A life well lived,' he added.

'She was lovely,' I said.

'I'm curious, though, about what she wrote about ghosts and all that. Bit of a strange message, don't you think?'

Iris and I had initially been surprised by her note, but after finding out that she had left us the means to leave New Zealand and travel to London, we had been overly ebullient and had somehow brushed the subject aside in our enthusiasm to arrange the journey as soon as we could manage.

'I suppose so.'

'What could she have meant? Was she a believer in the supernatural?'

'I haven't a clue. Iris neither. Though I doubt it. She scoffed at religion, I know, so I can't imagine her putting much faith in ghost stories.'

Gwillam had explained earlier in our rambling conversation that as part of his training for the Bar he had become something of a specialist in hunting down lost heirs and estate beneficiaries. It was like detective work, he said, and he was already an avid fan of crime and mystery books anyway, so it felt like combining his job with his hobby.

I'd even found out that he had seen our Jack the Ripper play at the theatre, although it had been a week before I had begun my work as an usherette there so our paths hadn't crossed.

'Maybe I could look into it?' he suggested. 'Find out more about her life here and why she jumped ship?'

'Would you? Could you?'

'I feel I'm obligated to do so now. You know, I'm like a dog with a bone once something catches my attention!' He chuckled. 'Here you are, a hitherto unknown cousin from the other side of the world, bringing your own mystery along with you. How could I resist?'

He took out a small notebook and wrote down the details I could recall about Joan and her time in London, and the stories she had regaled us with, and quizzed me about what I knew about Iris's family background.

He was still methodically interrogating me and I was running out of answers when I realised, by the increasing flow of punters into the pub, that time had flown, and with a quick glance at my wristwatch that I was soon due at the Princess Empire. Fortunately we weren't too far distant from Covent Garden.

I quickly excused myself.

'I'm so sorry, Gwillam. I have to go to work for now . . . By the way, what about you? Shouldn't you have returned from your lunch break?'

'No. I took the afternoon off. Just had a hunch that we'd need the time.'

We made arrangements for our next encounter – a new psychedelic music club was opening, called The Electric Garden, and he had an invitation – and I rushed into the commuter flow and made my way towards High Holborn, orientated myself and set off for the theatre.

I arrived just in time.

'You have colour in your cheek,' Clarissa said, greeting me in the foyer, herself straight in from the teeming street, dressed in a mannish white shirt with a stiff folded collar and matching grey pinstripe waistcoat and trousers. Her shoes were black brogues, well shined. She looked like an extra from the *Mary Poppins* set, as if she ought to be carrying a cane and might break into a tap routine alongside Dick Van Dyke at any moment.

'I've been running,' I explained.

'How wonderfully eager,' Clarissa said. And suggested we have a drink together after the show. Still buoyed by the unexpected comfort of my meeting with Gwillam, I accepted.

I busied myself between the seats more quickly than usual that night, impatient to meet Clarissa and put off my return to the bedsit. Each time I returned there these days, I feared what I would find. The loneliness of an empty home, or maybe worse, Iris and Thomas together relaxing in easy domesticity, or just Iris alone and the wall of awkwardness that had formed between us like a fortress, impenetrable.

A fog of blueness came over me at the thought, and I pushed Iris out of my head and tried to busy myself with the task at hand, picking up discarded sweet wrappers and empty plastic cups, but it was no use. I let my mind wander instead.

Gwillam had cheered me today. There was something soothing about the notion of a blood relative, distant though the connection might be. I often felt so alone in the world, with no particular family to speak of and the country of my birth so many thousands of miles away. I thought again of Iris and of the strange ties that bind us to others, whether through family lines, or romance, or friendship. How those chains could be at once so strong, and yet so brittle.

Finally I finished tidying my allotted corner of the auditorium, returned a silk scarf the colour of butter and a blue and red striped neck tie to the lost property counter, and tallied up the takings from that night's sales of ice creams and programmes.

It was nearing midnight, but I was by now used to the late work and had become something of a night owl. The witching hour, it occurred to me, as I prepared to fetch my belongings from the staff area within the dressing rooms and seek out Clarissa. I had half expected to find her waiting there, sitting on the low stool in front of one of the wide, gilt-edged mirrors, her face cocked to the side and her chin jutting out as was her habit, but the room was empty.

I was the last usher to leave. Only Gerry remained, somewhere upstairs, storing the receipts away in the safe and preparing to lock up.

The racks of clothes and array of headgear on the hat stand took on an eerie feel without the usual hustle and bustle of panicked wardrobe hands preparing for a scene change. I brushed my fingers along the clammy arm of a leather jacket. The costumes, with no one in them, had the same appearance to me as a room full of toys in the absence of a child playing. I was certain that when I turned my back, the boots would clomp, the skirts would rustle, the shirts would stretch out arms to one another, as if the props had a certain magic in them that they bestowed on the wearer instead of the reverse.

I had a sudden urge to dress up and act out a character, but who would I be? Femme fatale, in a long black gown and simple flat shoes, gliding silent down corridors in search of vengeance? Or damned young girl, wrapped up in belted red wool coat and crimson kitten heels, dark glasses and scarf obscuring part of her face, trembling in the shadows as her killer approaches? I picked up a wide-brimmed man's hat in tan felt, slipped it over my hair and looked at myself in the mirror. The addition of a prop did nothing to make me feel like a different person. Just the same old Moana, but with a hat on. I took it off and hung it back on the peg, leaving the magic of the theatre to the absent actors.

As I reached for my handbag, my hand grazed against a soft bundle wrapped in tissue paper and I recalled the tuxedo trousers that Clarissa had bought for me. I had not yet worn them, expecting that at any moment they might disappear from their hidey hole and reappear in Patricia's studio to be sold on to someone else. The garment still seemed far too extravagant a gift for me to accept, let alone wear. But tonight felt like the right time.

I tore off the wrapper and the trousers tumbled out, totally uncreased due to the silken nature of the fabric and Patch's expert packing technique. I removed my work skirt and stockings and pulled them on, tucking my blouse into the high waistband and stepping back into my shoes. I didn't look at myself in the mirror again to view the effect. To do so felt like bad luck.

The clock struck midnight, and I snatched up my bag, closed the door behind me and hurried down the theatre's long corridors to the exit. Again I thought of Gwillam, and his suggestion that he go searching for the ghost of Joan. Where would she haunt, I wondered? I guessed that whatever remained of her soul on this planet skimmed the waves still on Piha beach, spraying sea salt into surfers' open mouths, or dancing across the hot sand, black as coal dust and glimmering like a cloudless night sky. Or would she revert back to her youth and plague the stages of music halls, fluttering skirts and brushing the ankles of stockinged feet?

A board creaked beneath my hurrying feet and I jumped. What a crazy notion, I muttered aloud, shaking all thoughts of the supernatural aside and turning my mind back to the night ahead.

I didn't want to keep Clarissa waiting.

8th August, 1947

Sweet dear lover of mine,

My last two letters have gone unanswered and I have this awful feeling inside of me that I will never hear from you again. Gut feeling, you used to call it.

Even though this pitiless war has finally come to an end, and two long years have passed since, these are terrible times and I guess the world and its turmoil have reclaimed you in some way, as if the time we managed to be together was just a temporary gift.

I grieve for you, but in my own way. In silence.

I wish you were here and I could speak to you, but here I am confronting your absence and, as I am sure you would have wished, would rather celebrate the joy and pleasure we shared together.

You always said that pleasure was a holy gift, didn't you?

And oh, how we celebrated it!

You often asked me about my life before you, and I would evade your questions as if I knew already that we had to live in the moment, while the bombs were falling on the city and the secret life of London was so intense and alive as a result.

Now I will tell you, even though you are not here to listen to my words. Then, it didn't matter, because I felt that before you I was nothing.

Presently, I feel as if it is something I owe you.

I was living in Shropshire when the Great War began. Just another country girl.

My parents were farmers and I attended the parish school, but found it awkward to make friends, feeling I had little in common with my classmates. I was a happy soul but something inside me longed for more than the small world I lived in. A few streets, thatched roofs and rolling fields, farm work and of course the dances which occurred every few months, our small town way of blowing off steam in a flurry of brightly coloured if several-seasons-old skirts, painted on stocking lines and home brewed booze snatched slyly from hip flasks. At that age, I wasn't allowed to join the fray – my father was a kind and hearty man but horribly strict – so I was relegated to the sidelines and instead feasted on the unbound gaiety of others as they circled the floor in a frenzy of movement, the music, the loudness, the sheer joy that surrounded things. There wasn't much joy available to us then, so when we could, boy did we make the most of it.

Both my brothers died in the trenches and I was taken out of school and torn between the grief of my parents and long days of labour in the fields, trying in vain to replace the two sets of hands *we had lost with my small pair. Even though our holding was small, the amount of work required, keeping the crops going and tending to the few animals we had, managed to hold on to, soon overcame us. We could see no future and when an offer was made to purchase our land, my father accepted it. In truth, I suspected that they just couldn't bear to be in the same house that had birthed my brothers, to work the same soil that Andrew and Roley had toiled over. My parents decided to return to their native Ireland to join my grandparents until my father could find employment of some sort in the city.*

I, on the other hand, had no wish to travel to Ireland. I had been born in England, and on my rare trips back to the old country, had found it unwelcoming and drab. I know they say it rains here every other day, but at least English summers are long and hot. The sky even in Dublin is permanently grey!

But what was I to do? There could have been suitors, if I'd wanted them. It was not uncommon to marry young. But the men available to me were old and infirm or young and broken in some way or other and at any rate, I wasn't in love with them. I know you might think me silly and romantic, my dear – I never was the practical sort – but if I was to marry, I wanted to marry only for love. And I had not by any means decided that I wanted to marry.

Life, from what I had so far seen, was short and hard and full of grief, except for those nights of joy and music where even my father threw his cap into the air and took my mother by the hands and spun her like a top until she laughed as if she'd never worked a single day in her life. I wanted more of those nights, my lover. I wanted to take life by the middle and wring every drop from it. And that, I was certain, was not going to happen in Shropshire. Or in Ireland.

I had lost most of four years of schooling working in the fields after my brothers' departure and later death and I had reached adulthood with a patchy education. The local priest at the country church where we had worshipped — a short man with a bald head that resembled a moon, whose outer appearance was quite different from his inner sensibilities — had taken a shine to me, and had provided continuing lessons in English literature, mathematics, a smidgeon of philosophy, geography and the sciences and assigned me books to read from his personal library. I read about equations and astronomy, history and geology, the breadth of the oceans and the spread of the earth around me, and I read about love, in books that I imagine most members of the church would never even have allowed in the house. Books that challenged and opened my mind to possibilities far beyond the borders of our own hedgerows. There was never a religious message in his teachings, nor any apparent effort to win my heart. Maybe he saw a kernel of brightness in me and considered it his pastoral duty to help. Maybe he too was trapped within the confines of his birth and living his real life within the far broader walls of his imagination. Kindred spirits appear in the strangest places.

Little did he know where this would lead me to!

By the time my parents had made their decision about the farm and the journey to the home country, I had a mind of my own and was fiercely opposed to the idea of joining them.

There were few alternatives: remaining in the countryside and finding employment as a maid on a local estate or moving to the nearest village with hope against hope I could fit in, but I knew that was doubtful. Villages are the same everywhere and whenever I'd had to venture through our local township's constantly muddy streets, I invariably felt the villagers looked down on me, the country girl, the Irish lass, as if I were an inferior form of species, when I was all too well aware that the step they occupied on the evolutionary ladder above me was just an inch apart from mine and that their disdain was totally unjustified.

I wanted more from life.

That seed of pleasure was already working away at me, hidden, insidious, an appetite begging to be fed. It was still unformed but its power had been growing since the spectacle of the crowds dancing in the barns had opened a window into the pleasures of the world in which I loved, but did not yet participate.

When I revealed my plans to my parents, they were profoundly shocked.

This was in 1921.

It would be another seven long years before women would obtain the right to vote in Britain. By which time I was, of course, old enough to vote, make love, be dissipated, seduce, manipulate the hearts of men, be as wicked and unrestrained as I wished.

I informed them I intended to travel to London and live there.

My mother cried, my father roared his disapproval and the arguments continued well into the night and lingered for a whole week.

A terrible fate would befall me if I ventured into such a den of iniquity, I was warned. A place that no woman alone should even consider visiting. Let alone unaccompanied. Even the entreaties of our priest who was summoned to the farm, bemoaning how I would be wasting my life if I persisted in my decision, failed to budge my persistence. I still remember the way the light shone on his bald head, and I couldn't take any of his remarks seriously, knowing as I did that he had built me up to this.

I had always been a particularly obstinate sort of person, and the efforts to dissuade me from the path I had decided to take only served to reinforce my determination.

You see, I had read so much about London, and it felt like another world, one of attraction and danger, of noises and crowds and colour the like of which we country folk didn't even have an inkling of.

It was the hustle, bustle and heartbreak of Charles Dickens, the dark, inviting alleys of The Strange Case of Dr. Jekyll and Mr. Hyde, the glamour and passions of Marie Corelli's popular romances. It drew me in like a moth to a flame. As if I knew already it would be more fun being a good time girl and participating fully in its excesses.

Maybe then I was just an impressionable young girl, but my feelings went beyond mere curiosity and the superficial appeal of modern cities. After the perpetual silence of the country, the big city felt like a challenge I had to attack, come to grips with. I was aware of its dangers, and the way I look at it now, they attracted me, the 'bad' part of me, the wanton side that lurked under my virginity and my dormant desires.

Neither God nor the Devil could have stopped me once I decided that London was the place for me. Or maybe the Devil was actually whispering in my ear and I was mistaking his voice for my free will? Then again, I've never had any faith in religion. I put my faith in other things. In my heart, and my heart drew me relentlessly towards London.

So it was in October that I arrived in the capital.

I carried a hold all in which my few belongings fitted, two spare dresses, a corset my mother had gifted me with before I left, a woollen nightdress, a handful of blouses and skirts that I had darned again and again over the years as they kept on falling apart at the seams, some shawls I was attached to and an extra set of cotton underwear, as well as a few coins which constituted my total fortune.

I had no idea when I would sleep that night. Or where.

To cut a long story short, I of course survived.

I experienced joy. Some sadness too. Not everything I did was right, by my own standards or in the eyes of others but I regret nothing. Until we met, my love.

I miss you.

I miss the vigour of your cock inside me.

I miss your words in my ears, your hands on my body.

And I wish I had told you so, before it was too late.

The street lights outside have been dimmed and the sky is clear of clouds, but it's getting dark. And colder by the minute. London without you is a dull place, despite its many charms, and if, as I fear, I do not hear from you again, I am thinking of leaving Britain and the memories behind. Going South somewhere maybe. My heart pulls me again, this time even further from home, to lands beyond the great oceans.

I am not even sure if I will post this letter.

At times sadness overwhelms me and makes me question why I am even writing these lines. But I will always hold on to that kernel of doubt.

Because there has to be a future.

I am carrying your child. I became aware of this barely three months after you had left for Europe to see if any of your family had survived.

I know it is still a most dangerous place and the bleakness of the afterwar appears to have swallowed you up and I am prey to the fear of having lost you.

I write it again: I am carrying your child.

Warmly and wantonly yours, my dear,

Joan

Clarissa was leaning against a lamp post outside, her back pressed flat against the metal girdle, one leg forward and the other bent with the toe of her boot resting on the footpath.

Spring

A half-smoked cigarette hung from her lips. Tucked under her elbow was a worn leather satchel. She was the picture of casual chic.

Joan, I recalled, had been drawn into the Ball by a red-haired woman with hair down to her ankles like a long flame who had met her by a lamp post outside a music hall in Piccadilly Circus. I had the sudden sense that though separated by decades, our experiences were converging, as though time were folding in on itself and drawing our worlds closer together.

I coughed, and Clarissa looked up.

'Well, well,' she said, examining me up and down, her eyes lingering on the silken sheen of my tuxedo trousers. 'Don't you look wonderful.'

'Thank you. I wasn't sure if you would like me to wear them, or not.'

'Dear girl!' she cried, drawing her body away from the post and standing at full height, 'of course I want you to. Did you think I bought them for you so they could sit in a cupboard? All you need now is a good haircut, but we'll leave that for another day. For now, let's drink, and talk, and be merry.'

She flicked the long nub of ash that balanced precariously on the edge of her cigarette and I watched it flutter like tiny grey snowflakes onto the footpath.

'Come on then,' she said, and proffered her arm to me. I

threaded mine through hers and we walked along Shaftesbury Avenue and into Soho, dancing between late-night drunks, couples walking hand in hand and occasional raucous groups of youngsters in search of the next best thing. I instinctively scanned each face that passed mine, searching for Iris among the crowds. She would have stood out here, a lone pale star amid the busy glittering throng, her quiet graceful beauty gleaming all the more bright against the gaudiness that surrounded us.

Clarissa pulled me towards the doorway of a basement bar that I would never have even noticed under ordinary circumstances. The steps downward were rickety and poorly lit, and inside it wasn't much better. Bare electric bulbs hung from the ceiling and cast a yellowed light not much more powerful than the flame of a candle. The room was oddly absent of any proper tables, but instead furnished with a mix of small coffee tables, most of them in carved Edwardian style with tall, curved legs and bulbed feet that gave them a Daliesque appearance, like an army of wooden spiders that might come to life at any moment. A wide, long bench seat ran along three walls, dotted with cushions and throws in shades of pale pink, yellow, and deep red with gold trim on which a handful of customers lounged. Painted wooden screens set up at irregular intervals interrupted the geometric straight lines of the place and added some booth-like privacy that could easily be removed when the tables were pushed aside and the bar was turned into a dance floor. Posters affixed to the walls advertised themed discotheques, thankfully occurring on other nights of the week. I was not in the mood for loud music. Tonight, music was notably absent, and just the low murmurs of whispered conversations filled the air. There was not even a jukebox.

'Not elegant, I know,' she told me, 'but intimate. Just what we need. You settle in, and I'll fetch drinks.' She pushed me towards at the back of the long, low-ceilinged room and I tucked myself onto the bench, rearranging my limbs several times until I found what I hoped was the most attractive position to any onlooker as I watched Clarissa order at the bar. Her waistcoat highlighted the squareness of her hips and sharp angularity of her broad shoulders, and her cropped hair elongated her neck. She swept her long fringe back behind her ear with one hand and then took the wine glasses that the bartender presented to her, one in each hand, and turned towards me.

The other patrons didn't even glance at her. I was astonished by this. To me, Clarissa brought a stage with her everywhere that she went. To see her walk across a room was to see her lit by an invisible light that cast the world around her into shadow. She was a butterfly in a sea of moths.

'Thank you,' I said, relieving her of one of the glasses so

that she could sit down without spilling the contents of the other.

'Now,' she said, 'my melancholy Moana. Tell me something I don't know about you. Tell me a secret.' She ran the tip of her finger around the length of her glass and I noticed for the first time that evening that her nails were painted bright red.

I thought of all the secrets I could tell and nearly laughed.

'What kind of secret?' I asked her.

'The kind that you're too afraid to tell anyone. Tell me and I'll forget I ever heard it, right away.'

'You might write it into a play.'

'Only if it's a very entertaining secret.'

'I'm in love with my room mate,' I blurted out. 'I watched her make love to a man. And now I can't think about anything else.'

A wide smile spread across Clarissa's lips and she leaned back against the sofa cushions.

'Oh. I confess, that is vastly more entertaining that I was expecting. Perhaps I shall indeed make you into a play. Tell me more. Tell me all about it.'

I told her first about growing up with Iris and how my feelings had been lustful from the outset. Of the nights that we shared huddled together in a single bed ('How charming,' Clarissa remarked), and the bedsit that we shared now, in Hammersmith, and Iris's job with the legal firm and how

Thomas had inconveniently appeared in our lives out of the blue.

She just sat and stared straight ahead into the distance, as if my words were playing out in front of her like a film on some invisible screen, and carried on playing the tips of her fingers against the wine glass. All of a sudden, as if it were nothing, she put the glass down and relocated her hand to my knee.

My voice faltered for a moment. Her touch was so warm, as if she had been standing too near a radiator. It crept right through my clothing and entered my veins, and like a candle flame blown by a gust of wind I felt my own heat rise up in response.

I told her how I had arrived home, the night after I had first met her and we had visited Patch's studio, and how Iris had been waiting for me, perched at the end of the bed in her borrowed outfit with that terrible look on her face and she had asked me to watch her with Thomas. I told her about the squat ottoman stool at the end of his bed that gave me such an obscene view, focused almost entirely on the lower part of their bodies, and how that particular angle seemed to throw them out of proportion in the low light, like a pair of tall shadows. The way that Iris had looked nude, like a lily flower with a single blossom. As if I were seeing her truly for the first time. Thomas, standing straight and tall in front of me as she sat, and my first true view of a man's cock – so smooth and rigid against the softness of his balls, and the firm pertness of his arse. How her lips had parted as he touched her, and she had turned pale and awkward, like a schoolgirl with her first crush.

'And is she very fond of you?' Clarissa asked me. I recognised the expression on her face as I had seen it on the faces of others many times before. Pity. Mixed with something else though, recognition and a kind of hunger. It cast her face into a strange masque and made her look older than she was, as though she had experienced too much already for her years.

'I don't know ...' I faltered. 'I think so.' I tried to remember the last time that Iris had told me she loved me and came up short. I could not recall the last time that I had spoken those words aloud to her either. More often I whispered my feelings to her in the privacy of my own mind, fearful that my tenderness would be unreturned and I would be made a fool. But I felt like a fool now. Why had I not told her how I felt? We shared a bed and a flat together but no longer the deepest recesses of our hearts.

It wasn't until Clarissa handed me a tissue that I realised I was crying.

She wound an arm around my shoulders and pulled me close against her and I was further overwhelmed by the heat of her body and richness of her fragrance and began to sob, my face pressed against the short crop of her hair as the tears fell. Clarissa hugged me tighter until I had cried myself out.

'More wine?' she asked. I had barely noticed finishing the last glass.

I shook my head.

'I suppose I should be going home.' I glanced around the room looking in vain for a clock, and noticed for the first time that the sketched charcoal drawings that decorated the walls were pornographic in nature and depicted men and women in various states of undress. I was no wiser about the time.

She squeezed my shoulders. 'Why don't you come back to my place?' she asked. 'It's perfectly warm and comfortable on the couch and I can't send you out into the night like this. Or indeed home. Iris will think we're mistreating you at the theatre . . .' she joked.

For a moment I thought of how Iris might react if she woke up alone and realised that I hadn't come home, and had not let her know my plans or left a note. I could hardly call the home phone now – it must be two in the morning, at least. And what would I say – that I was in a Soho bar with Clarissa, with another woman?

'Come on,' she said, 'a few more hours won't make a difference. I can call a cab for you before the sun rises. And you're not rostered on tomorrow, are you? You can sleep in, laze around all day.'

She brushed her fingers under my chin and lifted my face towards hers, and then she kissed me. I kissed her back without even thinking of Iris, such was the heat of Clarissa's mouth and the insistency of her touch.

The pads of her fingers arrived lightly on my hips, finding their way beneath my blouse and caressing my waist. Her grip was as gentle as a breath of wind, so gentle that it crept past the barrier of my guilt. Or perhaps it wasn't in fact guilt that I felt, but just the knowledge that I was not free. Despite the fact that I had witnessed my lover in bed with a man, the ties of my relationship with Iris bound me to her. Clarissa had deftly loosened those bonds.

I shifted in my seat and the pressure of her touch grew firmer. Her palms ran all the way up my body to the base of my neck and she pulled me against her.

A light alongside us began to flicker and I was struck by the illogical impression that somehow our rising energies had affected the electrical current. Or was it the spectre of Iris, physically absent but present in spirit? Clarissa's lean body cast a long, dark shadow across the pale hardwood floor. My tempter, in both body and spirit.

Clarissa guided me up the stairs ahead of her, with one hand pressed firmly against my tailbone, narrowly avoiding grabbing my arse. She threw her arm into the air the moment that we exited the bar into the now chill night, and a taxi skidded to a halt in front of us. The driver glanced at us once in the rear view mirror as Clarissa instructed him to take us to Brick Lane, and then he lit a cigarette and turned his attention back to the road. Clarissa gripped my knee, and I felt a sense of claustrophobia mixed with my rising arousal. I wound down the window an inch, seeking relief from the lingering scent of late-night takeaway snacks, cigarettes and cheap perfumes battling against upholstery cleaner in the small cab. The streets of the inner city, and then the East End unravelled before us and for a moment I forgot where I was and watched it all rush by, caught up in the sheer romance of London.

Brick Lane was eerily quiet. It was by now too late for all but the drunkest of partygoers, and too early for the market traders. We had arrived in that strangest of times between the night and the dawn when time seems to stop for those few who are awake when the rest of the world sleeps. A bird chirped, as if letting us know that we were not the only two out-of-place souls in the neighbourhood.

Clarissa took my hand, and pulled me along to her front door. She pressed her fingers to my lips.

'Shh!' she said, as she turned the key in the door. 'My partner is upstairs. He won't mind of course, but we'll need to be quiet. And keep the lights low.'

We stepped inside.

'Your p-partner?' I remembered at the last moment to

keep my voice down and the words came out in a high pitched hiss.

'Yes,' she whispered, 'Edward. He has an early start tomorrow ...'

'Oh ...'

I must have sounded surprised.

'Just because I fancy women, my dear,' Clarissa pointed out, 'doesn't mean I must deprive myself of male comforts ... We're even married, but partner is a much better word, isn't it?'

Her voice had a velvet quality to it that made her able to speak perfectly clearly in a low, hushed tone that would more easily lull a man to sleep than wake him up. I tried to do the same, but my shock made it nearly impossible not to shout.

I heard the flick of her lighter, and then the soft light of a candle appeared on the counter top. She removed my purse and set it down on a shelf alongside her own.

'I thought ...'

'As some would put it, I play on both sides.' Her grin was gloriously impish. She bent down and removed a liquor bottle from a wine rack that stood near the front door, and poured two strong measures into shot glasses. 'Why deny one's self anything good?' she continued. 'Wouldn't life be absolutely boring, if we just stuck to woman and woman, man and man. Mix it up, I say. Pleasure can be reached in so many different ways, you see.'

Spring

She handed me the drink and raised her own glass into the air.

'We don't have long. The sun will be up soon. Here's to pleasure . . .'

'To pleasure,' I replied, and knocked the shot back in one.

There was nothing soft about Clarissa's lovemaking. She was as different to Iris as night from day. She took my glass away as soon as I had swallowed, set it down on the counter and then took me into her arms and kissed me forcefully, her tongue edging between my lips and her fingers tangled in my hair as she walked me backwards until my legs knocked against a sofa and she pushed me onto it. I took in a vague impression of the room as we stumbled across it; the thick rolls of fabrics piled up, prints and pictures covering the walls and hung at haphazard angles, albums and books stacked in random piles around the room, no apparent order to anything. In the half-dark candlelight with everything blurred in shadow it seemed vaguely unreal, as if the contents of her mind had tumbled out onto the floor and morphed into her studio.

She unbuttoned my trousers and pulled them down and off in one swift motion. I felt her nails scrape against my hip bones as she hooked her thumbs in the sides of my knickers and yanked them down to my calves. Before I had a chance to even think of stopping her, she ducked her head down and placed her mouth on my slit. Her first lick was long, right from the base to the top. She ran her tongue lazily between my folds, sucked my lips, paused when she reached my nub and pressed there until I lifted my hips up in response and she grabbed my arse and held me against her face.

'Oh, god,' I muttered.

I had always felt a vague sense of discomfort around the thought of Iris going down on me. Iris's licks were tentative and gentle, and I harboured the suspicion, and the fear, that she did not enjoy giving oral sex. I always felt like I ought to be the one giving Iris pleasure, and not the reverse.

Clarissa ate me with such gusto that I forgot my fears. When I instinctively closed my knees together to cover myself, vicing her between them, she spread me open again. When I drew my palms over my face, covering my mouth to quiet my moans, she reached up and grabbed my hands and directed them to her head, silently directing me to press her against my groin. When I complied, winding my fingers into her hair and applying gentle pressure to her head, she responded by burying her tongue deep inside me. I pushed harder, clamping her against me, and began to grind. Muffled sounds escaped from her lips.

Now, I no longer felt as though I was in a position of vulnerability, submitting to Clarissa's demands on my body. A thrill ran through me, warming my veins and freeing my inhibitions. I held her down and drove my pussy against her face and the more firmly I did so, the swifter and deeper her strokes became. Her saliva mixed with my juices, a cocktail of lust, and ran down the valley of my cunt where it pooled on the sofa beneath me, wetting my buttocks. My heat rose as I listened to the sound that our bodies made, the slap of damp skin on leather, the low humming growl she made in her throat, the scraping of my fingernails clutching the furniture.

She paused, giving me momentary relief from the onslaught of sensations that her caresses elicited. I teetered on the brink of overstimulation, caught between intense pleasure and pain. I exhaled, felt my muscles relax and just as my heightened arousal began to ebb she wet her finger and slid it gently into my arse. Her tongue returned to my clitoris, trailing around my fully exposed nub in a slow, circular motion. My whole body tensed again and I shuddered and came and she ignored my attempts to pull her away and held me to her, licking me over and over until the first wave of my climax subsided and another built up, layer over layer, and I came again.

Finally, she released me, and I lay back against the couch, spent. Before I could properly catch my breath, she flipped me over onto my front. I wriggled, pushing myself up onto my knees and turning to face her and she placed her hand onto the small of my back.

'Stay still,' she whispered. 'We're not finished yet.'

She leaned over to one side and pulled a wooden box out from under the sofa. Its hinges creaked when she opened it. She lifted out the object inside as delicately as if she was handling a dangerous weapon. Squinting in the half light, with Clarissa's body partly blocking my view, I could not make it out entirely, but I could see that it was dark, and phallic-shaped.

'Have you ever been penetrated, Moana?' she asked me. She didn't look at me when she spoke. Her eyes remained fixed on the dildo in her hands. As she held it up, I was struck by its size and glossy black sheen. I had never even seen a dildo, though of course I knew such things existed and had even fantasised about using one on Iris.

'No,' I told her.

'Would you like to be?'

Again, I thought of Iris, but my thoughts of her were tinged with bitterness as well as guilt. I knew that she would never penetrate me, what was the point in saving myself for her? Especially since I had come this far already.

I nodded. 'Yes,' I said.

Clarissa's eyes gleamed.

'My harness is upstairs ...' she explained. 'Another time, I will fuck you properly. For now, a gentle introduction ...'

I could not imagine a gentle Clarissa.

I positioned my body in the same way that I had seen Iris

do when Thomas took her from behind. On all fours, back dipped like a cat's, sucking my stomach in. I tensed, waiting for the pain. My mind raced, expectant.

'Relax ...' she murmured. Her voice was soft, soothing, but it was almost impossible to let go. I felt as though I was on the edge of a precipice, about to fall over into another world. As if the next few seconds would alter the course of my life.

The dildo inside me felt better than I had ever imagined. I groaned.

'That's it,' Clarissa said, 'you like to be fucked, don't you?'

'Oh god yes, yes,' I replied. I pushed my arse back against her as she thrust inside me. In my mind it was Clarissa fucking me. Her dildo was just as real as any cock. That it was not physically attached to her and made of flesh and bone made no difference at all. I clung onto a cushion and bit into it to stop myself from screaming. She pushed it inside me, her thrusts alternating short and long, hard and gentle, until her arm began to tire.

'You're an insatiable little slut,' she remarked, as she withdrew the toy. 'Hard to imagine that you're a virgin.'

'Was,' I corrected her.

'True enough,' she said. 'I suppose that depends on your definition. Have you ever thought of fucking a man? Would you like to?'

I remembered the vision of Thomas standing in front of me, his buttocks firm and his dick hard. It wasn't an unpleasant thought, although I found his naked body an unfamiliar sight. I never fantasised about men. Physically, they just didn't attract me in the way that women did. And yet I was curious about how a penis would feel inside me. If it would be warm, softer than a dildo, I assumed, less rigid. If it would feel different to be taken by a man.

'I might consider it, I suppose,' I told her.

'Maybe we could arrange it sometime,' she said lightly, as if she was talking about arranging a dinner date or a card game.

I wanted to ask her more about her relationship with her partner and what arrangement she had with him. Questions tumbled onto the tip of my tongue. Did he too have sex with other women? Or other men? Did they have sex with other people as a couple? Had she just invited me to a threesome? I blushed at the thought, and I wondered if Edward had heard our maybe not so muted cries. It was possible that he had even come down the stairs to investigate, perhaps even watched us from above while we were entirely preoccupied with each other and unaware of his presence. A surge of excitement rushed through me at the thought that we might have been witnessed by Clarissa's husband, in flagrante.

But now was not the time for more questions. I stretched

my arms lazily over my head and looked up. Rays of sunlight shone through a high window. I sat bolt upright, suddenly aware of the time.

'Shall I call you a cab?' Clarissa asked.

'Please,' I replied, glancing at her warmly to convey my gratitude. She was still fully dressed. A sheen of sweat coated her brow. Her eyes were tired.

'I ... I'm sorry,' I said to her. 'I've been terribly selfish. Would you like me to ...'

She laughed. 'Very sweet of you, but the moment has rather passed now, I think. And besides that, no. I very much enjoyed introducing you to the joys of sex ... and no need to worry about me. I will have a nap, and then seek Edward out later.'

She handed me my clothes and a banknote for the taxi ride.

'I would of course offer you a shower, and breakfast, but time is ticking on, and I know you must get back to your love.'

The clock on the cab's meter read 6 a.m. I told the driver that I was in a hurry, and he sped across London, through mostly clear streets. The early morning traffic had not yet begun to pile up.

I turned the key in the door as quietly as I could manage, thankful that Iris was a heavy sleeper.

Her head lay still on the pillow as I removed my clothes

and slipped into bed alongside her, hoping against hope that I smelled only of a night out – cigarette smoke and a note of alcohol that might have come from anywhere – and not of Clarissa.

She didn't stir, and when I woke again, her side of the bed was empty.

4

Ghost Dancers

Summer came.

His parents were spending the time in the Caribbean and Thomas had opted to stay in London, but had access to their house in the Chilterns. For several weeks now, he had been singing the praises of the mansion, with its vast grounds and nearby woods, outdoor heated swimming pool, inviting nooks and crannies and luxurious amenities. He had allegedly been planning the garden party for several weeks already and had, naturally, invited Iris, and by default, me.

I was reluctant to go, if only for the reason that it would mean missing out on two whole days of work at the Princess Empire, which I could ill afford to do. But then I was also wary of Iris being away for a whole weekend with Thomas. Maybe I feared she would not return and would move in with him if I were not around, a constant reminder of what

125

we still shared, emotionally and physically, despite his increasing, obtrusive presence in our lives.

When she heard about it, Clarissa insisted I go.

'The theatre will still manage without you,' she said. 'You haven't taken a day off ever since you began, anyway. You're owed. It will do you good. A change of scene. Some real-life glamour, away from our tinsel-lined imitation game.'

Sensing my reluctance, she suggested I take Gwillam along. She had been particularly amused when she had learned the story of my reunion with this long-lost cousin.

In addition, Iris genuinely appeared keen for me to join her, as if she was still uncertain about the true state of her relationship with Thomas. 'I might like him but I still need you too,' she confessed. 'You're my anchor. Maybe it means I'm greedy, but what the hell; who ever said it was wrong to want one's cake and eat it too?'

I called Gwillam at his law firm but was told he had a few days off and I had no other way to contact him.

We left London as night fell. Both Thomas and Iris had hurried home from their workplace to pick up hastily packed holdalls with clothes for the weekend. I'd had all day to prepare and wait, and already felt unsettled at the prospect of the next two days. Iris had mentioned that the party would be quite glamorous, with politicians, celebrities and even film stars present, and seemed taken by the idea. I wasn't.

Spring

We heard the sound of the horn of Thomas's small double-parked Renault 4CV below our window, the signal we had agreed, and rushed down to the street where we fitted ourselves into the vehicle.

'Ready for an adventure?' Thomas asked.

'Absolutely,' Iris replied, ignoring me and settling in the left front seat next to him, while I sat at the back crowded into a corner by an uncommon amount of luggage. How much stuff did Thomas need?

We crossed the river and crawled past the West End through Holborn until Camden Town. Beyond was unknown territory to me. Thomas pointed out Hampstead and the outskirts of the Heath as we climbed a steep hill and then the passing vistas outside the open car window blurred into darkness and a twisting maze of tree-lined roads until we finally emerged into the countryside and a straight road that seemed to continue forever. It was rush hour and the traffic was heavy.

An hour later, we turned off the busy main road and found ourselves driving down a narrow lane between a canopy of leaning trees that made me think of the entrance to a fairy-tale wonderland, and still the journey into darkness continued.

'This is it,' Thomas cried out. On the passenger seat at the front, Iris stirred back into life. She had been dozing.

There was another lane, narrower than the first, on our

left, with just enough space for a car to advance in single file. We ventured down it at lesser speed. I wondered what would happen if another vehicle came towards us; there was just no room for two cars to manoeuver without scraping against each other. The lane was boarded with high hedges behind which a vastness of fields stretched into the night.

For ten minutes we drove down the exiguous lane. There was no light, but Thomas's driving was assured and steady.

Then, the path broadened and we were moving on gravel, a crunching sound below our wheels shuddering through the car's thin bodywork and vibrating across our bodies. Ahead, I could distinguish the squat shape of a huge building, with just a few random lights on. The mansion looked like something out of the movies, regal, tall with a rampart of whitewashed stucco dotted by an infinity of windows. There were half a dozen cars parked in front. Each one more luxurious than the other.

'Home, sweet home,' Thomas said, parking the diminutive Renault on the gravel drive at a right angle to a sleek, shiny, fire-red Italian sports car. 'My sister's chariot,' he said.

'What does she do?' Iris asked.

'Something in fashion,' Thomas replied. 'It's just a hobby, though. She has rich lovers . . .' And laughed.

He had never mentioned having a sister before, that I recalled. Not to me at any rate. Maybe Iris was aware of her existence. But my friend remained silent, visibly in awe of the building in front of which we now sat.

'Actually,' he added, 'Tilly's the one who is organising the party ...'

A further revelation.

'Is she older than you?' I felt compelled to ask, my curiosity tickled.

'Oh yes. Four years older. Tilly stands for Matilda. I've always called her that. She hates the nickname, which is why I keep on using it. But best if you refer to her by her real name when you meet,' Thomas advised.

We picked up our stuff from the boot and filed up the short flight of steps that led to the mansion's main door, which was held open and revealed a bonfire of light beyond the darkened threshold. I heard the purr of further cars advancing across the gravel path behind us and parking at random angles. Large and expensive ones, I knew, just from the cushioned rumble of their powerful engines.

Thomas's own pieces of luggage seemed to weigh a ton and he advanced with mighty caution.

'What have you got in the cases that's so heavy?' Iris asked him.

'Evening dresses for both of you,' he said. 'I don't assume you had brought any along, had you?'

Neither of us even owned an evening dress. Anyone could have guessed that, but his presumption annoyed me.

We followed him haltingly through a network of boulevard-like staircases followed by a criss-cross of identical narrow low-ceilinged corridors winding their way under what appeared to be the roof and finally reached our room. We were being housed together, we discovered. Somehow, I (and Iris?) had previously assumed we would be lodged separately, and that she would be staying with Thomas.

Noting our surprise, 'Propriety . . .' he said with a faint smile passing his lips.

We stumbled into the room, hunting for the light switch and dropping our holdalls to the floor, while Thomas struggled further along the corridor.

'I'm down the end,' he indicated, his back already to us.

I was about to slam the door closed behind us when he shouted out: 'Be ready for midnight!'

'Midnight?' Iris queried.

'In those lovely evening dresses, ladies, remember! As soon as I've unpacked, I'll bring them by your door. Don't forget . . .' He faded away.

'I wonder what they're like,' Iris remarked, visibly excited.

'I just hope he has taste and we don't have to parade like floozies,' I added.

Iris was freshening up in the bathroom when I heard the shuffle of feet behind the door.

'I think he's dropped our outfits off,' I said to her when she stepped back into the room.

She rushed to collect them.

'Incredible!' she shouted out, tiptoeing back holding two large Biba carrier bags under her arms.

I knew it was not only a classy label but the hippest around according to the fashion magazines scattered in the dressing room that I sometimes leafed through on my breaks. How much had this cost him? Or were the dresses just hired? And the thought then occurred to me: had he got our sizes right?

Iris excitedly threw the bulky bags down onto the bed and tipped them over to empty their contents on the dark chenille throw.

The glossy garments that tumbled out came in two colours and the styles appeared identical. I opted for the pale yellow confection and Iris for the pink one.

The material felt like cotton to the touch, but stretched across the skin in an uncommon manner, highlighting every curve and dip of our bodies. And the dresses were an uncanny fit, adhering to our frames as if tailored to be a second skin. Strapless, cut in a sharp V at the front unveiling a long, thin valley of flesh, the dresses held our breasts in place in an invisible cup of reinforced material giving the illusion of defying gravity. Then the expensive material descended all the way down to our waists with the grace

131

and elegance of flowing folds of lapping waves, where it held us firmly in without the ungainly visible constraints of a corset. The midriffs were cinched and below the dresses flared out like flowers, all the way down to our knees. The shoes that also dropped out of the bag Thomas had left for us matched in colours, stylish and elegant, shiny, evidently brand-new, perilously high-heeled too.

We helped each other into the garments, marvelling at the silkiness of the material, how sensual it was both to our touch and against our bare skin.

'It feels too good to wear,' Iris said. After the initial try-out, she'd shed the dress and was now standing in her knickers, having jettisoned her ill-matching brassiere which couldn't been worn under the dress without exposing its clumsy straps and plain pattern. 'I wish I had something else I could have on underneath.'

I picked up the crumpled Biba bag from the bedspread and turning it upside down anew, shook it, hoping there was still some treasure left deep in its bulging depths. As if by magic, a breeze of yellow and pink silk, translucent lingerie floated down.

I couldn't believe that Thomas had such feminine foresight. Surely it must be his sister Matilda who was at the bottom of all this.

Again, the panties fitted us perfectly. They were so light that it felt as if we were wearing nothing and, at the same time, that our skin was sheathed in a fabric made of air.

'We're going to be princesses,' Iris giggled, recalling past childish games in New Zealand. I smiled, although inwardly I was gritting my teeth. I wasn't a princess kind of girl, and felt awkward, out of place and over-exposed in such frippery.

I caught a glimpse of my watch.

'There's barely an hour to go to midnight,' I noted.

'Oh dear,' Iris said. 'We must wash. Do something about our hair. We can't go looking like this, can we?'

Further surprises awaited us in the bathroom. An impossible selection of lotions, creams, perfumes, combs, shampoos, conditioners, brushes, make-up compacts, lipsticks and powders straight out of a Hollywood movie and an avalanche of mirrors in all shapes and sizes in which to perfect our looks for tonight. Nothing had been left to chance.

We dived in and pampered ourselves outrageously.

Iris washed her hair and I brushed it for her. She was bubbling with barely suppressed energy, excited and vibrant. I wanted to pull her into bed right there and then, intoxicated by her urchin beauty and the thousand new smells of her. Stroke after stroke of the ivory-handled hairbrush travelling across her delicate scalp, me standing above her and observing how the tips of her nipples were so visibly hardening with every additional movement of my hand. There are times when you wish that the world would freeze and stay that way forever. This was one of them.

Then it was my turn and Iris scrubbed me, washed me, rubbed me clean and sculpted my hair into a shape we hoped would be sophisticated enough to match the garment I'd be wearing.

'I want you to be psychedelic,' Iris exclaimed, her excitement just short of erupting madly. Thomas had taken her just a couple of weeks previously to a concert in a theatre on Shaftesbury Avenue by a new American guitar ace called Jimi Hendrix who had ended his set by setting fire to his guitar. Since then she referred to everything as psychedelic!

She began foraging through the bathroom cabinet's cave of wonders, hunting for glitter and colour, but I stopped her.

'I'm not going to the party as a rainbow,' I warned.

'Oh . . .'

Her eyes begged me.

'It would be so much fun . . .'

'No way.'

Even I had limits.

October 31st, 1921, London

Dear diary; I have neglected you these past three weeks – can you believe it's been just three weeks? It feels so much longer, as if

134

time takes longer to pass here, each minute an hour because I'm sucking the marrow from every second.

So much has happened in that short time.

There was a terrible chill in the air tonight, a prelude to the coming winter. But oh, I didn't care a bit, because I was in London, properly in London for the first time. Not just physically here, but out in it, the whole city whirling around Gladys and me like a tornado revolving around the eye of a storm.

Mrs Moorcroft didn't suspect a thing when I snuck out. And why should I need to justify my movements to the landlady? So long as I pay my rent on time and keep the place clean, that should be all that matters. The room is about as big as our larder was at home, the bed is so short that my feet hang over the end (even though I'm only five foot four) and the mattress is so sunken that I feel sometimes like I'm resting on the floor. I know I ought to be grateful for it because even in this modern world it's not easy to find suitable accommodation in London, especially when you're a woman, and with no husband or father in tow. I am sure that Mrs Moorcroft thought I was a working girl, when I first arrived.

'No funny business is allowed,' she said, as I followed her up those rickety stairs, praying they wouldn't collapse beneath the weight of her enormous backside. 'You could rest your tea cup and saucer on that,' my father would have said, of course when he thought that I wasn't listening. You would never have believed she's been on rations. She must have been hoarding butter and sugar in her apron skirts.

Mrs Moorcroft's lodgings also shelters five other tenants, a mournful war widow, so thin she is almost invisible, two middle-aged and red-faced cooks from up North who toil together in church kitchens near Clapton Pond, another Irish lass whose family has fallen on bad times and who is studying to become an articled clerk, and an elderly relative of our landlady, ever dressed in black and lurking in a corner, watching us as we go about our business.

It is not a cheerful environment.

It is easy enough to pretend that I too am a youthful war widow and pull on Mrs Moorcroft's heartstrings and I do so unashamedly, although it hurts me to use the lost lives of our loved ones in vain. Especially for a cramped little wardrobe of a bedroom in unfashionable Islington such as this. But at least there is a basin where I can wash my face at night without needing to walk all the way down the corridor – so narrow it feels like the walls are preparing to swallow me up – to the house bathroom, and a crooked shelf where I can set a pot of flowers to brighten the air and store my books. I've brought precious few with me, since they made my case so heavy and it seems like madness to fill what little space I have with novels and poetry. And yet, I do anyway, for what use is worrying about clothing the body, if the soul needs feeding? I often pick them up and run my finger down the lettering on the spine and put them back on the shelf again. I had agonised over which volumes to bring more than anything else. In the end, I chose three. Edith Wharton's 'Age of Innocence', a falling-apart, battered copy of which I had found abandoned on a train seat just weeks previously, L. Frank

Spring

Baum's 'Magic of Oz' – even though I was a little ashamed of reading children's books, still, I loved that tale, a belated one but my favourite in the series – and a popular romance that I won't even tell you the title of, my dear diary, in case you should think me silly, or worse, immoral. Reading certain pages of it makes me even warmer at night-time than sitting in front of Mrs Moorcroft's fireplace in the plushly carpeted living room, even though I blush to admit it.

Before I left home, Father Kelly had given me a page that he'd torn from a magazine – sent to him by a relative, all the way from New York – with a poem by Robert Frost that I had pinned next to my bed.

I roll the sweet, affecting words of the poem around on my tongue as soon as I wake each morning, and before I am overtaken by sleep each night. Now I feel as though I can taste desire, or at least I might, if given the chance. London is on my doorstep at last, and desire is on the tip of my tongue. It was such an odd choice of poem to gift me with; I wondered, and not for the first time, what it was that Father Kelly saw in me that led him to educate me so, but I was grateful for it nonetheless.

I sleep with the window open, no matter what the weather. It's only the size of a handkerchief so doesn't let in much rain, and mostly the wind just slides by under the eaves. I like the sound of the sputtering cars rushing by, and even the scent of the traffic fumes from Islington High Street below.

Do you think me odd? I asked Gladys, the first time I showed her my room, and she flicked through my books, stared at my poetry on the wall, and stood on her tiptoes to peep out of my little window. She wore a bright red, fringed scarf and had pulled it up around her neck and cheeks to ward off the cold, blocking her face from me.

'You just are who you are,' she replied.

I thank my stars that I met her on my first day, arriving into London's teeming Euston, the London and North Western Railway mainline station, at last with my old striped suitcase, a hand-me-down from my father, so battered that the clasps broke apart as I tried to drag it up the stairs. She appeared right then with my scattered smalls in her hands, like an angel out of nowhere, though if there are angels, I doubt they are even shorter than I am with ginger hair and freckled complexions and voices that would have better suited a market trader in the East End. Without her, I'd have been on the street that night I suppose, instead of tucked safely alongside her in her single bed in the room she rented, just a few blocks up from the Angel and right alongside St Mary's Church. 'I don't go to church,' Gladys told me, with her shoulders back and her chin jutting out, 'I don't believe in all that God nonsense. I make my own luck. And besides, it's creepy, that big tall spire looming over everything.' I decided that we would be friends, right then.

What a strange feeling it was, sharing a bed with a woman. I wondered if that was what it was to have a sister. And yet my heart tells me that lying alongside a sister wouldn't have felt quite like

*that. Gladys's hair so soft and with that strange fragrance to it —
she told me she used raw egg as conditioner. That seemed so daring
to me, I could only imagine what my mother would have thought
of wasting good eggs on hair. 'Think of all the hungry children,' she
would say, tutting at me when I didn't manage to clear my dinner
plate.*

*The work at 'Butler and Butler, Garment Repair and Tailoring'
is hard, harder even than work in the fields, since there's a sort of
closed in feeling of being stuck indoors and the whole place smells
acrid, like it needs a good airing. Sitting down all the time at a
sewing machine is more tiresome than standing up, even more tiresome than turning earth over with a hoe. But Gladys is there too,
and I'm grateful she got me the job. Chatting to her takes my mind
off things, and it's only up in Highbury, a half hour's brisk walk
along Upper Street and left at Highbury corner. Next door there's
a cake shop painted all red and white that sells the most delicious
lardy cakes, even better than those my mother makes, although I
would never admit that to her, and even the nicest cake in London
wouldn't take my mind off the work as a seamstress. When I close
my eyes at night-time, I still hear the whirring of the needle moving
at such a pace, and sometimes my foot twitches up and down as if
I'm making a shirt in my sleep.*

*Gladys is friendly with Harold Butler Jnr, the son of Mr.
Butler who owns the shop where she works. He's a horrid creature
with a flat face like a pug dog and a squat round body with bandy
legs that make him look like a frog walking upright. He hadn't*

been allowed to sign up, or so he said, because of his legs, and he carries a cane everywhere he goes to aid with his 'condition' but he never seems to use it. He lets Gladys call him Harold, but the rest of us have to say 'Mr. Butler'. He was never 'Harry', even to his own father. The shop was originally called just 'Butler and Co.' but Mr. Butler junior had insisted on the change, which was why half the lettering on the sign that hangs outside is now faded, and the other half black and bold. To save money, they'd only repainted part of it.

I couldn't understand why Gladys bats her eyelids modestly at the young Mr. Butler when he leers at her, which of course makes him leer at her even more. We had our first row over it. 'Don't encourage him!' I hissed at her, and she called me a jealous little fool and a country girl, and told me to shut my trap. Then he promoted her from the machine line work of men's shirts and trousers onto the more delicate, tailored luxury items, and put her pay up to boot. I was still angry with her, and angrier still with myself for being so naive.

Of course, there's no other way we could have put our Halloween costumes together. Despite her rise, neither of us had a farthing clear at the end of our outgoings, and me least of all since I'd had to wait a fortnight for my first pay packet.

She was using him, I knew that, and took some satisfaction from the fact that she didn't really fancy him. 'Why would you care if I fancied him anyway?' she asked me, and I couldn't answer her. 'I fancy loads of lads,' she insisted, and proceeded to *list them until I growled at her to stop. The butcher, the baker, the candlestick maker – she recited the rhyme to me, turned on its head. 'We need to introduce you to some gentlemen, country girl,' she told me. 'Not just men – I'm going to introduce you to the world.' She had a plan, she said. A secret. 'What is it?' I asked, 'Well it wouldn't be a secret if I told you, would it?' she mocked me.*

Finally, she confessed what she'd been up to.

'You're stealing,' I hissed at her, as she prised up the loose floorboard in the lunchroom – I'd heard it creak dozens of times as I walked over it and never even thought to guess at what might lie beneath – and she'd showed me the pile of fabric she'd stealthily accumulated. Sequins that would have been affixed onto expensive dresses and sold up West in swanky stores to rich women. Yellow and pink chiffon, can you imagine! A proper treasure horde of the stuff.

'Rubbish,' she retorted. 'I'm just topping up our wages. You know we don't get paid enough. There's men sweeping the streets who take home twice as much as we do. Besides, these are last season's colours, the stuff didn't sell well. No one will miss it.' I was still unsure. 'You won't tell, will you, promise me Joan, you must promise me?' she begged. Well, of course I had to go along with it, she was my only friend in the world.

'There's enough for you too,' she said, 'if we're careful with the stitching, and make the skirts short.' She giggled.

Even after a whole day at work, sitting and sewing by hand in

141

the dim light in my quarters didn't feel like a chore. We made masks, too, from cardboard with a tiny piece of precious silk glued on, and pink feathers from Mrs Moorcroft's feather duster.

We could only make the costumes stretch over both of us by cutting them terribly low, and frightfully short. If there had been a large enough mirror in my room, I don't think I could have glanced in it without blushing. I could only look at Gladys with her hair swept up into a knot and her earrings dangling – she'd made them so cleverly, with buttons fixed to regular hoops – and a daring coat of rouge over lips, and imagine that I was the dark haired version of her image. She had taken the yellow, and me the pink. We looked wonderful, I thought, but dear me how my heart raced as I imagined being seen like this by someone I knew.

For one night, tonight (yesterday now, since it's the early hours of the morning, diary), I became a different person. And oh what fun it was. The day Joan and the night Joan. It was like meeting a whole new version of myself that I had never even known existed. And a whole new version of London. As if the inner city with all its pomp and ceremony, the calm and grandeur of St Paul's Cathedral and Westminster and all the horror of the Tower were just a day-time spectacle and after dark she lifted up her skirts and displayed her underbelly to us.

We had no spare coins for the bus so put our sturdy working boots on (the only pair of shoes I owned, in fact) and walked up the Gray's Inn Road and through Bloomsbury to Drury Lane. Gladys carried a small hold-all with a pair of shoes for each of us to change *into, heels and all (I didn't dare ask where they had come from!). We were both shrouded in long white workman's coats that Gladys had 'borrowed' from her father who owned a butcher's shop near Epping Forest and we had wrapped scarves over our heads to hide our elaborate hair dos. We must have looked a sight to behold, like a pair of fishwives set loose from their market stall.*

Nobody minded us though. It was Halloween! Even the moon was full and bold tonight, shining overhead like a stamp of approval on our planned hijinks.

'I want to be an actress,' Gladys announced, as we walked over the Holborn Viaduct, its ornate red-painted iron work casting strange, gothic shadows onto the road beneath our feet. The winged lions crouching at either end paid us no attention at all. 'I'll be Gladys Nightingale,' her voice rang out, 'the next Betty Balfour, but better.' She pirouetted on the spot, as if her heavy shoes were dancing slippers and her white coat a ball gown. 'That's not your real name,' I scolded her. 'How do you know?' she asked me. 'It's my real name from now on, because I say so.'

We would both be women of the world ... no, actresses, we decided. So much more glamorous than the life of a seamstress. No more pin pricks, no more whirring sewing machine dreams, no more Harold Butler Jnr.

'We'll go to the West End and audition, seek out one of those fancy theatres and dazzle them with our charm and beauty,' Gladys said. 'But first, we'll go dancing.'

And oh, how we danced.

We were just about ready when there was a knock at our door.

Thomas.

'Wow! You both look great . . .'

He was wearing a sober, traditional black tuxedo with shiny lapels and a purple bow tie, with his hair severely combed back. The sort of proper young man you could take back to your mother, had it not been for the glint of mischief in his eyes that kept on annoying me.

He led us anew through the maze of corridors and imposing staircases until we reached the mansion's ground floor, but this time around we ended up at the back of the building, at the opposite end to the high ceilings of the entrance hall facing the gravel-laced area where the cars had arrived and parked.

The room was large enough to function as a dance hall, but it was empty. Just a wilderness of crystal chandeliers, bottomless mirrors and an endless swath of bay windows, all opened and leading into the sloped gardens beyond.

Trees, a field of torches burning bright illuminating the landscape and a chessboard of white tents fluttering in the night breeze.

Couples were dancing, like ghosts in the flickering, shadowy darkness, weaving patterns across the gardens, knitting shapes and drawing unseen hieroglyphics into the freshly mown grass in their wake, its distinctive aroma rising through the night air towards me, reminding me of home and raising a torrent of memories. Most of the women dancing wore diaphanous gowns that put our own outfits to shame and moved with a nonchalant grace to the strains of the light jazz music being piped out through unseen speakers. The men led, with a quiet authority, their backs rigid and unbending as if on parade, and some even wore uniforms while the others were a symphony of black evening wear, tuxedos, dinner suits, tunics with not a fold out of place.

'Ah, those must be your little friends . . .'

The voice was sharp and crystal clear, both ironic and detached.

I turned round. Still holding on to Iris's hand for dear life, as if conscious of the threat approaching us.

She was terribly tall and her deep even tan held the perfect balance between London pallor and sunburn; her lipstick was a slash of fervent scarlet across thick, greedy lips. Her eyes were concrete grey. Her dress ran across her body like a shroud of silk, cobalt blue, shimmering with every movement she made, and her long black hair trailed all the way down to the small of her back, catching distant reflections of moonlight in its straight, shiny lines as it did so. She was striking, in a feral sort of way, I felt. The sort of beauty that came with centuries of breeding and an endless source of money.

'Tilly!'

'Dear brother.'

She looked down at us, haughty, critical.

Disappointed.

'I'm Matilda.' She introduced herself. Then as an aside to her brother, 'Oh Thomas, they're so cute, but I don't think you'd make a very good pimp, would you? I concede they might be jolly fun between the sheets, but it's just not the standards our guest are accustomed to. Really.'

Thomas blushed, was about to say something but she disdainfully moved on to greet another couple who were making their way from the mansion into the gardens, her voice now effusive.

'What did she mean, Thomas?' Iris asked him.

'Don't worry,' he attempted to reassure her. 'She has it quite wrong. I brought you here as friends, not in any other function.' But there was something about the hesitant tone of his voice that failed to convince me.

He pointed to a large marquee a hundred yards further down the gardens.

'You must surely be hungry,' he said.

We stepped away from the improvised dance floor towards it, leaving the geometric waltz of the assorted dancers behind us, caught in their repetitive rotations, slaves to the music.

My stomach rumbled. I was actually starving, not having

had a bite of anything since breakfast now fifteen or so hours ago.

A huge trestle table was laden with breads of all type, cold cuts, cheeses, sumptuous slices of smoked salmon, chicken thighs, and even caviar. I made a beeline for it, seized a large porcelain plate and piled samples high on it and retreated to a wicker chair to stuff myself like a pig. Iris and Thomas stood in another corner, seemingly arguing, neglecting the bountiful manna.

As I sat eating, I watched guests wandering in and out of the breezy tent. The men always appeared older than the women, I noted. There was also something submissive, almost obsequious in the way most of the women, the girls, were responding to the conversation or words addressed to them, giggling, smiling, feigning coy. All the female guests I could observe, during their brief passage through the food tent, were undeniably beautiful but in a too-perfect sort of way, it appeared to me. As if they'd been gleaned, brown-haired, auburn, blonde, night-black, leggy, sporty, lanky, curvaceous, from the anonymity of a luxury catalogue.

That was it, I realised: as if they were hired out for the occasion, or even on sale. Something about the way they walked, held their heads, reacted to the men on whose arms they paraded.

I recognised the face of one of the men passing by. I was

certain I had seen his features in the newspapers, several times; but I struggled for his name.

Iris and Thomas had now ceased their minor altercation and came over to me, each holding a plate with merely half the amount of food I'd amassed on mine.

'Drinks?' Thomas suggested and it dawned on me that I'd been so famished I hadn't even noticed the absence of liquid sustenance in the marquee.

'Oh yes. Where is it kept?' I looked around.

'Not here. A bar has been set up by the pool, I gather,' Thomas said.

I was mighty thirsty. All the smoked salmon I'd stuffed down my gullet had opened a chain reaction in my mouth that called for water, or better.

'Tilly always chooses the best champagne,' he added.

'That sounds just delicious,' said Iris, whose mood had radically improved. What could they have been discussing, I wondered? Juggling our plates, we left the marquee and headed further down the immense gardens, following the trail of burning torches until the path turned into a row of high bushes garlanded with fairy lights in an assortment of bright colours.

Arriving at the swimming pool felt like emerging from a maze, as the bushes grew closer and closer, carving a passage that grew increasingly narrow as we approached.

'There is a more direct way,' Thomas revealed as we

caught a first sight of the large kidney-shaped pool, 'in a straight line from the house, but this is so much more quaint, isn't it?'

'Unless you're dying of thirst . . .' I complained.

Isolated couples stood around the pool's perimeter; others lounged on white deckchairs, deep in conversation or haloed in silence. At the far end stood a low marble table on which white sheets had been draped and a crazy assortment of bottles had been scattered. A tall, shaven-headed black valet was dispensing the drinks.

'Champagne for all,' Thomas ordered.

The attendant set to serving us, uncorking a new bottle with deft ritual movements.

He handed us our drinks. The liquid bubbled happily, generously flirting away with the rim of the delicate, elongated glass.

'Is this crystal?' Iris asked, pointing to her champagne glass.

'Nothing but the best,' Thomas confirmed. 'Crystal glasses for Krystal champagne . . .' Back home in New Zealand, the few pieces of crystal in our family home were only brought out for special occasions like birthdays, marriages and funerals.

I took a tentative initial sip. It was divine. Fizzy, sweet and sharp, flowing past my tongue, lingering and reluctantly making its way down my throat, and I was instantly ready to take a second sip and taste it even longer. I briefly tried to think of further occasions when quality champagne could be savoured from now onwards, already a potential addict.

I looked up. The liquid gold was having a similar effect on Iris. She shone in the pale moonlight, her dainty silhouette a shadow within her dress, the shape of her body a mass of yearning for my senses and sensibility. But she was looking up at Thomas, with a look of adoration that, I knew, was only partly due to the quality of the champagne. He had an arm around her waist. Claiming her for tonight, I realised.

With reluctance I guided my gaze away from them. All of a sudden, I felt empty, with only the caress of the champagne on my tongue keeping my spirits afloat.

The sound of splashing and laughter down in the pool.

I turned to watch them. Two young women were lazing in the water. One had dark, long hair, floating across her shoulders, and the other was closer cropped and blonde. They looked as if they didn't have a single worry in the world. They were also both stark naked.

I kept on watching them, admiring the ease with which they bobbed in the water, so natural, and how their naked skin caught the moonshine.

The blonde girl noticed me and swam towards the edge where I was standing.

Holding on to the pool edge, she looked up at me with a smile. 'Why don't you join us?' she suggested. 'I'm Mandy.'

'I'm Moana.'

'What a lovely name. Are you Australian?' She'd mistaken my accent, as so many did in England.

'From New Zealand,' I corrected her.

The other nude young woman in the swimming pool lazily pushed herself through the underlit aquamarine waters towards us. 'She's Christine,' Mandy said.

'Come on down.'

'I'd rather not,' I said. I was becoming somewhat self-conscious. I looked around and noted that Thomas and Iris were no longer with me.

'The water's lovely,' one of the girls said. 'They keep the pool heated, night and day. It's why we always come back here, not just for the work.'

My high-heeled shoes were feeling tight, so I kicked them off, lowered myself down, sat on the ridge and dipped my feet in the water. It was indeed unpleasantly tepid. The lakes and sea back home were colder; this felt like being in a bathtub.

Christine took a hold of the pool's kerb and pulled herself up. She was skinny but her breasts were full, her nipples in the semi-darkness the colour of ripe cherries. Out of the water from the waist upwards, she threw up a leg and briefly caught her balance before her other leg followed and she raised the rest of her body onto the ledge.

Dripping, she stood facing me, her genitals generously exposed to my eyes. She had no pubic bush. She picked up a towel and began drying her hair. I felt breathless. At first, I was confused. I had never encountered a full-grown woman whose sex was so smooth before. Was it a birth defect or something, I wondered? The outline of her opening was both straight and sinuous. Then, as I focused and my gaze fixed on her mound in almost microscopic enquiry I noticed here and there minute dark dots, hair growing back. She had shaved.

My confusion was replaced by lust. How would it feel licking a sex as smooth and unencumbered as this, parting its lips with my tongue and fingers? My face must have reddened or she noticed my terrible fascination.

'Do you like it, darling? I'm told it's going to be all the vogue. Lots of European women do it. Show everything off, eh?'

I was frozen to the spot and tongue-tied.

By now, Mandy, the young blonde woman, had also exited the pool. She was not a real blonde.

From a group at the other end of the pool, a tall, thin, balding man in evening dress and a large bow tie had detached himself and was walking towards us.

'Ah, it's the Minister,' Mandy remarked. 'He's caught a sight of the goods . . .'

Spring

Neither of the girls seemed in any hurry to dress as the older man reached us. They were actually flaunting themselves. I found this difficult to believe. He ignored me and gallantly kissed both Christine and Mandy on the cheek, quite undisturbed by their unavoidable nudity. I was too overcome by the circumstances to hear the few words that passed between them.

Whispers.

The Minister nodded and both the young women spun and took him by the hands.

As they were about to leave, Mandy called out to me.

'Maybe you'd like to join us? He's good fun, John is, and likes a bit of variety.'

The words stumbled out of my mouth.

'I don't think so. I'm waiting for a friend. Anyway, I'm just a guest here.'

'Aren't we all?' one of the women chuckled.

They were swallowed by the nocturnal darkness as they headed back towards the illuminated mansion. He clad all in black, the two girls pale and naked in the flickering of the burning torches under the moonlight, holding on to his arms.

'Your loss, girl,' either Mandy or Christine shouted out.

I stood there on my own. The water in the pool lapping across my ankles, the beautifully obscene vision of Christine's bare cunt still fixed in my retina and the way it made my blood simmer with a thousand cravings.

I don't know how much time passed. Shadows moved around the pool area like fireflies, dancers hovered, twirled and moved on, the tall shaven-headed black attendant the sole fixed point in my landscape. I was beginning to feel the cold. I resolved to walk back to the main building and seek out our room, although I was under no illusion I would find Iris there tonight. I rose, shook the droplets from my feet and grabbed the shoes in my hand. I would walk back barefoot as my feet felt swollen.

But first, I wanted a final glass of that delicious champagne. It would warm me up, I knew. The valet saw me coming and held out a glass at the ready.

'Madam.'

'Thank you.' We were the only ones around and I wanted to appear polite. 'What's your name?' I asked.

He didn't answer, retreating behind a wall of silence, as if instructed not to mix with the guests.

I brought the glass to my lips, anticipating the buzz, the fizz of the drink and the way it would electrify me.

Then retraced my steps back.

And got lost.

A sense of panic overtook me.

Stepping rapidly through a deceptive avenue between a parade of oak trees I thought I had traversed earlier I reached a low wall of thick bushes, and experienced a dreadful sense of déjà vu, picturing myself as Alice no longer in wonderland but in a place of discombobulating evil. I began to run. I dropped the high heel shoes. My breath came haltingly. I felt as if I were rushing headfirst through a maze, like a crazed automaton.

And emerged once again by the pool.

The coloured barman was no longer visible, nor was the table laden with beverages. Was it the same pool, or another?

In the distance there was the reassuring sound of music, a faraway waltz the ghost dancers must be turning and spinning to. But closer to me now was the muted whisper of other voices, moans, murmurs, almost animal sounds but lacking any sense of genuine menace. I squinted. There at the corner of the pool, movement. Had Mandy, Christine and the minister returned?

The light was weak.

The sounds increased as I approached. Frantic, breathless.

A woman was in the pool, standing in the shallow end, bare-breasted, her skin pale as moonlight. Sitting on the edge facing her was a tuxedo-clad man with his legs apart. And she was sucking his cock. Swallowing him whole. With appetite and fervour, the dark shape of his penis bobbing in and out between her lips. Her eyes were closed. His head was thrown back and the guttural sounds I had previously heard rushed from his throat. I was frozen to the spot and a feeling of utter despair overcame me as I imagined Iris, right now, in some room in the nearby mansion, doing the same to Thomas. On occasions, we had in jest discussed fellatio as girls do, always concluding that it was possibly the most disgusting thing in the menu of sex. Yet somehow now, I was convinced Thomas had convinced her otherwise and she was taking to it like a duck to water, feasting on him, tasting him, her sweet lips being stretched beyond repair by his long, thick cock. I felt sick, and more lost than ever.

My eyes fixed on the couple at play by the edge of the pool, acclimating to the surrounding darkness, I began to distinguish further shapes beyond them in the grass, slow movements, further sounds. I squinted. A woman and two men, she on all fours, one of the partly dressed men in her mouth, the other behind her thrusting with rageful, staccato movements, the sounds of lust cutting though the night air.

What was this place? What had I got myself into? I was both repelled and fascinated by the unfolding spectacle. Knew that if I now ventured further in the grounds I would inevitably come across even more tableaus of desire unleashed. A new world. Realised the elegant ghost dancers of earlier were just this night's hors d'oeuvre and I was now getting a glimpse of the main courses.

The shuffle of steps behind me. A voice.

Crystal-clear, nonchalant, superior.

'Ah, one of my brother's little playfriends! A taste for voyeurism, maybe?'

It was Matilda.

I turned round.

She looked even more regal than she had earlier, as if the surrounding spectacle of debauchery only served to enhance her looks. Her dress captured every inch of light the half moon above cast down at us.

She held a leather leash in each hand as she wandered towards me.

At the end of each leash, a naked man, on his knees, one stick thin and hairless, the other stocky and furry to the extreme. Between their thighs, their soft cocks and balls dangled, as if superfluous parts. Both wore masks, so I was unsure who they were or if I had caught sight of them earlier.

She noted my surprise.

'My pets,' she said and tugged on the leashes. 'They're very obedient, and love it when their mistress takes them for a walk, don't they?'

Neither of the men responded. As if insulted by their lack of reaction to what had actually been a question, Matilda turned a dainty ankle and dug her needle-thin high heel deep into one man's buttocks. He hissed in pain. 'Yessss, mistress, I like it . . .' She withdrew her heel. It had left a red dent in his rump. She raised her leg and presented her shoe to his mouth. The man obediently licked it.

I swallowed hard. Despite my jumbled thoughts, I had found the spectacle rather satisfying. Maybe right now, because of Thomas, I was angry at all men.

Somehow Matilda could read my mind.

'Darling, feel free . . .'

She pulled on his leash and the stocky, kneeling man turned and displayed his raised arse to me.

'Look at that worthless package between his legs, darling. Come on, make him cry a bit.'

I bent over and, looking up at Matilda for encouragement which her wide smile provided, took hold of the man's dangling genitals, and squeezed his ball sack as tight as I could. His body shuddered but not a sound left his throat.

I realised I had been holding my breath back.

'You can afford to do it harder,' Matilda intervened. 'He's a good pain whore.'

But my anger had already subsided. And I had no wish to inflict permanent injury to the helpless man. Aside from the fact that having handled his sponge-like ball sack, my hands now felt dirty in the extreme.

'What is this place?' I asked Matilda.

'It's where all desires can be purchased, my dear. As simple as that. Supply and demand.'

She turned on her heel and made to depart, her twin

submissive poodles behind her, crawling on their knees across the grass.

I had so many more questions to ask.

I stood in place for a while, the sounds of rutting and sex like the ebb and flow of a curious tide surrounding me. Ordered my thoughts.

The night was lightening and the glow of the burning torches close to the mansion finally guided me back towards it.

On the left of the building there was a red tent. All the other marquees scattered across the grounds were white. My curiosity was provoked. By now, I was eager for further revelations. I approached its drawn curtain flaps with some amount of trepidation and entered.

Carpets, couches, beds.

All occupied.

The sounds of sex.

Soft purrs, whispers, squelching, a peal of laughter, a groan of unbelievable pleasure, exhalations of pure relief and terrible yearnings, a veritable concert of the senses.

A tall man, with his back to me. White-haired. Trousers bunched around his ankles. Standing ramrod straight.

Someone on their knees, facing him. Naked, thin arms holding the man at his waist, as if pulling his bulk towards her mouth, to take his cock even deeper.

My heart stopped at the thought that this might be Iris

somehow. That Thomas had convinced her to enter this diseased dance of lust of her own free will. By now, I understood what Matilda had said about supply and demand. This was a place where the rich and powerful came for their pleasure. Where it was them and us, and people like Iris and I were only seen as instruments for that pleasure. I wondered how much the young women who made themselves available here were paid?

I sidestepped the tall man.

And gasped.

It was not a woman sucking his cock with gusto and greed, impaled on him.

It was a young man.

His eyes were glazed as he busied himself, on the verge of orgasm, his cock below at full mast, as he took the stranger's vigorous penis into the very depths of his throat.

It was my cousin Gwillam.

I took a step back. Confused.

As I did so, the stranger roughly pulled away from Gwillam's mouth, pulling him by the hair as he did so.

'Now, you little cunt. Now,' he said, his voice full of disdain.

Gwillam turned round and draped himself over the back of the neighbouring couch, offering his rear to the man, even obediently holding his cheeks apart. The stranger moved nearer, his cock seemingly enormous and throbbing to my untrained eyes and, in one swift, practised move-ment, pushed himself into Gwillam's rear like a spear through butter.

I know I should have really looked away, but I watched in dread fascination every single minute of my cousin being fucked by another man.

And, from the expression on his face, how much he enjoyed it.

5

Following the Ghost

Having satisfied his lust, the older man, after a final fearsome thrust into Gwillam, disengaged himself from him, bent down at the waist and pulled up the tangled pool of his trousers, buttoned them and, in silence, moved away.

Just a couple of yards from him, I stood motionless, still transfixed in both fascination and horror, cocooned in darkness.

Close by a bird sang a timid song of morning.

Gwillam, splayed, was laid out like a disconnected puppet, panting gently from the savage effect of the man's assault, catching his breath, as if badly wounded.

His continued immobility began to worry me.

'Are you alright?'

His head turned.

He opened his eyes.

'Who ...?'

'It's me.'

'What?'

He rose, quickly grabbing a dark blue towel that lay by the side of the pool and draped it around his waist in a by now futile attempt to partly cover up. I had seen enough, or too much.

He peered hesitantly at me.

A flash of recognition.

'Moana?'

'Yes,' I confessed, my voice no louder than a murmur.

Surprise rushed across his weary features.

'What the fuck are you doing here?' he asked me.

'Thomas brought Iris and me along as guests,' I said. 'But they've gone off somewhere and I somehow got lost ...'

'You too?'

'Me too what?'

He looked at me with an expression of resignation.

'Here as chattel, to please? Paid for it?'

'No,' I said. 'Or at any rate if we were, Thomas never made the terms clear. And anyway, no one specifically asked me, I suppose.' I briefly remembered Christine and Mandy's throwaway invitation to join in their revels.

'Good for you. Some of the customers here can be pretty rough and demanding ...'

'So I saw ...'

'You were present all the time? Watching?'

I bowed my head. 'Yes.' I could not admit to my horrible fascination for the spectacle he had unknowingly provided, let alone the mixed feelings of arousal it had given birth to in the pit of my stomach.

'Damn. There goes what remains of my dignity.'

'Why?'

'I suppose I could pretend that law studies sometimes require more than a poorly clerk's pay packet ... But I should also confess to the fact that there's a devil inside me who can't curb his attraction to anonymous sex too ... Please, don't think the less of me, Moana ...'

'I don't.'

'Good.' Gwillam sketched a feeble smile.

'Maybe it's reassuring to know that a taste for the same sex runs in our family,' I flippantly said without thinking. It was a feeble attempt at a joke, and he knew it.

His face darkened.

'There is nothing wrong about it, Moana. Wanting, having sex with someone of your own gender. It's natural. Who says what is right or what is wrong? The heterosexuals?'

'I suppose so.'

The burning torches were dying out all around the mansion's grounds as morning light made a timid appearance. Gwillam, wearing only the towel around his waist, began to shiver. He looked scrawny.

164

'Shall we walk back?' he suggested.

He'd been allocated a small room in the basement. Once the servants' quarters.

I watched as he dressed. A tired pair of jeans and a checked shirt with a button-down collar. He slipped the tight denim on, his long legs straightening its creases. He didn't bother with underwear. I couldn't help note how his slim, long cock bulged under the thin material. Not attraction per se, but a kind of puerile fascination.

He followed my gaze.

'It's the way I normally dress,' he said. 'I just have the one formal dark suit, which I only wear for work. I prefer to be casual the rest of the time.'

I sat there silently.

He noted my dreamy state.

'What is it, Moana?'

'Just thinking.'

He looked me up and down, as if really seeing me for the first time that night.

'Of what? That's a lovely dress,' he remarked, 'although I'm not sure it totally suits you, a bit girly-girly, I reckon . . .'

I looked him straight in the eyes.

'Gwillam? What does it feel like?'

'What?'

'When a man fucks you? To feel a penis inside you?'

'You never have?'

'No. Never.'

I considered telling him about Clarissa and her dildo but dismissed the thought.

'Well, I can't speak for the way it usually is for a woman, of course. But if you're curious, you should try. If only once. It's just so difficult to describe. Keep your mind open ...Your identity and who you choose to screw aren't the same thing, you know.'

'Does it ... hurt?'

'Sometimes.'

'But hurt is good sometimes, isn't it?' I ventured.

'Absolutely.'

He opened his arms to me and we hugged. Within moments, I felt sleepy. He brushed his fingers through my hair and closed my eyes. 'Rest,' he said. 'You seem even more exhausted than I feel, and that's saying a lot. Emotions can prove more tiring than action on occasion, I know.'

By the time we both awoke, I saw from my watch that it was already midday. We ventured out to the front of the house where some cars were still parked; there were only a half dozen left. Thomas and Iris must have departed earlier. The room I'd shared with her was empty and her stuff gone. I'd changed back into my normal clothes and left the extravagant dress behind.

As we stepped across the gravel, Gwillam peering at each car to see if he knew the owners and we could maybe catch a lift back to London, Matilda emerged through the front door of the mansion. She was still in her evening dress, and it continued to shimmer in the pale morning light. But she carried no more leashes and trailed no human dogs behind her.

She waved at us and a handful of other couples standing forlornly around and whom I couldn't recognise, signs of evident dissipation and tiredness spread across their bleary features.

'There's a hired coach arriving in ten minutes,' she declared. 'It will take you to the nearest train station.' Then she handed out envelopes to several of the stragglers, including Gwillam. Seeing me with him, she expressed no outward sign of recognition nor mentioned Thomas, or Iris.

We were almost the only passengers in the carriage of the London train and the non-stop journey would take just under an hour to Marylebone High Street. I was bursting with questions but Gwillam spoke first, possibly wishing to avoid further conversation about the events at the mansion.

'You know about Iris's grandmother Joan?'

'Yes?'

'I really think I've made progress.'

'Tell me.'

'I've scoured archives, newspaper libraries, even police records – you'd be surprised how easily the doors open to a request emanating from a lawyer's chambers – and you'll never guess what?'

'No.'

'An unbelievable coincidence. Did you know that Joan worked at the Princess Empire theatre too?'

'Really?'

'Yes. Apparently she used it as her last known address before she embarked for New Zealand.'

'That's amazing.'

'So the theatre should be our next destination to find out more ...'

'I'm ... friendly with someone who's involved in the management there,' I said. 'Maybe she can help us?'

'That would be super,' Gwillam said.

By the time our train reached the city, I knew I would barely have time enough to catch the Tube home and change for my evening shift at the theatre. Together with the fact that Gwillam felt and looked shattered from his mansion sexual travails, we agreed I would make some discreet enquiries and attempt to set up a time the following weekend for him to visit me, and Clarissa, there. We parted with an embrace at the station, each of us heading for a different line.

My mind was in something of a turmoil, still disturbed by the events and revelations at the mansion in the Chilterns and excited at the prospect of revealing the news about Joan to Iris. At the same time, there was an undercurrent of dread rushing through my veins as I approached our bedsit. An instinct that something was wrong.

Iris wasn't there.

The place was topsy-turvy, with coat hangers spread across the bed, where she had hurriedly emptied her side of the closet and pulled her clothes together. There was a hastily scribbled note for me: she had decided to move in with Thomas, as an experiment, she wrote, and asked to be forgiven. She knew I might find myself stretched for the rent, so had left her share of it for the next two months. I had no doubt Thomas had provided the money as Iris, like me, had little in the way of savings. She guessed it would be relatively easy for me to find a new flatmate and assured me we were still friends, but maybe this was best for the both of us.

It was not a surprise. Ever since she had met Thomas, I had blinded myself to the changes in her desires and my own, I realised. I tried to think back to the last occasion that we had really, properly made love, but came up with nothing.

There was little time for tears or to indulge in the blues though, as I had to make my way to the theatre. Even more so now that my meagre wages would have to stretch further.

Throughout the show, I had to fight the waves of anger

coursing through me and paint a fixed smile on my face as I led the patrons to their seats, encouraged them to purchase the overpriced programme and, at the interval, tramped around the auditorium peddling ice creams, Kia-Ora drink cartons, minuscule bottles of Babycham, sweets and pop corn.

Following the final curtain call, and having checked the empty rows for anything the audience might have left behind and coming across the usual assortment of umbrellas, a couple of cushions, eye pieces, scarves and even a forgotten handbag and deposited them with the cashier's office, I slumped on a chair in the claustrophobic staff area and felt the weight of the world collapsing over my shoulders.

It would be another half hour before the Princess Empire closed, and a pair of cleaning ladies were moving through the rows swooping for sweet wrappers and other detritus. They looked like mirror images of each other, both clad in the sky-blue, shapeless uniform of the cleaning company, their silken black hair tied into a tight bun held in place with a deep red hair band. One was much older than the other, I realised, and they might have been mother and daughter. The younger one stood on something unpleasant and lifted her foot to inspect her shoe, muttering, and the older one shushed her in a language I didn't understand. I was in no rush to return home. I felt I should cry, but the tears would not come, and I couldn't force them to.

Spring

'Something wrong, Moana?'

A hand on my shoulder. A familiar perfume.

Clarissa loomed above me with a look of concern on her face. She appeared like an earthly angel in her white chiffon jump suit, the same one, I realised, that she'd worn when we first met. It was cinched at her hips with a silver chain belt that jangled when she moved. Thick hoop earrings were threaded through her lobes and a grey trilby hat balanced precariously on one side of her head. She looked as though she had been raiding the wardrobe department and stealing the props.

I opened my mouth, but the words got stuck in my throat.

Her hand delicately swept through my hair.

'The blues, eh?'

I nodded.

'You do look tired,' she stated, 'and hungry, too. You shouldn't be skipping meals at your age,' she added. I realised she was right: the last food I had eaten had been at the mansion when I had stuffed myself much too fast with the plentiful snacks on offer. I felt as if they had quickly evaporated inside me and left me paradoxically empty.

'Come,' Clarissa said. 'Let me take you home and cook something for you. And I won't take no for an answer ...'

I wondered if the offer of dinner was a euphemism for altogether more primal appetites, but for once the look on her face was one of affection and care, not passion.

I stood up and followed Clarissa out of the theatre. Her trouser suit swam over her legs and arse as she walked, and I spent the duration of our walk through the corridors to the exit imagining what kind of underwear she wore underneath, if any at all. She hailed a black cab. In the back seat, we held hands, and stared out of the windows without saying a word, both lost in our respective worlds.

The moment I walked into the warm, lived-in atmosphere of Clarissa's two level studio off Brick Lane, in a converted warehouse with tall ceilings, red brick walls and wide bay windows, I felt at home and the pain inside began to ebb away. Of course, there was some degree of familiarity since it was my second visit. It felt different somehow, not least because I could see my surroundings in full light, but also because without the certain immediate distraction of sex, I was free to look around and absorb my environment in a way that I hadn't the first time around.

She worked on the ground level in a cavernous space piled with multicoloured rolls of fabric, railings heavy with garments, long tables, a scattering of large portfolios stuffed with photographs, prints and sketches, and rows of burnished metal shelves displaying a small collection of antique sewing machines. The plush leather sofa that we had so recently fucked on ran along one wall, scattered haphazardly with cushions and a cream-coloured fringe throw.

Spring

The living quarters were situated upstairs and could be reached via an intricately wrought circular staircase of art deco origin. The area was divided by thin partitions carved from silk and wood, most bearing Chinese calligraphy and images, or was it Japanese? But a striking oriental presence dominated and in an odd way reminded me of some of the splendours of the Ball, as if a tapestry of subliminal patterns and shapes repeated ad infinitum in the grooves of my brain and connected Clarissa's lair with the extravagant past I still couldn't banish from my mind.

She gently but forcibly installed me on the futon – a wide, low bed that doubled as a sofa – and offered me a glass of sickly sweet but potent liqueur with an aftertaste of pomegranate. It first burned my lips and throat before settling into an overall fuzz of warmth as it seeped lazily into my system and soothed my whole body from the inside.

'Relax. Just make yourself comfortable. I'll be cooking over in the kitchen. Call me if there is anything you want,' she said, throwing off her ballet pumps and moving barefoot to the far area of the space, beyond a set of dark curtains.

On a table nearby, an assortment of fashion and home decoration magazines were scattered. I began distractedly leafing through them, although my mind was still elsewhere and conflicted. After all, I had kept Iris in the dark about my frolics with Clarissa and maybe she had guessed that I had been, well, unfaithful, and could this have thrown her into Thomas's arms? I was undoubtedly attracted to Clarissa. But when I examined my feelings, I had to recognise that this attraction was purely sexual, that she did not make my insides flutter like Iris always had. My stomach clenched as I remembered the way Clarissa had entered me with the black, carved dildo and I had briefly imagined it was a man inside me, and experienced both lust and disgust. And then my unreliable mind pictured the stranger thrusting into Gwillam the previous night. Could I not control my feelings, my desires, my obsessions of penetration and not just watching others do it? I turned the pages of the magazines like an automaton.

Strong odours of food cooking wafted through from the kitchen area where Clarissa was busy behind the drapes.

'It'll be ready soon,' she called out.

I could hear the sizzling of oil in a pan, a strong smell of onions, garlic and frying meat. My mouth began to water and my stomach rumbled.

The food, when it arrived, was as delicious as the sounds and smells that preceded it. Clarissa brought out wide wooden trays and we ate while draped across the bed. It felt delightfully intimate.

'It's a Vietnamese stir fry,' Clarissa explained as I had to restrain myself from eating too fast and clearing my plate long before she was even halfway through her meal.

Thin strips of beef had been marinated in a cleverly blended mixture of spices, pungent enough but in no way aggressive, and then flash-fried in olive oil with an assortment of al dente vegetables: red and green peppers, baby corn, onion and invisible but undeniable savoury wafer-thin slices of garlic.

'It's wonderful,' I said.

'I learned to cook it in Paris when I lived there,' Clarissa replied. 'I made so many friends in the Asian student community when I was studying fabric at the Beaux Arts.' It all sounded so exotic to my ears. And the taste was quite divine.

The white wine she served with the stir fry was equally addictive, dry and sweet at the same time, flowing down my throat with the ease of tap water.

I eagerly wiped my plate clean with a piece of bread, not wanting to miss a drop of the juices the dish had left behind. Clarissa watched me indulgently.

Another glass of wine, plates set aside.

'So, Moana, care to tell me what this is all about?'

'Iris has left,' I blurted out.

Her expression remained impassive. She shifted closer and took my hand in hers as the words bubbled out of my mouth. I told her about the way that Iris had always just lain there when we were making love, and I had felt so ashamed of my desire for her. Like I was always pouring myself into Iris and hoping that I could fill her with so much affection that she would have some left over to return to me. Yet, yet, there was something else there, lurking in the darker corners of my soul and that was the fact that a part of me *liked it*, the way that she so passively allowed me to molest her, and what did that make me? There were things that I loved about Iris that I felt guilty for loving. Her fragility, the bird-like lightness of her body, the blank slate of her face when I drove my fingers inside her, the awful tugging need that encouraged me endlessly to stimulate her until I provoked some kind of response. Her response satisfied me because it made me feel as though I had won.

'I'm just like Thomas,' I sobbed, and Clarissa wrapped me up in her arms and held me to her. I appreciated the gesture, but Clarissa was not in the slightest motherly. Her scent was too sharp, her body too thin to be comforting.

'Shh, shh,' she said. 'You and Thomas do have something in common. You're both after the same girl, for a start. But desire, and the way that you choose to express it, the way that Thomas expresses it, are not inherently evil. Iris seemed happy enough with the situation until now and it sounds as though she has sought out the same with Thomas ... Had you ever stopped to think that maybe the parts of you that you're so ashamed of are the parts that attracted her in the first place? That maybe the very thing you're trying to hide from is the thing she wants?'

What she said made a dull sort of sense. I felt as though I

was on the brink of understanding something about myself that had previously been in shadow, but I still couldn't make it out, as though I was staring at my face in a fogged-up mirror that was only just beginning to clear.

I had already confessed so much to her that my feelings of shame began to dull and I just kept talking, telling her all about how I had felt watching Gwillam and the men that Tilly had dragged along on their leashes, the tornado of bruised feelings I could sense tearing me apart inside. When it came to the specifics of the party at the mansion, she raised an eyebrow and queried the events there and the type of people involved. She appeared to have an underlying reason for asking me these questions. I had to repeat myself several times over until she seemed to be satisfied.

'Good,' she said.

'Why is it good?' I asked her, puzzled by her response.

'Oh, it's just that for a moment there, I thought someone out there – Matilda you say was her name? – was attempting to pass a plain old, and nicely decadent sort of party off as an instance of the Ball . . .'

'The Ball?' My heart jumped.

'Yes.'

'You know about the Ball?'

That was the one thing I had kept back in my story, having only provided her with information about my life with Iris since we had arrived in London. Not least because

I feared that no one would believe the events that had occurred that night Iris and I travelled to Cape Reinga. Clarissa was the first person I had come across, aside from Joan, who knew of the existence of the Ball.

I was eager to question her further, when we heard the door to the studio downstairs open and sounds from the street briefly filter in before it closed again. Clarissa smiled.

'Ah, that must be Edward . . .'

I must have been staring at her like a fool, with my mouth wide open in an O of surprise.

'Oh, no need to worry, my dear, he knows all about our night together. In fact, I think he rather enjoyed the tale.' She winked at me. The caring Clarissa was gone, and the version that I was used to had returned, all hard edges and overflowing with gentle malice.

I heard Edward's steps coming up the baroque circular staircase, and looked round to him as he emerged.

He was a rake-thin man in his thirties, with flowing dark hair down to his shoulders that reminded me of a romantic poet in an old print. His square chin was dimpled and his eyes were a striking shade of dark green. He was dressed in a kaftan and jeans and wore scuffed knee-high boots. Had it not been for the fierce look of intelligence on his face he could have been mistaken for any old hippie from the narrow streets of Covent Garden and its subterranean clubs.

Spring

I had pictured the type of man that Clarissa might be attracted to. Someone handsome and droll, her equivalent in another body. I would never have picked Edward out as her physical match.

'Hi,' he called out. Sniffed. 'The food smells wonderful. Any left?'

'Tons, darling,' Clarissa said.

Noticing me, he waved. 'You must be Moana,' he said and walked towards us, pecked Clarissa on the cheek and extended his hand to me, with an air of interest spreading across his features.

'I need to clean up, ladies. See you in a jiffy.'

He pulled his heavy kaftan over his head and dropped it to the floor. He wore the tightest jeans I had ever seen on a man, the shape of his cock distinctly outlined beneath the thin material. I wondered how on earth he would manage to get them off without assistance. His chest was totally smooth and his body so lean that I imagined he and Clarissa, nude, were a similar shape. He lacked the broad shoulders and musculature that I associated with men. I pictured him in a shift dress – yes, he would look great garbed as a woman. He disappeared between a row of partitions at the far end of the living area and I heard the sound of water hitting the shower stall. I was arrested by the thought of what his smooth skin might feel like beneath a pair of soapy hands.

I looked tentatively at Clarissa.

'You told him everything? You and me ... about what happened?'

'Of course. Edward and I have no secrets. None whatsoever. We play apart ...' She raised an eyebrow. 'And together too, you know ...'

January 3rd, 1922

Ever since that night we went dancing and Gladys confessed that she wanted to be an actress, we have spent all of our time dreaming of the theatre. Gladys knows the name of every show, every director, all of the stars and the minor cast and even all of the chorus lines. 'The Gaiety Girls!' she said today, 'can you imagine how it would feel to be one of them?' She picked up her skirts and flung her leg into the air in a high kick, flashing me a glimpse of her thighs and the pale pink trim of her bloomers. We have both stopped wearing corsets and the freedom is delightful, and deliciously daring. When no one is watching, we dance, and revel in the glorious movement of our bodies.

Sometimes, I think that Mrs Moorcroft's mother – a corpse walking if ever I've seen one, just bones clad in a mourning costume – watches us dance. She seems perpetually in the shadows whenever Gladys visits, and probably when I'm alone too, forever peering around corners and appearing out of shadows and making me jump three feet in the air with her cold touch and soft breath. I try not to be too hard on her; she just wants to be near life, and youth.

Spring

Gladys says she's an old busy body, and probably wishes wrinkles on us both.

We have been living on nothing but tea and toast, saving our wages to see a show. Even the New Year we celebrated indoors, standing at my little window with our arms around each other and our cheeks pressed together, unwilling to let a single fire cracker go off outside unwitnessed. The Islington sky bloomed bright beyond the harbour of my humble room. It made me glad to live in London, and in a way, guilty that I don't miss home even a bit. I don't deny there's a quiet beauty in a sheet of stars shining bright over farmland on a still night, and many poets have remarked upon the fact – who am I to contradict them? But my heart is at home in the big, sprawling city, brimming with rainbow-coloured sparks of light and life.

January 15th, 1922

I live in hope that Harold Butler Jnr. may yet present me with a late Christmas bonus, and I'll use that to purchase my ticket. I doubt this hope will ever come to fruition, though he has not stopped supplying Gladys with little 'presents'. Jewellery and gloves and bits of fabric from the store that he always says are off-cuts to be thrown away anyway, but which seem far too fine to me for that.

I keep telling her she's asking for trouble leading him on like that, but she's stubborn as a mule and complaining too much would make me the worst sort of hypocrite since I have been happily receiving her old hand-me-downs – still perfectly good – while she makes room for a whole new wardrobe that would make even a girl of means jealous.

'I must go up West,' she excuses herself, 'or die! And not in the cheap seats either. I won't sit right up in the gods, behind a pillar at the back where you can barely see a thing.'

I worry that she has taken money from him, and I fear for what might happen if – dare I say when – he realises he's being taken for a fool.

But for now I try not to brood, and focus on the future.

We pour over newspaper reviews, deciding which show to see. You would think that Gladys expects a red carpet to be rolled out for us both at the box office, champagne poured into our glasses, and that the starring man might even spot us in the audience and invite us backstage to dine in his dressing room.

Maybe I will meet a 'Gentleman' during the interval, as Gladys keeps promising.

I'm not sure that I want to.

February 2nd, 1922

Tonight we attended the theatre, dressed like Parisian fashion plates, ready for the catwalk.

Gladys wore a cloche hat, deep red velvet with a ribbon around the middle, and a darling long white and blue gown with a low-cut front that she spent hours beading. When it was finished, we joked that it made her look like a sailor on a luxury cruise ship. We re-stitched my Halloween outfit for me, adding

*a cream lace modesty layer below the yellow chiffon, and alter-
nating pink and yellow ruffles at the bottom so that the hem
reached past my knee. I felt like a canary bird, just been allowed
out of its cage. 'It's not too much?' I asked her. 'You're an
original,' she told me. I had never seen anything like it in any
fashion magazine illustration.*

*She had chopped all of her hair off in a chic little bob, so high it
barely covered her ears and showed off her neck, so lovely and long.
We changed into our frocks in my room. Gladys strode right in
through the door and up the stairs as Mrs Moorcroft raced after her,
moving far quicker than I had ever given the large woman credit for,
tutting all the way, and telling us that if Gladys planned to sleep
here for the night then we had better not arrive back too late, crashing
and banging in our high-heeled shoes and disturbing Pansy and
Alice, who must wake early in the morning to boil potatoes in
Clapton. 'And if I catch either of you ladies drinking, you'll both
be out the door,' she said, 'this is a good Christian household.' Mrs
Moorcroft was a creature of misguided convictions, had even fiercely
opposed the suffragette movement before it had obtained all its
gains.*

*Temperance posters had sprung up all over the kitchen and the
hall. Of course, Gladys wouldn't have any of that. 'She's not
your mother,' she said, 'or mine,' and she pulled a dainty silver
hip flask out from a clever little pouch that she had affixed to her
garter. She tossed it to me and I took a swig and nearly choked
– it was brim-full of sloe gin. 'My Uncle Ted's Christmas brew,'*

she confessed with a wink, 'and he couldn't give a damn what I drink.'

The way she said 'Uncle' made me suspect that Ted was not a bona fide relation.

She continued to empty her pockets.

Kohl liner, powder blush, and even a strange black gloop that she told me was Vaseline mixed with coal dust to make our lashes long and black.

We were beautiful, and the show, it was every bit as wonderful as we had hoped.

Even the coating of snow that had fallen while we were inside, melting and causing such a jam on the footpaths as we made our way home, slipping and sliding in our Mary Janes, didn't dampen our mood.

March 25th, 1922

Gladys has met a man. Another one – but this time, one that I like. His name is James, and he works in the theatre, of course, and has bright raisin eyes and lashes like a doe and lips so full and red they could belong to a woman. He laughs like a horse, but I could forgive anything in a man with those dimples. Gladys is infatuated with him, and I think that I may be, too. I think I may be in love with them both.

Whatever am I to do?

Sometimes I tell myself that she must feel the same way – when, without guile, she undresses in front of me and shadows from the *candlelight play across her skin, just so, it seems to me that the cold has disappeared and spring has landed already, even if only in my bedroom.*

I dare myself to kiss her, every day.

June 30th, 1922

Oh diary, to think that only a few short months ago, I worried you might think me immoral for reading a romance novel.

Tonight, we made love, the three of us. I almost dare not write the words, for fear that somehow they will seep from the page and into the minds of my landlady or one of the other boarders – or, heaven forbid, the old woman who continues to stalk me up and down the stairs and down the corridor.

Gladys you know already, diary. I felt as though I knew her before, but now I feel as though I have barely begun to know her – to map out her whole body and memorise every inch of it, not with my mind but with my fingertips and my tongue, so that if I were ever to lose her I could blindly conjure her up again. I cannot even begin to grasp at the right words that might convey the honey taste of her lips or the soft silk of her throat. The way that we feasted on one another, as though throughout our whole lives until that moment, we had been starved.

And James – how avidly he watched us, and how I luxuriated in the knowledge that the sight of us together like that must be driving him into a frenzy, and yet he must abide by the agreement that Gladys had struck with him. That he could watch us together, but he must not touch us. There was such a strange sort of power in knowing the hold we had over him. It made me feel so alive.

Sept 18th, 1923

Tonight, diary, I flew.

James held the whip and I let him and with each blow that fell my soul lifted until I felt that I no longer needed a body, and all the games we played before seemed like nothing. How I imagine each time that we have travelled together to pleasure's epicentre and can go no further, and then the next time, I find that we can go further again. There is no end to pleasure, no point at which the end is reached.

Some appetites can never be sated.

February 1st, 1924

How cold I am, diary. Winter has come, not just in the wind that blows through every crack in the walls of this dreadful place but in every corner of my soul.

What a fool I was to think my little window at Mrs Moorcroft's too small. She would smile to see me now, and tell me that I have got nothing more than I deserved. A drunk and a slattern who could not be allowed to live any longer with Christian women, confined to a cellar room in the worst part of Whitechapel. How I hurry to and fro each time I must leave home – if I can call it that – in fear of the men who huddle together on every dark corner and call out to me as I pass.

Spring

Did I ever feel happy in London?

Gladys has married Harold Butler Jnr, and she will no longer look at me.

She carries a child – a child that I think of as 'our' child, for I am certain that it was conceived on one of the nights that the three of us spent together, James and Gladys and I, feeding one another's appetites with a lust sweeter than wine.

I have quit work at Butler and Butler. I cannot be near her and not able to touch her. My desire for her consumes me. It seeps from my every pore and I know that if her new 'husband' (I cannot bear to think of him that way) were to suspect anything then he would treat her badly.

I do not see James. We tried, once, but without Gladys we are nothing together. We agreed that we would each come to despise the other for lacking the power to bring her back. That we would spend every moment together thinking of nothing but the space between us that she filled.

I am nothing without her.

I do not know what I will become.

Edward returned from the shower wearing a silky navy blue dressing gown that I presumed belonged to Clarissa. It had oriental-style wide sleeves that draped down from his wrists like a wizard's robe, and a lace trim along the bottom that reached halfway down his thighs. He had tied the belt into a bow at his waist, so loose it looked as though it would fall open at any moment. He was a little taller and broader than Clarissa, though not by much. The pale, smooth expanse of his bare chest formed a sharp V, outlined in inky satin. His legs were more muscular than I had expected and covered in a coating of fine black hair. I guessed that his pubic mound would be thick and lustrous.

It occurred to me then that I had not yet seen Clarissa's cunt. I wondered if she would be hairy too, to match Edward, or if she might be fully shaved like one of the two good-time girls at the pool by Thomas's mansion. What were their names? Mandy and Christine.

He stood in front of us and briskly towel-dried his damp locks, rubbing his head furiously as one might dry off a wet dog. The belt that barely secured his modesty loosened the more vigorously he moved his arms.

'Couldn't you at least wait ten minutes before scaring the poor girl?' Clarissa asked him.

He laughed.

'She doesn't seem to mind,' he told her.

Clarissa looked over at me and raised an eyebrow, seeking confirmation.

I shrugged, feigning indifference, but truth to be told I was curious. Perhaps my increased exposure to nudity lately had made me more interested in the bodies of others.

I noticed that I had crept forward towards the end of the futon and was lying on my belly, apparently hoping for a glimpse of Edward's cock and balls. I tried to guess at his size. Long and thin, like him, and perfectly straight, I predicted.

I was wrong.

He walked back towards the bathroom and slung the towel over the door to dry, then returned. Clarissa took the bottle of wine from the low table at the end of the bed and topped up my glass, then poured the remainder into her own and held it out towards Edward. He stepped towards her and grasped the stem. His shins pressed against the futon's wooden base. Clarissa reached up and parted Edward's robe with her finger, caressed his shaft, and then cupped his ball sack in her hand. She seemed mesmerised by the sight of his dick, as if discovering it for the first time.

'Talk about the pot calling the kettle black,' he said, between mouthfuls of wine.

'It's your best feature, dear, why should I not wish to show it off?'

'Sometimes you can be such a bitch.'

He threaded his fingers into Clarissa's pixie crop and pulled her head towards his cock, holding her against him until she drew back, laughing.

I watched his face. His earlier expression of interest had morphed into something more. Hunger. Next time, I thought, he would not let her shift away so easily.

His erection jutted out between the flaps of the robe,

hard and long, and thicker than I had imagined. He had the sort of cock that belonged on a much larger man.

Clarissa tugged one end of his belt's bow. The satin slipped open easily, exposing his ball sack.

A memory popped unbidden into my mind; the men on leashes huddled at Matilda's feet, her encouraging me to clutch their testicles and squeeze them. How that must have hurt. I bet, too, that had Tilly been in my place, she would have dished out an awful lot more punishment than I had. Yet they were evidently cowering below her of their own free will.

There was something of the same power dynamic in Edward and Clarissa's relationship, but rather than one lording it over the other, they seemed to toss it like a ball between them. The ultimate give and take.

'You don't mind, do you, darling?' Clarissa asked me.

I wasn't sure whether she was referring to her husband's nudity, or to the public display of what appeared to be a private ritual in each humiliating the other.

I shook my head, no.

'Good. In that case, come closer.'

She wriggled forward and grabbed my hand, and I took her place directly in front of Edward's substantial package.

'Have you ever seen a cock before? Close-up I mean. In detail. Really looked at it.'

I hadn't, but I was doing so now.

Spring

The skin was stretched so tightly that it seemed thin, and as smooth as satin. His head was bulbous, with a thick ridge, like a mushroom. I remembered hearing once in the school-yard that the underside of the head was the most sensitive part, and I guessed that must be the soft piece of tissue that ran down from the tip to the shaft, like the cleft of a small peach. If I were to lick him, then I would lick him there.

He appeared to grow even harder under my steady gaze, his already pink skin turning a deeper shade of plum that grew darker towards the ridge. I watched, mesmerised, as a milky droplet pearled at the end and clung to his centre, defying gravity.

If Edward had considered forcing my face against him, he didn't indicate as much to me. He stood as still as a reed on a windless day, without making even the slightest motion of encouragement.

Clarissa, curled up by my side, was like the serpent in the Garden of Eden, luring Eve.

'Would you like to touch it?'

Doing so would at least assuage my curiosity, I reasoned. A tiny spark flickered inside me. I wanted to see if touching Edward would smother that spark, or if it would grow into a flame.

'May I?' I asked him.

'Oh, please do.'

I shifted onto my knees and stretched one hand out

towards him, grazing just the tips of my fingers from the base of his shaft to the tip, feather light.

He groaned.

I repeated the same motion on the underside, and heard him inhale, a whisper of breath whistling between his teeth.

His balls, a soft weight against my palm. His pubic hair, silken beneath the scrape of my fingernails. His tip, wet against the press of my thumb.

I lowered my head and opened my mouth.

Clarissa leaned forward and pulled me back.

'No, don't let him have that yet. I must admit, I didn't expect you to be so eager. You do get into the swing of things quickly.'

Edward groaned again, this time with an obvious note of frustration.

He bent down and took hold of Clarissa by the chin, forced her mouth open and just as I felt I ought to protest against his violence he released a mouthful of wine between her lips and they kissed. Clarissa's caught the liquid, swallowed, and wiped any stray drips with the back of her hand.

'Don't you dare spilling anything on this trouser suit,' she said.

He lowered his glass and waved it over the vivid white of her neckline.

'You had better take it off, I think. Not like you to keep your clothes on so long.'

'I think Moana should go first,' Clarissa replied. 'She hasn't yet seen me naked, and I want to make her wait a little longer.'

I felt acutely aware of my dowdy usher's uniform, creased and worn after a whole afternoon and evening's work.

'Actually,' I said, 'do you mind if I shower first?'

'Be our guest. But only on two conditions.'

'Yes?' I enquired.

She spoke in a hushed tone, directly into my ear as if she was imparting a secret, though I knew perfectly well that Edward was listening.

'First, you must return to us quite naked. Second, you must be prepared for anything.'

I agreed, and headed for the bathroom.

A large round mirror dominated the tiny room, and its frame, patterned like a flower with mosaic petals in shades of lilac, blue and indigo provided the only flash of colour against the spotless white of the walls and floor. It was all so spotlessly clean that I hung my blouse and skirt over the towel rail, to avoid soiling the shining tiles with my dirty clothes.

I washed quickly, eager to return to Clarissa to Edward and in their company, avoid experiencing the emotions that threatened to well up inside me again. If I thought of Iris, I might cry, so instead I concentrated on the physical action of lathering my body with soap suds. I ran my hands over my breasts and the hard, pointed tips of my nipples.

There was no mat to stand on, and having forgotten to ask where I might find the clean towels, I used the one that Edward had draped over the door. His scent lingered in the damp folds, something beyond the neutral odour of shower gel. A pungent, slightly bitter, masculine aroma.

Faithful to Clarissa's instructions, I left the towel, and my clothes on the rail and padded back into the living room naked.

Edward was still standing in the same position, but he had dropped the robe. Clarissa had removed her white trouser suit but donned another outfit altogether. She was smoking a cigarette, sitting on the futon and dressed all in black; patent stilettos and sheer stockings affixed to a skin-tight corselette with lace cups through which I could just see a hint of her nipples. Around her hips, a leather harness was fastened, and attached to that, a large black dildo. Whether it was the same one that she had earlier penetrated me with or if she had a whole collection, I wasn't sure.

They were engaged in conversation and did not hear me enter. I stood silently for a few moments and observed them. Edward's cock had half softened, and between puffs, Clarissa would reach out and stroke it gently. Once, she sat up and idly licked the full length of the shaft, then took the head into her mouth just for a moment and let it fall out again, then she leaned back and drew in again on her cigarette. He was playing with her lighter, flicking the top back and letting loose snatches of flame.

The main lights had been turned off and candles lit. One lamp in a corner remained on, casting a pleasant amber light through a thick yellow shade.

Clarissa turned to me.

'Come on back in then, lovely,' she said, 'and let us admire you.'

I walked towards them and stood in front of her, alongside Edward.

His cock immediately hardened again.

'You're beautiful,' he said.

I thanked him, although I didn't really agree. I was grateful for my body, glad that it worked the way it did, but I did not believe that I was beautiful. I did not possess Iris's delicate beauty, like a newly budding rose, or Clarissa's cool, languid elegance, or Matilda's striking form.

'She is a little gem, this one. Rough cut but so open to being polished into fine form.'

Clarissa spoke as though she thought of me not as a person but as a plaything, and implied that I might be one of many. This idea didn't bother me. It excited me. At least for tonight, I wanted to be Clarissa's plaything.

She stretched a leg out between mine, flexed her foot and ran the round toe of her shoe between my thighs, encouraging me to open them further. I shuffled my feet apart, obliging her.

'Good girl,' she said.

She traced a path with her fingertips, over the bump of my ankle and up the sides of my calf, the backs of my knees to the inside of my thighs, then around the neat mound of my bush. She dipped lower, outlining the shape of my lips, but careful to avoid dipping inside me. My pussy was becoming slicker. I could feel the slow rise of heat there, the gathering wetness that might make my panties damp, had I been wearing any. I imagined a drop welling up and pearling all the way down to the floor, following the map that Clarissa had earlier drawn.

Edward set the lighter down and took my chin gently into his hand, turning me towards him.

'May I kiss you?' he asked.

I wasn't sure if I wanted him to, but I nodded in agreement, reasoning that a kiss would make clear whether or not I was truly physically attracted to him.

His mouth met mine. His lips were full and wide, and close to him, I caught another whiff of his cologne – something generically masculine, but it had a warmth that suited him, although I could not pinpoint the particular fragrance. He tasted of red wine, a note of bitter tannin mixed with dark fruit. His arms hung by his sides and I took hold of his hands and guided them to my breasts. He kissed me harder, open mouthed, and his tongue touched mine, just a little. His palms were soft and dry, the brush of his skin against mine like an intimate conversation, our bodies communing beyond the barriers of our minds.

Clarissa nudged the round of her shoe against my opening.

'Very nice,' she said, 'and so unlike you, Edward, to be so restrained.'

Her lips formed a cupid's bow and a ring of smoke drifted lazily from her mouth. She took her cigarette into her left hand and with her right, picked up a bottle of red wine that was resting on the thick wooden bed frame, in between our two glasses. They must have opened it while I was in the shower, and between them, finished half already. She tipped her head back and swallowed a mouthful straight from the bottle.

'You've never been with a man, before, have you?' he asked me. 'Not even a kiss?'

'No,' I told him.

'Did you like it?'

'Yes, I did.'

There was something curiously genderless about kissing, I mused. I wondered if the same applied to sex, since as Clarissa so aptly demonstrated during our fuck on my last visit, a biological penis was not a requirement for penetration.

'So,' Clarissa broke in, 'you promised that you would be prepared for anything.'

'I am.'

'Good.'

She reached under the bedspread cover and pulled out another dildo and harness. Both the leather straps and the toy were a rich purple. The whole contraption looked heavy, and uncomfortable.

'You have two options,' she said. 'The first: Edward fucks you. The second: you fuck Edward. Either way, a virginity lost. Which would you prefer to lose first?'

Edward had moved behind me, and was still idly running his hands over my body. His palms grazed my ribs and my body, scooped up to my breasts and touched my nipples, then over my arms and shoulders to my neck. He lifted my hair back and kissed the hollow of my shoulder, the top of my collarbone. I was not accustomed to the manner of his caresses, and initially, was not sure how to respond.

'Just relax,' he murmured, sensing my tension.

Iris was also gentle, like Edward, but her touch always tentative. By nature she was much more comfortable as the recipient of pleasure. Clarissa had been rough and forceful; she seemed to prefer being in charge, as I usually did. Edward was somewhere in between. Languid, slow, but confident, lazily building my arousal as one might fan an ember into a blaze by blowing steady, patient breaths.

Clarissa picked up the harness with her middle finger and

dangled it in front of me. The dildo threaded through the centre swung from side to side like a pendulum.

I took it from her and then tossed it to the foot of the bed, out of the way.

'I want Edward to fuck me,' I said, and as the words formed on my lips I felt a surge of arousal flooding my veins.

I genuinely did want him to fuck me.

He pulled me back against him and his cock jutted into the back of my thigh, rock hard.

'Make her wet,' he ordered Clarissa.

She ran her fore and index fingers through the valley of my cunt and then placed them to her lips and sucked off whatever moisture she had found there.

'She's dripping. But a little wetter never did any harm . . .'

She stubbed her cigarette out on a silver ashtray that rested near the wine bottle and glasses and then shifted onto her knees in front of me.

Her tongue parted my lips.

I groaned.

Edward let go of my breasts and stretched in front of me, gripping Clarissa's hair and pulling her face hard against my cunt.

'Suck her,' he said.

Clarissa obliged.

I was sandwiched between them, struggling to keep my balance, the hard wooden edge of the futon's frame pressing uncomfortably against my shins. Edward kept one of his hands clamped onto the back of Clarissa's head, and the other he lowered to my arse. His finger travelled between the cleft of my buttocks to my opening. He pushed inside me, one finger, then two, as Clarissa's tongue teased my clitoris. I felt as though I might faint.

'Ohh,' I moaned.

Clarissa pulled away, gasping for air, and I crawled onto the bed on my knees, and kissed her. Her mouth and chin were sticky with my juices. I wanted to climb onto the dildo that still hung between her thighs and ride her, but instead I moved into the position that I had adopted for her when we fucked, the same stance that Iris had adopted when Thomas had entered her. All fours.

He promptly flipped me over, and pushed one of my legs into the air and over his shoulder. He raised himself up my body and I looked down and saw the head of his cock, millimetres away from my hole. It was covered with the thin, almost clear film of a pink condom, stretched so tight that it looked as though he might burst out of it.

'Look at me,' he said, and I did, and he plunged inside me.

'Oh, Jesus!'

I had seen it coming, yet his moment of entry was still a shock.

There was the sound of buckles unfastening as next to

me, Clarissa removed her harness and set it aside. She began to moan softly and I could hear the slip, slap of her finger rubbing against her own nub. She was watching us, masturbating.

I ground my hips against Edward's, trying to feel him deeper inside me. He grunted, pushed my other leg up so both were hooked over his shoulders and his cock was filling me completely, and yet it still wasn't enough. I grabbed his arse with my hands and pulled him against me harder with each thrust.

He bent down and kissed me again, wetly this time, our mouths open and clumsy, teeth knocking, tongues out of time, neither of us able to co-ordinate the rise and fall of our jostling bodies and the uncontrolled sounds of our pleasure.

I hung onto his shoulders, embracing him tightly, biting his shoulder, my legs tangled around the backs of his thighs, trapping him against me, willing him to drive inside me deeper and deeper again, never hard enough, unwilling to beg him to fuck me even more fiercely for fear of sounding ridiculous.

Clarissa let out a strangled cry. She was nearing the point of orgasm.

Edward's whole body tensed and I pulled him inside me and his sounds mingled with hers, a chorus of coming, and he shuddered and collapsed. I lay beneath him and continued to grind my hips against his until his cock softened.

201

He kissed my cheek, and rolled off me, then threaded his arm under my shoulders and I leaned against him. Clarissa scooted up and nestled into my other side, and we fell asleep together, the three of us, still wet and embracing.

6

Subterranean

I had mentioned the discovery of Joan's erstwhile association with the theatre to Clarissa, and enquired whether there was any way that Gwillam and I might obtain access to some of the Princess Empire's records to investigate further. At first, she had appeared reluctant. An initial sweep through personnel records proved inconclusive as only the previous ten years' were held.

'Might they be kept anywhere outside the theatre?' Gwillam asked. 'In storage?'

It appeared not and, apart from profuse bundles and dusty folders of mementos of previous shows, past programmes, photographs, cuttings, stage notes and financial papers, it seemed that the theatre had not retained anything of a practical nature about the people who had worked there over the decades and any information that might once have been retained had by now been disposed of or even destroyed. Living memories are seldom documented.

The news was immensely disappointing to Gwillam, as if a promising line of enquiry had been nipped in the bud. I was in two minds. After all, Joan was a relative of Iris's and the abrupt severance of my ties with Iris had made Joan's memory more distant, less immediate. In addition, all the events of the past few weeks, the questioning of relationships, the new bonds I was forging, the complications of sex, all of this still left me bewildered and confused.

Clarissa promised she would ask further questions of some of the older stage hands when the opportunity presented itself, and a week later she called me down to her office and informed me that someone who had once worked in the props department had a vague memory of Joan and there was a remote possibility she had left something of hers behind. She had, it appeared, departed the theatre's employment under something of a cloud all those years back, and not bothered to gather all her belongings in the rush to leave.

Clarissa suggested Gwillam and I come to the theatre the following Sunday morning and we would go hunting for the possible papers or clothing Joan had abandoned; the older backstage guy who had come up with the information was unsure what exactly Joan might have left behind, the news of its existence having only reached him second-hand.

It was a rainy early winter morning, the leaden sky heavy

with rolling masses of low clouds, and a bitter chill clouded our breath. Clarissa was alone at the stage door in the small alley that bordered the theatre and opened the door for us. The building was in eerie darkness, a sight I hadn't come across before, with just the faint glow of security lights flickering across the narrow corridors surrounding the auditorium, leading past a series of doors to the backstage areas. She had warned us to each bring an electric torch, but the illumination our trio of amateur explorers thus provided was notably insufficient, barely forming a slither of light in front of our feet before being smothered by the surrounding obscurity. I felt as if I were living through a Hammer horror movie as we made slow progress, reaching a concealed set of stairs that led to the theatre's basement areas and tentatively putting one foot forward at a time as we began our hesitant descent.

'Couldn't we switch the main lights on?' Gwillam asked.

'I haven't got access to the central electrical controls,' Clarissa explained. 'They're disabled when no one is around, to save on bills. We're not supposed to be here,' she added. 'The only reason we got in is that I did a deal with the night watchman and promised him I would keep guard on the place while he returned home two hours early.'

'Is there anything valuable stored here?'

'Not really. I suppose mostly the costumes. The remaining sets in storage couldn't really be used again elsewhere.'

By now, we had reached the third basement level. I had never been aware how far down the theatre's premises extended.

'I've only come down here once before,' Clarissa said, 'and that was years ago. I'm told there is a depository area of some sort. Stuff that's been sitting around for ages but no one can be bothered about getting rid of, let alone investigating. If Joan left anything, we should locate it there.'

The air was damp and dusty. Ideal breeding ground for mice. Or rats. I had an innate repugnance for rodents of all kind; even possums used to scare me to high heaven when I was a child. I dared not ask Clarissa if there was a chance of coming across any. I took Gwillam by the hand and held on to him tight. His palms were sweaty.

The wavering light of Clarissa's electric torch bounced between the walls and ceiling like a flitting will-o'-the-wisp.

We squeezed our way through a teetering maze of raised panels, old sets and separations, painted backdrops, and uneven piles of long redundant props: tables, sofas, curtains, framed reproductions of paintings, old clocks that had never functioned, vases. We had moved on from the horror movie to Ali Baba's cave. Everything was piled high, festooned with cobwebs that I guessed were genuine and anything but theatrical, while motes of dust danced through the air as we disturbed the accumulated layers carpeting the stone floor of the forgotten storage area. Clarissa stopped.

'If only we knew what to look out for …' she said with exasperation.

'I haven't a clue,' I indicated.

Gwillam's hot breath breezed against my cheek.

'What would Sherlock Holmes do?' I asked him. His hand tightened around mine and I knew he was smiling.

'If she had to leave her clothes behind, I reckon they wouldn't be around lying loose. They'd be in a suitcase or something, surely?' I ventured.

'Good point,' Clarissa said.

We continued our search.

We were no better off a half hour later, and even though none of us wanted to be the first to admit defeat, we all knew how close we were to giving up. The whole exercise felt futile.

There was a corner of the basement where the ceiling curved and to venture into it would require us bending uncomfortably. The recess was full of wooden pallets loaded with moth-eaten, rugged squares of thick material, like an old Arabian rug that had been torn apart and reshaped into asymmetrical squares and was now piled high, an irregular hill of detritus that would never see the light of a stage ever again.

I sighed, my gaze already moving away from the worthless rubbish stored in the corner. As my head moved, out of the corner of my eye, I caught sight of a dark shape peering out from under the lengths of rotting carpets. It was brown. Angular.

I stepped nearer and extended my hand.

Hard to the touch. Leather.

I disturbed the layers of material under which it was partly buried and the sharp corner of a large trunk revealed itself.

I wiped the surface clean with the back of my hand, diverting a thick cloud of dust that lingered briefly before floating down in slow motion towards the basement's floor.

Scratched gold letters engraved in the burnished leather of the trunk, carved into its geographical centre.

Two letters: J.N.

Joan Nutting.

I excitedly called out to Gwillam and Clarissa.

'I've found it!'

They came rushing, their torches blinding me briefly as they waved them in my direction.

'The trunk ...' I said. 'It can only be hers. It's what we were looking for ...'

'Well, what are the chances of that?' Clarissa said.

'Allow me.' Gwillam moved to my side and leaned over to reach the trunk's loose strap and pulled it towards us. More dust was freed. All three of us were overcome by it and began coughing.

Once he had cleared his throat, Gwillam remarked, 'It's

incredibly light. The trunk is so large I thought it might be rather heavy, but that's not the case. Not much inside it.'

Clarissa's voice was rough, the dust still bothering her throat. 'In that case, Gwillam, let's just carry the damn thing out of here and return to civilisation,' she suggested. 'I've had enough of dark places for a lifetime!' I doubted that was true. Clarissa seemed to me the sort of person who thrived in darkness, but I kept that thought to myself.

Five minutes later we had fully retraced our steps, and exited the theatre by the stage door in the alley. Gwillam pulled the trunk out behind him and Clarissa locked the door.

The rain was now sparser, the weather more clement, but still bothersome enough for us not to linger outside.

'So what now?' I asked the others.

'It's up to you,' Gwillam said. 'You wanted help in finding it. Only fair that you should open it first and see what it contains.'

I looked up at Clarissa.

'Your call,' she shrugged. 'I've never been a big fan of mysteries, anyway . . .'

It was agreed that I would take care of the trunk and transport it to my bedsit and let them know at a later stage what I came across inside: old clothes, priceless jewellery – which we knew was totally unlikely – baubles, anything of interest.

Clarissa hailed a black cab on the corner of Charing Cross Road. Gwillam kissed me on the cheek and took off home on his bike.

The trunk was not locked, just secured by a pair of straps that it was easy to loosen.

There were very few clothes inside: a couple of corsets, a nightgown that had seen better days, a moth-eaten summer dress and a pair of shoes that had probably been old-fashioned already a quarter of a century ago, and that I could not imagine someone like Joan having worn.

A meagre booty.

And underneath the thin layer of Joan's abandoned belongings, wrapped inside a single flesh-coloured stocking and secured with a wide red rubber band, a small book and thick envelope.

I opened the envelope first, pulled out a dozen hand-written pages. The ink, once purple, was beginning to fade but I recognised Joan's handwriting immediately.

As I pondered whether I should read the pages or was invading her privacy, I held out the small book and saw it was actually a diary. Page after page, in the same scrawl.

Would these pages answer my questions? Help bring Iris back to me?

I began with the letter.

I read it slowly.

Several times.

Spring

It was a letter to a lover. I felt like a terrible intruder, spying on someone else's deepest secrets. But by the time I came to its end, my mind was frantically piecing together the information in the letter with fragments of my own childhood memories, the childhood that I had shared with Iris. The way that she was so different from her parents, and how we often joked that she must have been adopted. Her mother's strange distance, the way that tension lingered in the air like a fog in her home. Her father's arms on the steering wheel of his beloved Valiant, stiff as two boards as he drove us to visit Iris's grandmother.

I noted the date on the letter. Did the maths.

Could it be true?

Was Iris actually Joan's daughter, and not her grand-daughter as we had initially believed.

I found it both difficult and painful to wrap my head around the notion.

It changed so many things.

What should I do? Contact and inform her? Would she hate me for doing so?

I needed time to think.

I would read the diaries later.

I wasn't ready for further revelations.

May 25th, 1928

I have been thrown out of my lodgings again, and this time I am entirely innocent – it transpires that I have been living in a brothel these past six months.

You must think me a fool, diary, for never having noticed the multitudes of strange men traipsing up and down the corridors, their tread hurried on the way in and jubilant on the way out. Perhaps I have become morally bankrupt, or think too well of my fellow humankind, since none of the women who roomed here ever struck me as anything but good and kind, and all of the men who visited seemed to me gentlemen.

I narrowly avoided arrest, having arrived home from the bakers at Spitalfield's market with a fresh loaf of bread for my breakfast, just as the police were storming the building. June Cooper, who occupied the room opposite mine and until today I had mistakenly believed was a Sunday school teacher (!) popped out from behind the shadow of a drinking fountain by the Vallance Road recreation grounds and warned me. She had been working at the time and run from the house in her night dress, if you could call it that, a tiny flesh-coloured slip of a thing that exposed her ample bosom entirely, and only just covered her backside, revealing the plump expanse of her dimpled thighs.

I gave her my coat as she told me everything (though I confess that I continued to picture her without it), cursing all the while about her client who had grabbed his hat and bolted the moment the first cry had been heard, without paying her fee.

For now, I am bedding down in the basement of the Princess Empire. I dare not let on about my troubles to my employer, lest he think that I might bring disrepute on the theatre, and I lose my job in the chorus line as well. I managed to sneak into Hughes Mansions after dark and collected just what I could carry in one case – a few clothes, my small book collection – but I dare not return again. My vase had been broken and flowers scattered, my mattress overturned, and the little purse of savings I kept there gone. All that I have in the world, and taken by the police I have no doubt. It's a topsy-turvy world when the whores show kindness and the authorities are thieves, but that is human nature for you.

Who knows how long I may stay here. Half of the city is still in ruins after the flood, thousands homeless and landlords being mostly a scurrilous lot, the rents have gone up outrageously. I have copied a key from the bunch the security guard keeps on his person – it was so easy to lift them from where they hung on his belt as I passed him in the corridor that I reckon I might have a career as a pick-pocket if dancing ever fails me.

October 19th, 1930

Again, my wages have been cut. These are not good times and the management have decreed that we women in the chorus line should be both fewer and less-remunerated. I agreed to the new terms. I enjoy the dancing and the gaiety it provides my life with, and the companionship of my fellow dancers, and cannot think of any other occupation which, though badly rewarded financially, I am now suited to. I just cannot see myself happy with the life of a cleaning maid, a shop assistant or working in a factory. It would be

213

like a living death, I feel, being away from the music, the lights, the effervescence of working in theatrical shows.

However, I just see no way I can continue to afford my Hammersmith lodgings, modest as they are, with my pay at the theatre and must endeavour to find another source of revenue to supplement.

The devil whispers in my ear and I am tempted . . .

June 19th, 1932

I would never have guessed the life of a prostitute to be so tiring.

Today I pleasured two prominent political figures – who shall go unnamed, even to you, diary, for a whore's discretion is her valour – and a bootmaker who could only afford one quick rut but offered to resole my shoes in return for a second go, and a short rest in between. I hope he brings my shoes back, else I shall have to track him down in my slippers.

The bootmaker was as short and round as a beer barrel, he had a beautiful cock, long and thick, and thank the gods, clean, for I had to sneak him into the back of the Empire without any chance to repair to a bathroom. I had him wear one of the costumes from 'Pirates' and pretend that I was a fair maiden, kidnapped and plundered along with a ship full of booty. He tied me to the railings and had me over the stair well, and oh, diary, how I loved the cut of the ropes that pinched against my skin. I almost offered to fuck him next for free.

Spring

September 25th, 1933

Today a woman paid me to make love to her for the first time. We did it in the back of her car, a sleek red and black affair with cream leather interior and silver fittings. Her driver watched us in the rear view mirror, smoking a cigarette all the while as if he were bored as hell.

'It's my husband's car,' she told me as I frigged her. That only made me frig her harder. I made her tell me about him while I rode her. We had nothing with us, no dildos, just our fingers and tongues and bodies so I had her lie back and I got her nice and wet then ground down against her until she came, still talking about her Gerald. I wonder if, miles away, in his spacious office, his ears were burning.

December 15th, 1934

Winter has come again. Somehow it feels colder this year.

I am afraid.

Not for my soul, no — I gave that up a long time ago. And not for my material possessions, precious few that I have.

The work goes well, mostly. The fervour I felt when I began has waned, and truth be told I sometimes miss my job on the chorus line although I still call the Empire home, and flit between the basement and the rafters. Should the theatre ever need an understudy, I know the lines to every play in production. But of course I can't let on that I am here.

There is a rumour that the place is haunted. I overheard the prop boys complaining. Shirts going missing and then reappearing, cleaned and ironed. Hats hanging from one branch of the hat tree popping up on another branch. Shoes polished in the night. Cufflinks put away in a drawer and now found on the countertop. Piles of rigging rope moved. Strange noises after dark. Grunting, groaning, a woman wailing. Well of course it is me, and the longer they go on believing that I am a phantom, the better, because they are all too afraid now to take the stairs any lower and discover my little cubby hole. My only home since the Hammersmith digs I was evicted from when my secondary profession was discovered since a travelling salesman who also lodged there recognised me exercising my other skills in a place of ill repute and took offence when I refused his entreaties to service him for free. I must just make sure that my noisy clients be still, or if they must cry out, cry out like spectres, for fear one of the staff suspects a ghost with rather more human appetites!

I do not fear for my conscience. I have grown convinced that there is no immorality in the pleasure that I seek, no crime in the pleasure that I provide for others. I do not fear for my livelihood – I am now over thirty and age has only heightened my talents in the dark art of sex and increased my popularity.

And yet I worry for my future. I am not so foolish to imagine that my fellow citizens forgive my sins as I forgive my own. My passions mark me. The strange shape of my desires like an ink blot that seeps from my heart and through my clothes, damning me in the eyes of others. Even when I am bathed and clean the smell of *sex lingers on my skin, in the curl of my hair, the twist of my wrist, the sway of my hips. They know. They hate me for it.*

I live on the fringes of society, always pretending that I am someone other than I am, else I may end up on the wrong end of a police constable's truncheon or worse, folded into a trunk and used as a piece of furniture to rest teacups on like the poor whore whose case is in the courts now, may she rest in peace. I am grateful that my body seems unwilling to carry a child, so I am spared at least the clumsy knives of back alley abortionists.

Yet I cannot bring myself to seek solace in a life of respectability. An unsuspecting husband, a permanent home, wealth. That would be a sin against my own soul, and far greater than any small hurt I might be responsible for in my profession.

For now, I continue to make my home in the Empire's basement, skulking in the shadows like a rat, sating only my lust. I long for love and friendship, and a home somewhere. A place to belong. A place where I might, if my womb allows, be able to bear and raise a child alone. I wonder if such a thing exists in another time, another city. Somewhere across the stars. Such things seem to me a feeble dream.

February 7th, 1935

I think I must be dreaming.

Tonight I walked the streets of Piccadilly. A light rain was falling, and the pavement was slick with water. Street lights burned like torches beneath a blanket; too dim to pierce their way through the thick smog that draped over all who hurried by as if we were wearing hats and jackets made of mist. It was the sort of weather that makes carrying an umbrella pointless, and so I had abandoned mine, since earlier gusts of wind had snapped half the spikes and rendered it of little more use than a newspaper held over only half of my head. Moisture floated like a haze in the air instead of falling down from above, and any attempts to block its path were therefore futile. I did not even bother to quicken my pace, since I had no engagements this evening, and was dressed in my thick red coat with the belt pulled tight and the collar turned up.

George, my faithful pirate, cobbler and rope extraordinaire, whose belly grows larger by the visit (I don't mind, so long as his cock doesn't shrink), had just reshod my favourite walking boots, and kindly padded the inside with a little sheepskin trim so my ankles were warmer than ever.

I stopped to admire the Eros statue at Piccadilly Circus, a lone crimson figure in a sea of rushing pedestrians and traffic, all hurrying towards hearth and home. Had I not been so acutely aware of drawing attention to myself, even in that crowd of blank, uncaring faces, I would have turned my face to the sky and opened my mouth to drink the rain. Then again, since even the mist is not immune to London's pollution, perhaps it is for the best that I kept my lips closed.

That was when I saw her. At first, I noticed just her cigarette. A steady pinprick of light in the fog, somehow still glowing despite the damp. I recognised a fellow traveller of the night. Something

218

imperceptible, like a shadow, that can never be erased or even entirely hidden. I sensed instinctively that the cigarette-smoker was watching me, and yet I felt neither the hunger that emanates from a prospective client, nor the disdain that pours in waves from the constabulary.

I stared back. Then I noticed her hair. A river of fire-red locks that flowed from her head all the way down to her feet, as if she had a silken cape attached to her scalp.

She was dressed in a full-length black coat with wide cuffs, a thick deep collar and a princess cut that nipped in at the waist and flared out at the skirt. Her boots were mannish: flat and knee-high with half a dozen silver buckles up each side. It was the sort of outfit that might be worn by a spy, and I wondered briefly if she might be concealing a dagger within its voluminous folds. I was not afraid. I was thrilled. She radiated something like electricity. The air around her was alive; she crackled. I wanted to be near her, in spite of (or perhaps because of) any danger.

She called me by my name.

'Joan.'

I walked towards her as though pulled by invisible strings.

She did not move to greet me. Just continued leaning against the lamp post, smoking her cigarette.

'Your work has come to our attention,' she said.

Her words reached me as a curious form of flattery and I responded like a puppy given a pat on the head.

'Yes?'

219

'Yes. We have had many reports of the ghost of the Princess Empire, the phantom whore of the theatre. All of them favourable. You have many admirers.'

Her kind words were like a warm balm and I shifted closer to her.

'I . . . thank you,' I stuttered.

'Such work cannot always be comfortable.'

'It is not comfort that I seek.'

My words seemed to finalise some lingering question in her mind.

'I come to you with an offer of employment,' she said.

'I am already employed.' (A little flattery had already made me arrogant!)

She dropped her cigarette to the pavement and ground out the ember with the flat of her boot. Then she looked me straight in the eyes. Hers were a strange shade of greenish gold, the colour of a deep stream in sunlight.

'You will prefer this work,' she said, 'and be handsomely rewarded for it.'

'Doing what? And where?'

'I work for an organisation that runs events. Exclusive events. Parties, if you will, though they are far more than that. We will pay you to perform. To fuck men and women. To dance. All over the world.'

She moved her hands as she spoke as though she were knitting a pattern with the rain.

Spring

'I will be a whore, then.'

'Yes. A very good, and a very well paid, whore. A pleasure bringer and seeker, rewarded accordingly.'

I accepted.

And expected her to vanish into the mist like a wraith, but instead she agreed with me a date to complete the necessary paperwork and begin my training, and then stepped onto the number 14 bus to Streatham.

Autumn soon merged into winter. The days grew shorter, and skies were overtaken by greyness.

The run of the Victorian slasher play at the Princess Empire finally came to an end and, a week later, a boisterous all-female version of a Shakespeare comedy was launched. It barely lasted a couple of weeks following a spate of unanimously bad reviews right after opening night and the theatre had to stay empty for over a fortnight. I was on half wages as a result, until a revival of a Gilbert and Sullivan operetta currently touring the provinces could move down to London and the theatre would become busy again.

Clarissa had been engaged on a freelance basis to assist with the costumes for the notorious Peter Brook *Marat/Sade* play soon opening at the Aldwych and became mostly unavailable, working all hours of the day in a studio in Stratford-upon-Avon with the rest of the director's team and never picking up the phone, while Gwillam was in the last throes of revisions for his law exams and not inclined to spend time gossiping with me.

Neither Iris nor Thomas had been in touch with me and I felt awkward contacting them. Maybe I was secretly hoping that their relationship would run its natural course and she would, of her own accord, return to me, having miraculously come to her senses. It was like a minuscule seed that I harboured inside my heart and protected quietly, in the hope that it would inevitably flower and grow beyond the daydream into full-blown reality.

London was effervescent with excitement. I wandered Soho's music clubs and the Covent Garden venues, which seemed to sprout overnight and then disappear as quickly as they had arrived, overcome by the talent of folk singers, bands and musicians, mostly my age but already wrapped in an aura of myth that I knew deep inside my heart I would never attain. I was not creative, merely a follower, a fan among many, and the suns of others burned bright and made me feel inferior, even worthless.

I had been rationing the pages of Joan's diaries, reading just a few entries at a time, as if to make the story last forever. It entranced me, made me want to be a fly on the wall of this fascinating, now lost world she had moved through. It also touched me deeply, making me think much too much, setting off triggers in my mind that I didn't always know had been there.

Spring

The experience with Edward had shocked me. Not so much the fact that he was a man and had expertly known where to touch me and originated a chain reaction down in the core of my body and, to my utter surprise, managed to elicit pleasure in ways I had not known possible. But with Clarissa absent, I had no way to reach Edward again; I knew he was part of a couple, and that one would not move without the other's accord.

Joan's writings evoked similar feelings, proving there was nothing unique about me, let alone my reactions and enjoyment of sex, or my occasional feelings of confusion and shame of my own desire.

I lay in my bed at night assaulted by cravings, some of which even surprised and shocked me, had me yearn for even more extreme situations into which I could plunge head first.

The romance of the whip.

The yearning for defilement.

The often disgusting pleasures of men.

The masks. The games. The exhilaration of dark rooms and unknown beds.

The pleasure. The pleasure.

I was confused. Yearning. Scared by what I was finding out about myself.

I needed someone to talk to. And didn't believe Gwillam was that person right now.

Maybe Iris. But then how could I broach these matters with her after the way we had become estranged? Would she become irredeemably angry at me for unveiling the secret of her origins?

There was a cellar bar on Dean Street which I had been given to understand catered to women only. By the time I arrived, it was crowded. Dimly lit and low-ceilinged, a suspended haze of cigarette smoke floated across the bar counter. I ordered myself a shandy. Looked around. Even though it was apparent that the majority of women present indulged in the same sexual preference as I mostly did, by their looks or the way they dressed – although many appeared quite girlish and, should I say, so normal – I felt invisible.

Ordinary.

And too timid to engage in conversation with total strangers. Most appeared to be part of existing groups anyway. I was somehow hoping someone would approach me first. But none did.

Even the two barmaids remained distant and sullen, busy dispensing beverages, their gazes never alighting more than a second on any given customer, a perfect portrait of indifference.

My drink tasted watered down and I left. Walked down Shaftesbury Avenue towards Piccadilly Circus. The theatres were disgorging crowds onto the pavements, all apparently so much busier than the momentarily shuttered Princess Empire. I zigzagged my way through them.

Remembered one of the adventures Joan had written about. One that had profoundly shocked me. An early occasion when she had been penniless and unable to meet her rent, let alone purchase food. I recalled the tale and the name of the hotel. The Regent Palace.

The lobby was a mass of humanity. Tourists, provincials, a characteristic blend of old and young. I headed for the bar. The lights were set low and the room was warm. Unlike at the Dean Street club where I had felt invisible, I felt normal here. Here, I belonged in a paradoxical way.

I was unsure what to order as a young grey regulation waistcoat-wearing barman with long, lank hair and a CND badge pinned above his heart asked for my order. In the background, Mantovani and his Strings could be heard playing the theme from *Exodus*. I could recognise the tune with one ear closed, as it had been a favourite album of Iris's father – or at any rate, her adopted one as I now knew – who would invariably play it repeatedly on Sunday afternoons while smoking his pipe, the acme of his leisure time.

I settled for an apple juice.

Retreated into daydreams, barely noticing the ebb and flow of the customers entering and departing the bar, the couples cuddling in the alcoves, the singletons checking out the competition and the business men in tweed suits, white shirts and ties, the crowds milling in the lobby beyond the bar's swing doors.

I was awoken from my reverie by a desultory rap by the barman on the counter in front of me.

'Uh?'

'Someone wants to buy you a drink. Another apple juice, or maybe something stronger?' he asked me. For a moment, I even thought he was winking at me.

'Who?' I looked around. No one stood out.

'The gentleman at the far end.' He nodded in the man's direction.

I peered at the stranger. He was caught between two opposing sources of light as the bulbs illuminating the bar area cancelled each other out and I had difficulty clearly making out his features. All I saw at first was a quiet wave of the hand as he identified himself. I had to squint. Hoping as I did that the man would not think I was actually smiling at him.

He was of indeterminate middle age. Wore a dark suit with stripes, either black or navy blue, with a regimental tie of some sort. He was neither ugly nor attractive, just average in looks. A slightly hooked nose, full mouth, tanned complexion, as though he had just returned from holiday and his hair was combed back.

I ordered a scotch.

He watched me take my first sip. Then rose from his stool and walked over to me and sat down. He was taller than I had initially thought, and even when he was sitting alongside me I had to look up at him.

I instinctively looked at his hands. He wasn't wearing a wedding band.

'Cheers …' he said. I couldn't get a grasp of his accent.

'Thank you … for the drink …' I muttered. The liquid burned my throat, albeit in a pleasant way.

'I'm Zander,' the man said.

'Zander?'

'It's short for Alexander.'

'Ah,' I nodded.

'You?'

'Me?'

'You have a name, I assume …'

'Joan. It's Joan.' No way was I going to tell him my real name, and right then it was the only one that sprang to mind.

'Nice to meet you, Joan.'

'You too.'

'Call me Zander. I see you're from the colonies?'

'That's one way of putting it,' I said.

We fell into an uneasy, pointless sort of conversation. He was a Sales Director – not a salesman, he loudly insisted, although it made no difference to me whatsoever – for a company based outside Brighton manufacturing bespoke soft furnishing and was in London for an exhibition at Earls Court.

By our second round of drinks, I'd moved on to white wine and in a gesture of familiarity his fingers were grazing my knee. I let him. I felt nothing. Tried to think of myself as a blank slate.

I agreed to yet another glass, but resolved not to drink more beyond that point. Whatever happened, I wanted to be lucid. An impartial observer. I disliked how Zander's hands kept on surreptitiously touching me. My knee, my elbow, my side, as he tried to make rhetorical points. He seemed more intent on talking about himself than enquiring about me anyway, splendidly unaware of my total lack of interest in him as a person.

But he was a man.

And I was coming to an uneasy realisation that maybe a man was what I wanted right now. To find another form of fulfilment, anonymous pleasure. Something normal, uncomplicated. To be passive. Was it my mind or my body talking? Between the semi-monologue that came in one ear from Zander's direction and promptly flew out of the other, my certainties oscillated wildly.

'... my room?' Zander's voice faded back into my consciousness.

'What?' The look on my face must have betrayed the fact I had been faraway.

Spring

'I was saying how nice it is to be able to chat to someone. Maybe we could repair to my room and raid the mini-bar, no?'

'Why not?' I found myself answering. Zander offered me his hand as I slid off my stool. The waistcoated young barman smiled at me, as if approving the total indifference of my decision.

We shared the lift with a family of German tourists who gave us disapproving sideways looks as if they well knew the purpose of our upwards journey.

Zander unceremoniously grabbed my arse as we walked into his room. Because of the prestigious location of the hotel, I was expecting something large and luxurious, but the space was narrow and dimly lit, not much larger than the bedsit I had shared with Iris and still occupied on my own.

Flipping the light switch with his free hand, Zander pulled me towards him and pushed his lips against mine. I had to stand on tiptoe to reach him and closed my eyes. Up front, he smelled of cheap deodorant or cologne. Our noses clashed. Why did this never happen when I used to kiss Iris?

His fleshy lips parted and his tongue forced its way into my mouth. He tasted of booze and other things I would rather not think of right then. I passively bore the brunt of his embrace, coming to the realisation that every man was different and that this one, Zander, the Sales Director, was

229

in no way comparable to Edward and his elegance and refined attention to the way his partner of the hour reacted, or even Thomas and his innate forcefulness when he was with Iris.

Locked into the kiss, I felt his hands move across me, grope randomly, dig into me and his growing cock strain against the wall of his pinstriped trousers as he aligned his body against mine. His breath quickened. I felt limp and detached from the whole predictable rigmarole unfolding.

Almost a spectator.

He parted briefly from me and threw off his jacket, then loosened his tie and unbuttoned the front of his shirt.

'Do the rest,' he asked.

When I had pulled his shirt sleeves off and he stood there topless, pale hairless white chest and uncertain abs on display, he kept on gazing at me.

'Trousers,' he ordered.

I fumbled with his belt, pulled the zip down and revealed his Y-fronts. And froze, knowing there was now no going back. Is this what I was really seeking tonight to alleviate my loneliness and confusion?

'Let me see you,' he continued.

In a daze I began to shed my clothing until I quickly stood facing him in just my non-matching underwear. A sly grin animated his lips.

'Nice,' he remarked.

He moved closer to me, spun me round and began fiddling with the clasp of my bra. He was only partly successful and, after a short while, he gave up and pulled the straps down towards my waist and uncovered me. I unclipped the bra and let it fall to the floor. He turned me again to face him, got down on his knees and pulled my knickers down. I held my breath.

'Very nice,' he stated. Was he comparing me to others he had known or was he just being polite? I was adrift on the etiquette of the circumstances. Trying to recall whatever comments Iris might have made in the past about my body. Or had she ever done so?

He rose. His erection straining against the fabric of his white pants, a ramrod shape whose outline appeared fiercer than if it had actually been unveiled and mere hard flesh and veins.

'Suck me.'

It was now my turn to lower myself down to my knees, though not before noticing with no small amount of irritation that he had only looked at me, not made any attempt to give me pleasure. I slowly approached his crotch, holding my breath, and my lips met the thin, warm material and roamed briefly against the cotton hill of his unfurled penis. I extended a tongue, puckered my lips and took his covered cock an inch or so inside my mouth.

'Not like that,' he remarked and pushed me briefly away

and pulled his pants down, allowing the cock to dangle out and extend to its full length.

'Now.'

His smell was unlike Edward's. Where Clarissa's partner's long and languorous cock had retained a faint smell of lime from his previous shower, Zander's shorter but significantly thicker appendage emitted a suffocating, musky odour and a curious pulsing heat that quickly faded.

Again I opened my mouth and tentatively seized the glans of his cock between my lips, licking its extremity, tasting the velvet smoothness of its raw skin, pushing back his short foreskin. His cockhead felt rough against my tongue, but altogether pleasant in a soothing sort of way. I circled his ridge, delineating it, exploring its borders. As hard as he already was when I had taken him into my mouth, I could feel the penis growing still harder as I partly swallowed it and moved cautiously, attempting to match my ministrations to the rhythm of his cravings, communing with the growing tenseness of his body and the fingers now sweeping through my hair.

'Not so fast,' he cried out as I settled into a quick/slow/quick sweep of my tongue across his bare skin and began elevating his levels of sensitivity. 'I want to make this last ... Get value for my money ...' he snickered. I presumed that he was talking about the wine, not that it had seemed very expensive.

He withdrew from my mouth and nodded for me to get to my feet and brusquely kissed me again. His tongue deep inside me, reaching for the back of my throat, as if mapping the emptiness his cock had just abandoned.

I held my breath.

His fingers roamed across my body, weighing my breasts, kneading my arsecheeks, pinching my nipples until I was forced to exhale if only to control the rising pain this provoked.

Unlike the thousand kisses I had exchanged with Iris, there were no emotions involved in his frantic embrace, just something both feral and mechanical which my body blandly accepted and refused to acknowledge as a trigger for sensations of pleasure. Perhaps he was just not very skilled at lovemaking, but I felt myself too inexperienced to be an adequate judge.

We parted.

'Let's fuck. Now,' he said.

'Okay.'

'I hope you're clean.'

'Of course,' I said. 'I showered earlier . . .'

He laughed. 'Very funny . . . I meant you're clean of any diseases?'

I blushed.

'Totally,' I blurted out.

He stepped out of the pool of his trousers, bent down to

reach the jacket he had shed and extracted a small, flat cardboard box from one of its inside pockets.

'Better safe than sorry,' he said, pulling out a condom. He tore the envelope and handed it to me. His cock stood straight and rigid. 'Put it on.'

I tried not to panic and to puzzle the delicate manoeuver out, stretching the plastic skin open and attempting to place it over his hood. But the elasticity of the material and my nervousness worked against me, and I failed. Zander shrugged and took over, sheathing his hard cock in one swift, practised movement. I stepped towards the bed.

'No,' he stopped me. 'Not there.'

I stood looking at him, nonplussed, noticing with dismay that he had kept his socks on. They were black and reached just above his ankle.

'I want to have you on the floor.'

He gripped my shoulders and brusquely forced me down onto all fours. I felt the bulk of his body looming over me as with his foot he swiftly spread my legs open and lowered himself. His fingers parted my lips, noting my lack of lubrication.

'Damn it, you're so dry . . .'

I heard him spit on his hands and wet his cock.

First the squishy contact of his soft balls pressing against my buttocks, then the tip of his cock exploring the rim of my hole and a sudden thrust and he was inside me. Filling

234

me. Stretching me. Impaling me. The initial pain was intense. Edward and Clarissa had caressed and played with me endlessly, prepared me with kindness, before Edward had finally entered me, finding me open, welcoming and eager. This was brutal, invasive.

The salesman began to thrust, a loud exhale of breath with every repetitive movement, animalistic, greedy.

He grabbed my waist with both hands to steady my wavering position and continued his attacks. I felt my bowels loosening, my insides turning to mush, my borderline hurt inevitably retreating into a diffuse sense of arousal.

But before I was anywhere near ready to climax it was all over.

'Fucking hell!' the stranger inside me cried out. 'You fucking slut. You're so tight. Aahhh . . .'

He bucked, dug deep and hard into me with a final violent thrust and orgasmed with a mighty roar of pleasure. Then collapsed onto my back, short of breath, still panting.

We never exchanged any further words.

His lust sated, he eventually pulled out of me in silence, retreated to the bathroom at the far end of the narrow hotel room, ignoring me all along, and hurriedly washed, then dressed and left the room, slamming the door behind him, as I lay on the floor, mute, naked, breached and incomplete, still in a daze, trying to process the experience.

When I finally rose and looked around, the hotel room was singularly bereft of his possessions, cupboard empty, bathroom free of toiletries, as if he had never stayed here.

I looked around for my clothes. On the pristine bed Zander had left a couple of banknotes. For me.

I swallowed hard.

It seems I was worth a whole week's rent.

He had hired me, bought me, used me.

Was that why I had ended up here, I wondered? And I recalled the stories in Joan's diaries of the sex she had sold, her mixed emotions around the fact.

And I tried not to feel bad about it.

The second time was easier.

And the third and fourth, and the times after that, easier again.

I remembered what Joan had said in her diaries, about travellers of the night carrying a certain aura with them – a shadow – that was recognisable to others of the same ilk. I had no wish to walk the streets, for fear of my safety, nor to join any kind of brothel that might give me some harbour and convenience but end in my being caught in a raid and treating myself to an unwanted criminal record.

There was something more than that, too. Each time I pretended that I was just going to try it the once, and then one more time again, each occasion planned to be the last, until my curiosity was piqued once more or my loneliness reached an even lower ebb. Joining a bawdy house would have cemented my place in a world of whoredom, in a way that lingering in hotel bars did not.

Nobody ever mistook me for anything other than a prostitute, no matter what I wore. I began to wonder what it was exactly about me that gave men that impression, since my skirts were not short and my blouses not low cut. I had never thought of myself as coy, or a particularly good flirt. Perhaps it was just unusual for a young woman to spend time alone at the bars of upmarket hotels.

My second was a man younger than I was, only eighteen, and a virgin. I did not believe him at first, until his hands began to shake when he undressed me. He was dark haired and pale, with pointed ears, and a wide mouth and he asked me to teach him how to bring a woman pleasure. I told him that to teach him that, I would need to demonstrate on the body of another woman, for I could give pleasure in others, but I was still not sure how to elicit my own.

'We don't have another woman,' he rightly pointed out.

He didn't have any money for a hotel room either, having only cobbled together enough to linger in bars like I did, hoping to come across someone either cheap, or easy.

That night, I was both, so for a little more than the price of a nice dinner I led him into an alleyway and ordered him down onto his knees and under the shadow of my skirt, and I held his face against me and had him lick me until I came into his mouth. I had to help him up again, since his legs had gone numb beneath him.

The third and fourth occurred at once. Two men whom I met in the American Bar of the Savoy paid me ten pounds each to have them together. I had hoped to see them make love to each other but was disappointed. Instead they wanted to both penetrate me at once, and I let them, on the proviso that I could see the cock of the man who intended to fuck me anally first. He dropped his trousers in the elevator, and I gave him a blow job for free, having first decided that his penis was sufficiently small to enter my arsehole.

The fifth was at least three decades older than I, and could have passed for my grandfather. I returned again to the Regent Palace and encountered the same bartender, who this time looked at me with disdain.

The man's name was Harry, and he worked as a podiatrist. 'A foot doctor,' he said, when I admitted my ignorance of the term. He had a flat rump and skinny legs and his ball sack was pale and wrinkled. He paid me to simply stand over him and shout obscenities as he crawled at my feet, but after a few feeble attempts, I had to tell him to get up again and confessed I couldn't do it.

'Touch me if you like,' I told him, and I lifted his hands

to my breasts. He began to cry, still holding my breasts. My nipples grew hard. He tipped me more than any of the men before him.

There was a red-haired man from Missouri who told me that he was travelling the world and intended to try a different woman in every city.

'It's kinder for me to fuck whores,' he told me, as we shared a cigarette afterwards. 'Saves breaking hearts.'

I could barely understand a word he said, but I liked him all the more for it.

Another was the son of a policeman, who claimed to be trying to break as many laws as he could without ever really hurting anyone, just to piss off his father. His cock was as small as my thumb, and stayed perfectly limp the whole time, but he brought me to orgasm twice with his tongue, and slipped a finger into my arse.

The last one didn't tell me his name – only his wife's. Maureen. He showed me a well-thumbed picture from his wallet. A pretty blonde with a blunt fringe, grey eyes and a wide smile, wearing a pale blue blouse buttoned all the way up her throat. Her arm was nestled around a young boy with the same colouring, dressed all in red. They both looked awkward captured by the lens of the camera.

'She looks nice,' I said. 'And your boy.'

'Not my boy,' he replied, and slapped his wallet shut.

He fucked me hard, and pulled my hair until I asked him

to stop. The next day I found bruises on my thighs where he had gripped me in the missionary position.

Their faces and hair cuts and smells all blended into one another, until I began to try avoiding any real personal contact altogether and just getting straight to business. I developed a desire for cocks, without the men attached to them. I wished that I had X-ray vision so that I could look through a line of trousers standing at a bar and see whose was largest, straightest, longest, thickest, smoothest, without being so enormous as to actually cause me pain. I longed for Edward's cock, which had been perfect to my mind, in all of these respects.

I avoided repeat customers. The virgin who had gone down on his knees for me in the alleyway came back to the Regent Palace looking for me. I told him I couldn't help him, and he offered to take me to the pictures instead.

'I don't want to be alone,' he said.

We watched *Here We Go Round the Mulberry Bush*, a lighthearted comedy about suburban youth on the make which bore no resemblance whatsoever to my reality, because someone had once told me I looked a little like the actress Angela Scoular who featured in the film, and I let him hold my hand. His palms were sweaty. He had to hold his jacket in front of his erection as we exited the theatre. He paid for a cab, and I took him back to Hammersmith with me, and rode him in the garden, underneath the lemon tree. I told him to never contact me again.

I often returned home sore, but never sated.

I was so terribly lonely.

7

The Romance of the Whip

Gwillam was aware of my whoring. Or was there another, better word to describe my recent unconventional sexual entanglements? Several times a day, my feelings about what I'd fallen into veered between shame, horror, resigned acceptance, using curiosity as an excuse, and many more thoughts and back again. I knew I wasn't doing it for the money, surely not? So why did I keep on doing it?

I had to talk about it with someone, and there was only Gwillam who could lend a sympathetic ear and not be judgemental, I reckoned.

'Hmmm ...' he said, after listening to my story. I'd provided him with a digest version and none of the crude details. 'I just hope my own dubious example hasn't proved a bad influence.' Somehow he appeared to find humour in the situation. Certainly more than I did.

I repressed a smile.

'It's just a phase I'm going through,' I said.

'Exploring possibilities?'

'Exactly ...'

'Well, if like me, you don't see it as a permanent sort of activity, I'd say there is no harm in it,' Gwillam stated. 'It's all experience.'

Since Iris had left to shack up with Thomas, Gwillam had become a true friend. Like a brother, almost, and because of his own sexual inclinations didn't feel in any way like a threat.

I nodded. But then I would have done so whatever justification he had offered me in the circumstances in my unspoken search for forgiveness.

'Talking of experiments,' Gwillam said, 'I've been invited to a rather particular celebration tomorrow. Should be something of an eye-opener. And I'll be off-duty, so to speak, so in a better position to enjoy the fun. Care to join me?'

I agreed.

Rain was pelting down outside the tall Belsize Park two-storeyed mansion and we'd rushed from Chalk Farm underground station optimistically hoping our flimsy umbrellas would not be blown away or torn apart during our hurried progress to the house, carting along our surprisingly light shopping bags in which Gwillam had packed our outfits for tonight.

There was no one at the door to greet us. Beyond the open front door was a small well-lit hall and an umbrella stand already bursting with dripping brollies packed tight in an architecture of calculated chaos. The house had a welcoming warmth to it.

I followed Gwillam in, shook the rain off my jacket and undid the shawl that had, not entirely successfully, kept my hair dry. Gwillam pulled back his hood. He looked at ease, if out of breath from our frenzied uphill run from the Tube to the house.

He caught his breath.

'Have you been here before?' I asked him.

'I have,' he replied. 'But I was otherwise accompanied on that occasion, if you know what I mean.' He sketched a weak smile. I instantly recalled, heat surging into my wet cheeks, the spectacle at the party in the Chilterns of him being used by the other man, his thin body shaken by the vigorous thrusts of the stranger fucking him. 'But I'm not working today,' he added quickly, seeing the confusion on my face.

He had warned me earlier that this was an occasion where we would have to dress up. 'A fancy dress party?' I had asked. I hadn't been to one since I was a child, and still remembered the choice I had then been given to be either a fairy princess or an evil sorceress. I had chosen the latter, while Iris had opted for the side of virtue versus evil.

'Not quite.'

I hadn't questioned him further. I trusted Gwillam.

The door to the street swung open behind us as we stood there brushing off the rain, and I glimpsed a cab driving off as an older couple sheltered under voluminous capes stepped in to the hall and silently acknowledged us before quickly divesting themselves and laying their sodden outerwear on the wooden bench to our right.

I gasped.

Under their travelling clothes, they were both encased in thin, black leather bodysuits that shadowed every inch of their form, capped off by knee-high boots. Hers sported thin, rapier-like, heels and his, thick wedges that added a good few inches to his height. Both looked unnaturally pale, making me think of vampires in a bad Christopher Lee B-movie, and their eyes were an eerie shade of green. Must have been contact lenses, I reckoned, as they were strictly identical in colour, and I didn't believe in coincidence.

Seeing them emerge in all their thin, leather-sheathed splendour, even Gwillam lost some of his assurance and stood there gazing at them, his lips half-open, as if uncertain what to do next.

The man rapidly looked us up and down, disapproval on his emaciated features.

'We had to travel here on foot,' Gwillam blurted out by way of explanation, and pointed at the wet carrier bags we had set down on the ground.

The man blinked. The woman standing by him smoothed the creases in her outfit, her long fingers travelling lazily across her curves.

'Over there.' He pointed at a recessed door. 'You'll be able to change,' he said.

He turned his back to us and stepped to the end of the hall and into a dimly-lit corridor. The woman followed him.

Once again we were alone. Gwillam picked up the bags and pushed the door open with his foot. It was a small windowless room. There was a built-in cupboard which was open and in which an assortment of clothes were hanging or draped across the closet's floor, and a dozen or so shoes were scattered in a corner. Other guests had come in here prior to our own arrival to also change into their chosen outfits. There were two narrow wooden benches on either side of the small room, on which we could sit.

'Good,' Gwillam said. 'Now to blend in better.'

He passed one of the bags to me and busied himself emptying the other onto the bench on which he perched and proceeded to pull off his sodden shoes. I walked over to the other bench at the opposite end and did likewise, and kicked off my flats. I looked up, seeking a mirror or something in which I might be able to adjust my make-up. There was nothing. How was I expected to look good?

Opposite me, Gwillam had by now taken off his shirt,

revealing his anaemic hairless chest. As I was pulling off the tight Electric Garden T-shirt I was wearing, tugging it past my ears, I realised with dismay that I was wearing underwear that didn't match, a pair of simple white cotton panties and a red, lacy padded bra. Then, as I my hands delved into the shopping bag and found nothing but a pair of heavy metal-tipped boots, a long thin stretch of narrow black satin and an instruction sheet folded in four indicating a myriad ways in which the ribbon might be tied to constitute an outfit, I knew instantly that the state of my lingerie was of no consequence tonight as I was unlikely to be wearing any.

I unclasped my bra, allowed it to fall to the ground and began the laborious exercise of untangling the slippery piece of fabric, and was puzzling out how this curious if abbreviated outfit should be worn properly, standing there in just my jeans, when Gwillam called to me, and snapped me out of my reflective daze.

'I need your help, Moana.'

I looked over at him. He had risen from the bench and was now stark naked. He stood upright, his thin pink cock hanging between his legs, cushioned by the soft, seemingly elastic sack of his balls and the slim outline of his white thighs. It was strange how I could peruse Gwillam's naked body with neither attraction nor repulsion. I was entirely indifferent to his nudity.

'I have to get myself into the outfit,' he said, pointing at the pool of black latex he held out in his other hand. 'Can you talc me over?'

I must have looked confused.

'If you cover my body with talcum powder, it will make it easier to slip into the suit,' he explained. 'I'd do it but I'm bound to miss a bit and then make it tear. Latex sure is a bastard.'

He extracted a plastic Boots baby talcum container from the carrier bag and held it out to me.

'All over,' he advised. 'Start from my feet.'

I shook the container and a fine mist spread across my hands like a suspended cloud of dust. I began by coating the raised soles of his feet, and then methodically spreading it upwards across his ankles and calves. The natural whiteness of Gwillam's skin now took on a cartoon-like unnaturalness as I reached his knees and distributed the baby powder onto his thighs. Just a hand away from my fingers now, his cock imperceptibly twitched.

At that same moment, the door to the changing room opened and a tall woman barged in, throwing off a wet green mackintosh and kicking it into a corner.

I looked up. And recognised Matilda.

'Ah, the young playthings!' she said, peering down at us through a sodden fringe she promptly combed back with her fingers.

I felt defensive, struggling for words to justify being

caught massaging baby powder into a naked guy while squatting down uncomfortably on my haunches.

'It's for the costume,' I muttered. Gwillam stared at her with a look of deference. He also knew who she was.

'Yes, I know, dear,' Matilda said. 'Latex outfits can be a bitch to slip on, can't they?'

She looked away from us. She was wearing a thin white silk tunic, Japanese in appearance, which starkly revealed every curve of her body beneath its shimmering looseness, the outline of her hard nipples beneath it dark hillocks pointing upwards to her swan-like neck. Her lipstick was crimson, her eyes lined with a strong frame of darkest kohl. She looked imperious. And dangerous.

'Don't stop because of me,' she added, fussing with her hair, her long nails streaking through it in an attempt to order it back into the shape she preferred.

Gingerly, I shook the container and the mist floated momentarily in front of my hands before settling down on Gwillam's exposed skin, the top of his thighs, his cock and balls and, my mind a deliberate blank, I began to spread it across his whole midriff. Even though not at full attention, his penis felt hard to my touch. I tried to remind myself that we were related. I heard him hold his breath as my hands washed across his body and his parts.

I kept on liberally coating his skin with talcum powder, finally making my way past his stomach and now generously spreading the white cloud into his chest, neck and thoroughly under his arms. Gwillam thanked me and took hold of the latex costume, wriggling his way into it, first forcing his legs into the second skin and then, with difficulty and a measure of studied contortion, his hands followed by his arms. I could see how the coating of talcum powder made the exercise easier; without it, even slow progress would have been almost impossible to achieve, as well as decidedly comical to witness.

Finally, he stood encased in the black costume from neck to toe. I saw a hood in similar material waiting on the bench, with small circular eyelets and a zip where his mouth would fit. He picked the hood up and, holding it open carefully, squeezed a few puffs of talc directly inside.

'Saves spreading it over my face and probably into my eyes,' he explained.

I nodded, and resolved never to wear such an outfit myself, not that I would be likely to ever require anything in latex. I couldn't imagine how Gwillam would manage to go to the toilet during the evening. Hopefully he wouldn't ask me to assist.

'Your turn,' Gwillam intimated, pointing to the long satin ribbon. I was still staring at the instruction sheet, trying to decide which of the various configurations would look good and actually stay in place all night. I had rummaged all through the bags, but didn't find any trace of sewing kit or pins. With a nod of the chin, he indicated the panties I was still wearing. With Matilda still present, although too busy right now seeing to her own adjustments to pay any attention to me, mussing her hair, smoothing her silk tunic, I felt terribly self-conscious, painfully aware of the cheap nature of my Marks & Spencer cotton briefs and the fact that my body could in no way rival hers for curves and innate elegance.

I quickly slipped off the knickers and stuffed them down inside the carrier bag, and turned, preserving what was left of my modesty from her gaze and possible scrutiny.

'Let's puzzle this out,' Gwillam said, picking up the untidy array of what was supposed to be my costume and holding it up to me. There was a moment of silence as he studied the instruction diagram with rapt attention, and I heard a swoosh as Matilda left the room, finally leaving us alone, openly wounding us with her indifference.

'Raise your left arm,' Gwillam suggested, passing the length of satin over my shoulder, running one extremity over my breasts and frowning in concentration while he repeated the manoeuver around my other shoulder and breast and attempted to fix it into place without any fastenings. 'Hmmm,' he reflected, observing his work. 'This is worse than architecture . . .'

It took another few minutes for him to complete his construction of the diminutive costume and dressing me into a state of relative undress. The endless black strap was finally in place, circling me like an octopus, my whole body criss-crossed with a series of interconnected satin strips, and creating artificial curves that I felt did not belong to me, highlighting every single imperfection I was aware of. Not that it was much of a costume anyway, as over three quarters of my skin was still bare and on flagrant display. It almost felt worse than being naked, like being trussed up for a slave auction. At least there was no mirror in the room for me to actually witness the spectacle I would be making of myself.

'Rather fetching,' Gwillam remarked as he gazed at me with a faint smile spread across his lips. 'Now, the boots,' he said.

They reached to mid-thigh, and fitted me like a glove, their metal-tips burnished and fierce. But the heels were higher than any I had worn before and I would have to walk most carefully with them to avoid toppling over and appearing even more ridiculous.

'Good,' Gwillam appraised me. 'I think we're ready.'

'I suppose so,' I said.

'Time to rock 'n' roll, then ...' Taking me by one hand and holding his talced black hood in his other hand, Gwillam opened the door and we followed in Matilda's footsteps. I doubted, though, whether I was about to shake my bones or blissfully body sway to the sounds of Jimi Hendrix or the Incredible String Band, let alone Pink Floyd ...

Spring

A warren of rooms opened up on both sides of the lengthy, carpeted corridor.

Had I been expecting an atmosphere reminiscent of the Hellfire Club, all underground grottos, naked stone walls dripping with the accumulated sweat of decades of excess and flickering torches, I would have been sorely disappointed. The rooms were dimly lit, but the fixtures and decorations were pleasantly anonymous if not even suburban in their plainness. Furniture straight out of high street displays, imitation art deco lamps and fixtures, brocade curtains, pastel-coloured throws and coverings.

Folk were gathered in small groups, standing about in clusters, talking in low, hushed voices, leisurely sitting on long sofas, deep in conversation, balancing glasses of wine, or moving at random between the set of available rooms with no particular destination in mind.

Where matters parted from everyday reality was in the way everyone was dressed. If I had thought that Gwillam and I would stand out, I was wrong. We were even unremarkable. My revealing network of black satin geometric strips was actually modest in comparison with the way some of the other women, and men, were clad. My eyes ran frantically between the gathering's motley participants as we strolled along, unable to register all the details without lingering too long on the way. Sumptuous and regal sets of breasts were cupped high, as if held in vices and offered for wanton display, jewellery-adorned or actually painted, or the inescapable size of the frequent metal-like codpieces fronting the men's fierce leather garments where there was actually a barrier protecting their genitalia. Some of the male standers-by had even dispensed with the formality of cock shields or cups, a circle cut into the fabric of their breeches unveiling the jutting of their cocks and the weighty back curtain of their ballsacks. I tried not to stare. Especially at the rings and small metal bars that sometimes decorated their cocks.

Modesty was not the order of the day, but, paradoxically, most of the people here wore diverse masks, so that few of them actually displayed their features. I was one of the rare open-faced persons present. I looked around at Gwillam; he had slipped on his black hood, so all I could see were the pinpoints of his eyes and the slash of his thin lips peering between the zip.

'Quite a party,' I whispered to Gwillam.

'A birthday,' he remarked.

'Whose?'

'Just an acquaintance,' he answered. 'A male friend.'

A murmur of sounds reached us as we arrived at the end of the corridor and walked into a large conservatory situated towards the back of the house. The light here was even dimmer and it took me a while to get the lie of the land and pick out what was happening in one corner where some form of activity was taking place. A short man dressed in a Pierrot costume was trailing a whip in his right hand and demonstrating to another how to wield it properly. The man he was teaching wore an elegant white dinner suit, a shocking-red bow tie like a splash of blood around his throat, and his face was obscured by a Pulcinella mask topped off by a matching hat. There was something sinister about the cartoon headgear and the contrast with the clean lines of his tailored suit.

As I observed them, my eyes were captivated by the swish of the whip and the way it caressed the dull brown leather of the stool he was practising on. A small crowd observed them, standing in a circle around the two men.

A flash of recognition drove through my mind, recalling Joan's tales of whips and punishment, and the way those stories had perversely excited me when I had read them.

Pierrot corrected Pulcinella's stance and his dark, painted lips smirked with satisfaction.

A buzz of anticipation ran through the small audience.

The circle parted and a tall, stocky man, also clad in dark leather and weighed down by intricate patterns of metal straps, stepped towards us. Arriving by our side, he ignored me, made a beeline for Gwillam and kissed him smack on the lips. I froze while the kiss endured.

'Come,' the stranger said to Gwillam, his hand cupping Gwillam's latex-sheathed arse with much familiarity. Gwillam nodded.

'You'll be okay,' Gwillam said to me as he began to walk away in the wake of his acquaintance. 'Enjoy yourself . . . Do whatever pleases you. The word "no" here always does mean no . . .' He faded through the crowd, abandoning me to my fate.

I turned back to look at the Pierrot, but he had moved aside, and two women in evanescent silk shifts were sliding a small but sturdy wooden saw-horse across the floor to place it in front of the white-suited Pulcinella, who was now holding the whip aloft. From the back, the whip-wielding man looked familiar but I couldn't quite place him. The Punch and Judy hat covered his hair.

He parted his legs, steadying his position.

One of the women in sheer transparent silk, her breasts hanging heavy behind the material with a glint of sparkling metal teasing her nipples, returned, gently leading a short, fully naked young woman towards the saw-horse's frame and delicately arranged her across the padded beam. As they moved, I noted the vulnerable girl was wearing thigh-high boots similar to mine, the dark shine of the leather a striking contrast to the milky glaze of her pale skin.

My heart tightened.

The girl was now lying on her stomach and the other woman slowly parted her legs as she disposed her, exposing the pinkness of her cunt lips.

And I could not but recognise Iris.

I shuddered. Blood running hot and cold in my veins as I stood rooted to the spot. My initial impulse was to call out to her, but the words froze at the back of my throat and all I heard was a strangulated groan.

The other spectators pressed behind me and by my sides, all eager for a better view of what was about to unfold. I had no choice but to move indecently closer.

My eyes unavoidably directed their stare towards Iris's beautiful arse and the visibly wet lips of her sex.

Pulcinella moved between us, raising the whip.

Now I knew who he was: it could only be Thomas.

I was unsure now where to look first: the sheer beauty of Iris's exposed body, the elegant line of Thomas's movements as his arm rose and the whip flew or the actual whip itself – soft in appearance, multi-threaded, seductive, snake-like, so full of promises.

The whip cracked and I jumped.

A hoarse sound rose from Iris's depths as she seized up. I held my breath, as if wishing to delay the impact of the whip against the delicate surface of her skin. A sigh of satisfaction ran through the small group of onlookers.

Thomas's arm rose again. Out of the corner of my eyes, I caught sight of Pierrot, following the angle of rise and descent of the whip, a teacher approving his pupil.

Again, the thin leather threads bounced off the bared skin of Iris's arse and she trembled imperceptibly, still courageously holding back the sounds inevitably birthing in the back of her throat.

I wanted to rush to her side, kneel in front of her and hold my hand out, wipe the sweat from her forehead, soothe her discomfort with a kiss, show her that I was with her in spirit and shared the pain, but I couldn't budge. I watched as the whip inexorably rose and fell, the angle of its descent ever more perfect as Thomas grew accustomed to handling it, absorbing Pierrot's earlier lessons in a trice, even adding variations to its waltz of speed and pain.

Soon, my whole body tightened as I witnessed the tension present in her face, her brow tight with apparent distress as the assault relentlessly continued, but, to my terrible surprise, I also couldn't avoid seeing that a faint smile was curling its way across her lips, betraying how the discomfort, the pain was morphing into pleasure as a bevvy of chemical reactions exploded inside her body and brain.

My anger burst its dams.

It wasn't so much directed at Thomas, but towards Iris herself, for having allowed such a situation to present itself. But was it truly a surprise? After all, even when with me, Iris had displayed all the characteristics of submission, or at any rate a certain form of passivity. I recalled all the previous instances of Thomas's natural sense of domination, even when I had been present. The way he had conducted the scenario on that initial occasion when they had first made love, albeit with me being present, the quiet orders, the prompts. And I had silently approved. My cheeks were flushed. My annoyance was also turning to envy, a whole symphony of conflicted feelings long-distance running inside my heart. Thomas had intuited this streak inside her and taken advantage of it, or at least indulged her – while I had ignored all of the signs that had been right in front of me. Had I ever been capable of raising that enigmatic smile of pleasure across her lips? Because Thomas certainly could.

I snapped out of my own trance, as Thomas paused, took a deep breath, dropped the whip and stepped towards Iris. Her body was quite limp, spread over the saw-horse. His fingers caressed her chin, moved to her lips, wiped some involuntary drool away with obvious tenderness. The small crowd surrounding the scene began to disperse.

Thomas kneeled in front of Iris and kissed her.

Tears were running down her cheeks.

The kiss seemed to last forever.

I was rooted to the spot.

Very soon, it was just the three of us left in the room, as the bystanders had moved on to other attractions elsewhere in the house.

Their lips finally parted and the lovers realised they were not alone and both looked up and saw me.

'Oh . . . Moana,' Iris whispered.

I was momentarily struck dumb.

She shone.

The pleasure the whip had triggered inside her was like a halo surrounding the pale nakedness of her body, transforming her, electrifying her.

'If only you knew how it feels,' she said.

The look in my own eyes must have been murderous. Thomas opened his mouth.

'It was her idea,' he defended himself.

'Oh, was it? And I wonder who suggested it?' I asked him.

'I would happily have switched,' he said. 'But it's not in Iris's nature . . .'

'Would you really?' I replied, disbelieving.

'I would.'

I reached for the whip.

'Let's see, then . . .' I suggested.

I stepped over and helped Iris rise from the saw-horse. I could not avoid my eyes lingering on the red streaks crisscrossing her arse cheeks and my throat tightened. She stumbled, and I held her up.

'What do you mean?' Thomas asked.

Iris had realised what my intentions were before he did.

'No,' she pleaded, her teary eyes gazing at me. 'Not while you're angry.' Her voice was quiet, barely even a whisper.

Naked but for the shiny boots, in the dim light of the room, her pale skin glazed with sweat, she seemed so small and vulnerable. My heart dropped. But I would not lose my resolve.

'Drop your damn trousers,' I ordered Thomas.

He loosened his belt and pulled the cream-coloured suit trousers down and stepped out of them. He was wearing checked boxer shorts in shades of blue.

I nodded. 'Those too ...'

Without a sound of protest, he obeyed.

I had half-feared he would be erect and this would stimulate my anger even further, but his cock just hung limp and useless there, like an anonymous extension to his body which no longer held any power. Over Iris. Over me.

He kicked off his shoes, without unlacing them and made to take his dark socks off.

'Don't,' I said. 'Keep them on.'

He, or the protocol surrounding the scene, had allowed Iris to keep her boots on. I could do no less, I reckoned. Aside from the fact that I felt there was something profoundly ridiculous about a bottomless man wearing socks.

'All of it. Everything,' I said. 'Except those socks.'

Thomas shed his jacket, then his shirt and necktie.

He was left with only a thin white vest which stopped just above his navel.

'You can keep that,' I said. I was seething, determined to humiliate him.

Now in the shadows, Iris was silent.

261

His head bowed, Thomas walked over to the saw-horse and positioned himself across it, his arse raised and offered. I tried to retain my composure as I raised the whip. It felt lighter than I had expected.

August 10th, 1935

It has been six months now since I joined this strange circus of erotica. Already I have visited more countries and fascinating cities than I could previously identify on a map, but I couldn't tell you anything about them, since my circumstances are so unreal that I sometimes wonder if I have woken in a dream, or just lost my mind.

In July, we travelled all the way from Brest to Vladivostok, leaving the train only once, to swim in Lake Baikal. 'The sea!' I cried out, when at last we stepped from our carriages. Hilda laughed at me. 'It's only a lake,' she said. 'Shall we swim in it?'

I have become so accustomed to nudity that the sight of her body ought not to have moved me, and yet it did. There was poetry in the curve of her arse, I swear. Her red hair hung over her breasts, just her nipples visible, as if peeping out from between stage curtains. Her bush was red too, and so thick and curly. When she emerged, water dripped from each strand, and I wanted to drink it.

Later, I did.

September 12th, 1936

Back in London again. I do miss this beautiful city and all her contradictions. My purse is full enough that I could buy a room of my own now, never mind renting one, and yet I feel nostalgic for my old home and so am bedding down in the Princess Empire. Today I wandered all of my old haunts. Covent Garden and Piccadilly Circus and the Strand, soaking up the smog and the traffic jams. Westminster and St Paul's, and the view from London Bridge, that murky ribbon of water that keeps floating on without a care.

I have a few days leave before I am off again.

I even considered tracking down my old friend Gladys, and telling her that there is a place where we can be free, and I've found it. I always thought her to be so worldly compared to me. I was wrong. And yet I am jealous of her domesticity. To have a permanent home and a permanent lover – can such a thing exist without entrapment? I always wanted nothing but the freedom to roam, and now I long for the safety of a cage.

Working with the Ball, and the myriad of unusual people who make up the enterprise – the whores and the subs and the dommes and the gymnasts and the dancers and the sluts and the just plain strange folk – I am surrounded by kindred spirits. We are all of us hungry for something. Money, notoriety, family, sex, love, a place to be oneself. Here we apparently have it all. And yet I haven't found happiness. I wonder if there is more happiness in loss, because those like Gladys always have the hope that there is something more, something other to strive towards. They live in the knowledge that if they could only indulge their one secret greed then they would be content. But for those of us who have sought to quench our thirst, only to discover that one kind of hunger, once satisfied, fed, only begets another, I fear that contentment can be but a dream. We drink from a river that leaves behind it a drought.

As to what we do, that is another matter altogether. We seek pleasure, chant its wonders, perform, play, all things that the common man would frown upon but none of us have any shame. It is a continuous celebration.

We succeed in making the holy spectacles of bodies in motion an ever fantastic representation, assisted in no small part by the rope wranglers, the magicians and all the shadowy denizens who run the Ball. I am, of course, not a part of the elite, of those who determine its annual climax. Apart from the night when everything turns into sheer beautiful madness, I only see them from afar: the dazzling images on the body screen of the Mistress, the budding beauty of her Mistress-in-Waiting, the muscular energy of the stallions they have attached themselves to . . . Yet again here I am part of the chorus, but it's a whole universe from the life I lived before.

At times, I wonder what it would be like to be like them. But the feeling always passes. Being a companion of the Ball, on the road with it, preparing for it, participating in it, immersing myself in its folly, is reward enough.

Listen to me, diary! So full of foolish melancholy. How I envy those born with simple minds and hearts.

I think I will go dancing.

Spring

January 1st, 1937

I met a man last night. New Year's Eve and I was standing alone, watching the fireworks over the Thames from Blackfriars Bridge. I had both hands stuffed tight into my pockets to ward off the cold, since I had earlier left my new fur muff – the one that I bought in Paris! – in a café by the riverside where I had stopped to eat an early dinner of pie and mash.

At the moment he passed, my face was turned away from the celebrations, and staring at the young girl who adorns the drinking fountain on the North side of the bridge. Temperance, they call her. I had stood on that spot many times without really paying any attention to her small and graceful figure. There was a note of sadness in her face, and I wondered if she wanted to cast her water urn aside and dance in the fountain, instead of be forever tasked with filling it for others. A silly daydream.

'A penny for your thoughts?' he asked me, and gave me quite a fright. I jumped a few inches into the air and straight away pulled my hands from my pockets.

He wore a tan fedora, and a navy wool suit. His tie was the colour of fresh butter. Under one arm, he carried a newspaper, tightly folded. His hands were encased in dark blue leather gloves.

At that same moment, it began to snow. It was like a sign, something that would happen in the movies.

We stood still for several seconds, just looking at each other.

He was about six foot tall and lean, with short dark blond hair that had been combed back, besides a cow-lick that threatened to drop forward on the right side of his forehead. His eyes were nei-ther brown, nor blue or green, but a mixture of all three. He was clean shaven without any sign of shadow, and had a dimple in his chin.

'Don't mind if I smoke, do you, while you think about it?'

'No, of course not.'

He shifted his newspaper from one side to the other, pulled a cigarette and lighter from his breast pocket, and carefully cupped his hand over his mouth to protect the flame.

He offered me a smoke. I shook my head.

'I was wondering if the lady Temperance here would rather be paddling in the fountain, than filling it.'

He laughed.

'I suspect she would. Though maybe not in this weather.'

He wiped away a snow flake that had landed on his eyelashes.

I blew on my hands to warm them up.

'You must be frozen,' he said. 'Take my gloves.'

I have them still.

February 16th, 1937

We stayed in bed for three days and did nothing but talk, smoke cigarettes and make love. He has a little maisonette overlooking Blackheath, but also likes to fuck me in the basement of the Empire – strange, strange, wonderful man. He likes the ropes, and the costumes, and the thought that we might be chanced upon by one of the staff. He wants to do it on the stage, in front of an audience.

Spring

Just once, he says, just once after dark and we'll pretend there's a crowd watching. Wicked man, I told him, you're wicked! But he insists that he is not so wicked as I.

He sells pianos, and hasn't any money. The flat belonged to his parents. He has no children either, nor any previous marriage.

'Why have you never married?' I asked him.

'Why haven't you?' he asked me back.

'I never met a man I wanted to marry.'

'Until last month,' he teased.

He is the most beautiful man that I have ever seen nude. I light the candles around the bedding, and he sits nude on the coverlet, reading, his cigarette dangling on his lip. And I just watch him. The way the shadows flicker across his skin. I lie next to him and trace my finger over every inch. Muscles like a strong man, but not so beefy. 'Lifting pianos,' he told me, when I asked him how it is that he has the physique of Adonis.

He hails from Europe, he says, his foreign accent ever so faint. Came to this country a few years ago. He is well-educated but will not speak of his past and he evades my inevitable questions. I don't follow the newspapers but it is impossible to remain unaware of the torment and climate of fear holding the continent in its grip. There are terrible rumours, turmoil, talk of war. Having lost two brothers and seen the break-up of my own family because of the Great War, I can't but wonder why people never learn from experience.

The other night, I snuck up the stairs to where the costumes are kept and slipped into one of the chorus outfits – petticoats, bustier, stockings and all, and we played a game, pretending that I was a dancer, and him a punter, and that we were meeting and making love for the first time. He lifted my skirts and buried his face in my bush and licked my clitoris until I climaxed into his mouth, and then he just kept on licking. At first it hurt, but he refused to let me push him away, and after a time, I felt the joy rising inside me again.

He gives me even more pleasure than I am able to give myself.

I told him that, and he made me wait a whole week without touching myself until I saw him again, and I thought that I would die without an orgasm.

In a few weeks, I must return to the Ball and engage in the preparations for its next manifestation. It will be in Bristol, so I will not be far from London and we can still see each other on my breaks from training.

I have resolved to tell him all about the Ball. I am confident he will accept the news of its existence and my connection to it and not spurn me as a result. As to my life before that, I remain unsure.

June 1st, 1937

Robert, Robert – how I feared that I would lose you when I told you what I have been.

For so long I told myself that the past didn't matter. He didn't need to know. Or that he did know, he must know, for what kind of woman knows the things that I know, and does the things that I do? Certainly not a virgin. Definitely a whore.

Spring

I told him everything. I even told him that I had once sucked a man's cock in exchange for new soles on my winter boots.

He laughed.

He laughed and he stroked my hair and he said, 'Do you want to know all the things that I have done?'

His first time with a woman, he said, he was thirteen years old, and she was twenty-two. She taught him how to lick a woman, how to make them orgasm. She was married. 'I told her I was sixteen,' he said. 'I doubt that she believed it.'

He told me that he has been with a man too and I asked him to tell me everything. Everything. And I lay next to him as he spoke of their first meeting, how he felt when their lips met, the way his partner's body pressed against him, the sensation of being on his knees for another man's cock. I touched myself while he talked, and when he was done talking, he sucked my nipples and I kept on playing until I peaked. We fucked twice that night. The second time, he rode me, and hugged me so tight against him I could barely breathe. I didn't want to breathe.

He says he wants to see me when I am part of the Ball. Assures me he will not be jealous. States that even with another man, or women, or multiples of men, I will be a thing of beauty, a creature who comes alive with the tide of lust.

What a wonderful man.

December 20th, 1937

It has nearly been a year since we met, and still we cannot bear to be apart from one another more than a week at a time. I cannot live without his body joined with mine. I want to drink him as soon as I wake. Sometimes when he is sleeping, I wriggle down to his hips, and I rest my cheek on his thigh, and I lick and suck his cock while it lies still and soft and so trusting, curled against the pillow of his balls. I love the way that he comes to life in my mouth. Then groans, and opens his eyes and sighs. And when he is hard enough I slide on top of him and fuck him quietly until he wakes, and tells me that it's the best kind of morning, when the first thing he feels is my pussy on his dick.

March 11th, 1938

He has attended the Ball. Seen me there. And still wants me. Madly.

Last night he asked me to tie him.

I knotted my silk scarves around his wrists and his ankles, and bound his eyes too.

How he moaned when I slipped my finger into his arsehole. I am going to buy a dildo and a harness – or take one from the Ball. I have never fucked a man before but I want to know how it feels to slide inside Robert, to see the expression on his face when I fill him.

He looks so handsome when he is helpless.

November 28th, 1937

We have been so drunk on each other that neither of us has even *thought of how it might be to let in another. Robert always told me how he dreamed of having an audience.*

And yet, such a thing didn't seem so risqué to me. I have seen so many orgies with the Ball and while they are often beautiful, such events lose their glamour after a time.

I wanted to be one with a person. To be a pair. And we have been so intimate, we have practically lived inside each other's skins. I could only be closer to him if I were to crawl inside him somehow, if he were to actually consume me.

I have invited Hilda to be with us.

To watch us, to touch us if she wants to. We have talked of nothing else this past week but the many variations of how the three of us might fuck when that night comes. The way that her red hair will sweep over our bodies. Our breasts rubbing against one another. How Robert wants to slide inside me from behind while I press my face between her thighs and drink her nectar.

Feb 4th, 1939

Robert was travelling on the underground yesterday when I heard news of the explosions. My world went dark. Bombs. Had the war we all expected begun and we had not been told? He must be safe! He must be because without him I cannot live. I had not thought to even ask him where he was going, which stations he would pass through. I waited at home, wearing his jacket because it smelled of him, praying as though I had never fallen out of touch with God. Oh, the things I promised Him if only He would bring my Robert back. And then when I was done with God, I promised my soul to the Devil, if he doesn't have it already.

When I heard his footsteps on the stairs at last I thought I would faint.

I thought of my family for the first time in years. My mother and father, Ireland. I had stopped writing to them when I began to feel that they would no longer be proud of me. When I began whoring, I felt as though I were hiding something from them, and that they would hate me if they knew what I had become, and I couldn't bear it. Now, I imagine that they are gone, but if they are living, I wonder what has become of them and what they make of all this.

The world is changing. I can feel it. There is a wind rising all around us and I am so afraid that it will take my lover – my love – away.

July 15th, 1939

I have told him that if we go to war again, and he joins up, then I will join the Women's Air Force and go with him. I will not let him leave me. He just laughed, and ground his cigarette out on the pavement, and said that he wanted to fuck me right then and there so we crept into the churchyard by Waterloo Station and made love on a bench in the garden. On the way home we bought vanilla ice cream and tasted it on each other's lips.

Spring

May 1st, 1942

I do not know when I will receive another letter from him, or indeed if I will ever see him again. He is somewhere in Europe and is not allowed to reveal exactly where or what he is doing. I know it must be terribly dangerous.

He told me to not to wait for him. To make love to others. I cannot, without you, I said, and he laughed, and asked me what stories I would have for him if I remained a nun? Make love to them, and write to me. Write me everything. Send me letters so dirty that you make the censors pass out.

I promised him that I would, but the fire of my lust burns only for him. I touch myself and I think of him and it hurts. I cannot even bear to do that.

September 15th, 1944

We had three days together. Three glorious days and he has gone again. We spent them in bed.

He has changed, we have both changed. We are older, thinner, hungrier for each other than we have ever been before.

He jumps and cries in his sleep.

I promised him I wouldn't let him sleep.

I am consumed every moment by the thought that this will be our last together.

September 9th, 1945

This monstrous war is finally over.

Maybe our future can now unfold.

And the Ball will call me back and Robert and I can join it forever, wander the world, experience joy.

January 4th, 1947

I have just discovered that I am pregnant with child. I burn to tell him, but he is away.

He kept his commission even though this war is over and is now travelling through the devastated no man's world of Central Europe, working for the government. How I detest them, all of them. Leave it be, I want to shout, let our men come home and just leave the world be. He will never tell me about the true nature of his activities but I know it must be dangerous. He has been gone this time over a month. Normally he is back within a fortnight.

I worry.

I write him letters.

I fear I will never see him again.

That he will never set eyes on the child I am carrying. His child.

If the worst happens and Robert does not return to me, I have decided to leave this place. I want our child to come into this world away from the greyness of London and the austerity that now surrounds it.

I will go journeying again and find a new world beyond the stars.

Spring

I wanted to hurt him.

As the whip descended, it took on a life of its own. Its multi-threaded wing flying through the air with both grace and ire, forming a curve that defied the laws of geometry and gravity combined, at first suspended, then briefly floating on air before finally colliding with Thomas's bare buttock with all the unstoppable dynamics of a runaway train.

I was unsure what sound reached me first: the sharp swish as the leather made contact with his skin, or the muted sound of his teeth gritting and a deep moan taking birth in the pit of his stomach and riding through his lungs up to his throat.

I heard Iris sigh deeply behind me.

'Jesus Christ, that fucking hurt,' Thomas hissed.

My arm rose again.

I was aware of the fact I was not holding the whip right. Pierrot earlier, when he was instructing Thomas, had been careful to demonstrate the angle at which it should be wielded, and how the holder should angle his body. I followed no rules.

I paused briefly.

Thomas was catching his breath. He knew there would be more. I would not disappoint his expectations.

My wrist relaxed and the whip cord took flight again.

This time, it struck just an inch away from the previous

line of impact, flashing against Thomas's right side, instantly drawing a welt.

Thomas's whole body spasmed, a shock wave of delayed pain racing through his splayed limbs.

I wanted to see into his eyes, but standing behind him all I could peruse was the bruised landscape of his exposed arse and the darker valley of his crack. My anger was receding, gradually being replaced with an invigorating feeling of power instantly followed by helplessness, as I quickly realised that I wasn't necessarily the person in charge. He could, at any moment, just stand up and walk away. By accepting my domination Thomas was in fact as much in control of the situation as I was, if not more. As probably Iris had been in the earlier play, using her tormentor to deliberately orchestrate the rise of her pleasure. The concept felt profoundly disorienting, rocking the foundations of my uncertainties. The more I thought about it, the more confused I became.

I struck again. His body bucked hard against the fixed saw-horse.

And again.

Iris emerged from the shadows and kneeled by Thomas and took hold of his free hand, as if wishing to commune with him and share his pain.

The whip rose again. But this time, there was no anger in my arm as I studiously attempted to control the glide of the whip's flight and downplay its violence so that its threads now caressed the young man's exposed skin rather than openly assaulting it. I found a rhythm. Settled my mind. And began to understand the dynamics of the play. I relaxed.

My wrist loosened and the whip became an extension of my arm, and I patiently began to draw patterns of pink across his arse as I could feel him impatiently now expecting every new stroke, anticipating them, transforming the sharp repeated impacts into something else which held no fear and was actually welcomed.

Still holding his hand, Iris looked up towards me and, for the first time in ages, there was gratefulness in her eyes, the knowledge that maybe now I was beginning to understand her true nature. Perhaps there was a way forward for us, I mused, even if it would now include Thomas too. Although I also knew that I was not yet ready for the roles to be reversed and finding myself on the wrong end of the whip or whatever other implements might emerge from this Ali Baba cave of sweet decadence. For now. But the seed had been planted.

My arm ached.

I stopped.

Set the whip down.

Silence fell.

Without speaking to each other, Iris and I helped Thomas

rise from his prone position and watched him dress. She embraced him as I looked on, then, with an expression that reminded me of the times that we spent alone together, before Thomas, she bid me join them and we all huddled, Thomas and I sheltering her nudity in our improvised harbour.

We were inseparable for the rest of the night.

After we departed the room, Thomas fetched Iris's clothing from a nearby closet where they had earlier parked it prior to their planned scene. She had arrived at the house in a confusion of crinoline layers that reminded me of the French queen Marie Antoinette in its opulence and fussiness but suited her perfectly, emphasising her wasp-like silhouette, and bared the milk of her shoulders and the onset of her small breasts to great effect. Iris and I located a bathroom where I helped her repair her make-up following the earlier tears and she suggested improvements to mine, drawing thick lines of black kohl around my eyes and adding a touch of rouge to my cheekbones, a part of the masquerade that Gwillam had wilfully neglected. The lightness of her fingers on my skin felt like the flutter of a butterfly and, yet again, I was feeling drunk at being so close to her.

Our eyes, for now, were doing all the talking.

Iris's gaze roamed over my body, lingering on all the exposed parts my maze of satin ribbon allowed. I blushed. I looked down and saw how hard my nipples were, dark, engorged and, further down, how the untamed bush of my pubic curls burst through the feeble web of material that framed it.

'I would never have believed I would see you like this, everything on show,' Iris remarked.

'I reckon we're not in New Zealand any more, Toto,' I giggled.

We hugged.

We were about to leave the bathroom and face the rest of the evening, when the door burst open and Matilda came rushing in. She was distraught, in tears, dark eye shadow rivulets skipping down her cheeks. Her silk tunic was crumpled, the seam under one arm torn and she was missing a shoe.

She saw us, recognised us and shielded her eyes, as if embarrassed to be seen in the dishevelled state she was in.

All her haughtiness had gone, wiped away in a stroke by some unknown event or person. She brushed away some hair from her forehead in an instinctive gesture and straightened her posture, ignoring us and heading straight for the sink where she plunged her hands under the running tap and brought them to her face to wash the distress away.

I wanted to ask her what had happened but I knew she

would choose to ignore me. Had her brother, waiting for us outside the bathroom, seen her?

It was a shock to encounter Tilly in this state, and it was puzzling to me to observe such a change in her personality.

Even though I wanted to linger, maybe offer my assistance, Iris, attuned to the mood and Matilda's obvious wish to be alone, pulled on my arm and we stepped over to the door and left her there.

Thomas had, in the meantime, moved to another of the adjoining rooms where he was waiting for us and sipping from a bottle of beer, unaware of his sister's appearance. Seeing us walk in, he beamed.

'My ladies,' he remarked, with a clear hint of mischief in his voice. Iris squeezed my hand as if to warn me not to comment, let alone tell him about Matilda.

I was hoping I would come across Gwillam again that night, but he was nowhere to be seen, and there were rooms with closed doors I had no intention of breaching. I'd experienced enough surprises already for a lifetime, I felt.

Emotionally exhausted, Iris, Thomas and I left together. His car, a Renault 4CV, was parked across the street and we packed in and drove back to his apartment on the other side of town.

Spring

That night, we all slept in the same bed, creating a cocoon of warmth in which we all sheltered.

We were much too tired for anything to happen.

Tomorrow would be another day.

8

In the Days of Aquarius

There came a period of peace as one season merged into another.

After much hesitation, I agreed to move in with Iris and Thomas. His flat was infinitely more spacious and comfortable than the bedsit I was camping in since Iris's departure and commuting to my work in the West End from there would prove infinitely easier – notwithstanding the fact that the Princess Empire was not having a great patch, with a series of loss-making shows that all closed early, which resulted in me and the other part-time staff having to struggle to live on our meagre, and unreliable wages. In addition, their invitation to join them provided me with a perfect excuse to cease my sexual experiments and the aimless whoring. Clarissa was no longer employed by the theatre as her freelance commissions now took up most of her time, so I was seeing very little of her right now. Anyway, I was also wary about investing more time in my relationship with her and Edward. As much as I did enjoy their company, I knew in my bones that they formed part of another world altogether, one I could visit on occasion but never be fully included in. When I was with them, I was their toy, and nothing more. Lavished with affection and embraces, but somehow always held at arm's length. A tourist in the sea of sex.

Thomas had a small spare room, which he had previously mainly used for storage, and with Gwillam in tow, Iris and I helped him clean it out and paint it in bright colours so it could become my own little bolt hole. It also had a bed, but most nights I slept with Iris and him. As to the nature of our carnal activities, nothing was ever planned in advance and we ventured down that path one day at a time, a hand here, a touch there, a kiss, a caress, accepting whatever direction it took us in, encouraging our bodies to do all the sensuous talking. I knew this couldn't last: it felt like an armistice between wars, but I was quite happy to allow fate and coincidence run my life for now.

One evening, joined for the occasion by Gwillam, joyous and exhausted, we'd all walked down the road to the nearest local curry house where Thomas had agreed to treat us. We were none of us great cooks, and our diet had become too reliant on beans on toast, ready-made meals and hastily assembled sandwiches drowned in gallons of tea.

A final round of lagers, and some of us were already tipsy. Gwillam nudged my shoulder.

'Have you told her, yet?'

Thomas was too busy mopping up his dessert plate of gulab jamun, but Iris was still alert and looked sideways at us.

'Told who what?' she asked, sipping slowly from her glass as if trying to make the beer last longer.

I shot Gwillam a dirty look. He lowered his eyes in response.

'Nothing,' I said.

Iris grinned. Kept on staring at me. Gwillam looked away.

'You know you can't keep a secret, 'specially from me,' Iris stated with a broad smile spreading across her delicate features, disturbing her normal aura of gravitas. We were saved by the waiter arriving at our table, enquiring if the meal had been satisfactory. We all nodded approvingly.

But once he had moved off, Iris's eyes were still focused on me and it was clear she was the least drunk of all of us; despite her petite size, she'd always enjoyed a strong resistance to booze.

'Back at the flat,' I suggested. Under the table, Gwillam was grabbing my knee.

'Let me guess,' Iris ventured. 'Gwillam and you have finally dug something up about the Ball, about Joan?'

Spring

She looked quite excited by the prospect.

Once we were home – Gwillam had since gone his own way – Thomas, pretexting tiredness and some important legal meetings early the following day, soon retreated to the bedroom and was fast asleep long before the kettle had boiled for the hot chocolate Iris and I liked to enjoy prior to bedtime.

We sat in the kitchen.

I was warming my hands on the hot mug, delaying the inevitable moment of reckoning.

'So?'

I briefly feigned ignorance and took a further sip from my mug. We had perfected our own brew over the years that varied according to the ingredients we had to hand and our mood. Tonight's mixture contained a pinch of cayenne chilli that sent a burst of warmth through my nostrils with each mouthful.

'It's not really important . . .' A final attempt to deflect matters.

Iris peered at me over the edge of her mug.

'I'm not moving an inch until you fess up. You're hiding something. It's written all over your face.'

Where to begin?

'Gwillam and I did come across some of Joan's stuff . . .'

'What sort of stuff?'

'Old bits of clothing, letters, a diary . . . nothing major.'

'Nothing major? That sounds totally major! Probably fit for a museum. A diary? Have you read it? Does she talk about the Ball?'

'Yes, and yes.'

Her eyes widened.

'Why didn't you tell me before, then?'

'It's not just about the Ball,' I said.

'What?' The rumble of a night bus rushing by outside the window and a fleeting roll of light unfurling along the opposite wall interrupted us.

Iris looked puzzled, trying to imagine what else we had uncovered. Since that day by the sea and the incredible events we had witnessed and, to a certain extent, participated in, the Ball had been an obsession of hers and she had often spoken of it and the possibility that we might track it down in London.

'It turns out Joan is your mother.'

'What?'

'Yes. Her diaries make it clear, though not exactly why ... Perhaps because she wasn't married. Or maybe she feared she couldn't raise you. I don't know. The Larks adopted you and agreed to pass as your parents at her request. I'm so sorry.'

Iris's mouth formed an O of utter disbelief.

There was a moment's silence.

'And do her diaries say who my real father was, then?'

'Yes and no.'

'What the hell does that mean, Moana?'

'She writes about him, even to him in one case, but only mentions his first name and no real details ... not enough to identify him. Gwillam did have a go but there's just not enough to go on.'

'Bloody hell.'

'I'm sorry. So sorry I didn't tell you about it earlier. But ...'

Iris shrugged her shoulders. 'It wouldn't have made any difference, though, would it?'

'I suppose not.'

I was expecting her to order me to deliver the diaries to her right there and then. They were in the bottom drawer of my dressing table, wrapped inside my shawls. But she retreated into silence.

I noticed my mug of hot chocolate was now tepid and still half full. Iris cradled hers in her palms.

'I have the diaries in my room. I suppose you want to read them?'

'Not quite now,' she said in a small voice. She looked deflated and so vulnerable. I dearly wanted to hug her and hold her tight against me, but somehow the correct etiquette of the whole situation eluded me. I felt useless. I had turned her world upside down and now didn't know what to do next.

The awkwardness of the moment was broken by a knock at the door downstairs. We shook ourselves out of our daze and looked at each other. Who could it be at this hour? I peered at my watch; it was past one in the morning.

We stepped over to the window and looked down. It had begun to rain outside, a thin but steady drizzle. Matilda stood by the door, her hair lanky and damp, wearing a long tan coat. She noticed us peering out from above and waved tentatively at us.

'I'll go,' I volunteered.

'I'll come along,' Iris suggested, and we both tiptoed down the stairs in our nighties and dressing gowns to let the prodigal sister in. 'What for heaven's sake does she want at this hour of night?'

I knew Iris was not Tilly's greatest fan.

We let her in.

Her normally impeccable make-up was a mess and she was a shadow of the imperious figure I had first come across at her parent's mansion when she had ruled the roost. Still beautiful, chiselled cheekbones and shocking dark eyes whose depths seemed infinite, but tonight her posture looked worn out by winds of defeat.

'Is he in?' she asked us.

'He's sound asleep,' Iris said. 'It is late, you know.'

I was expecting Matilda to come up with some witticism or other putdown about us two girls still being awake and about, but her quicksilver tongue was evidently dormant.

She shed her wet coat and hung it up in the hallway. She wore a dull grey sweatshirt and a pair of tight jeans. This was the first time I had ever seen her not dressed to kill.

'Don't wake him up,' Matilda requested.

'Fine ... I wasn't planning to anyway,' Iris retorted.

'I need somewhere to spend the night,' she explained. 'I couldn't think of anywhere else to go.'

Who were we to refuse her?

I offered her my bed. There was no other spare bedroom in the flat. She nodded and thanked me, not even bothering to query where I would sleep or the nature of our regular sleeping arrangements.

'I'll explain it all tomorrow,' she said and walked up the stairs ahead of us, her long, perfect legs and shapely arse sheathed in denim.

At least, with Tilly now occupying my room, neither Iris nor I had access right now to Joan's letters and diaries. Probably better we both got some sleep before opening that Pandora's box. I wasn't even sure I should show them to her at all, considering the X-rated content, but I couldn't see any way to avoid it.

We joined Thomas in bed. He grunted as we slipped between the covers. He always slept naked. Iris, who kept her slip on as was her habit, spooned into him while I threw my night gown to the side and fitted myself against her back, wrapping my legs around hers as we often did, sharing her warmth. I lay awake for a while longer, overcome by our closeness, puzzled by Matilda's silent presence down the corridor in my small closet of a bedroom and wondering how this would change things, as I knew it inevitably might. Nothing lasts forever.

Matilda had panicked.

It appeared that one of the many politicians who had attended her latest party had been the victim of a press sting and his extracurricular activities exposed. However, it was soon discovered that he had also enjoyed a relationship with a good time girl who shared her favours between him and a suspect representative from a foreign embassy and, as a result, had attracted attention from not just the press but also other shady government agencies and Tilly had been brought in for questioning. She had been let off for now but strong pressure was being applied against her to collaborate with the authorities and veiled threats made to make her activities public should she not follow instructions. She was distraught at the prospect of her parents and society friends finding out what she had been involved in.

She feared that her house was being watched and had run scared to us.

'I never began organising the parties for the money, you

know,' she pleaded as Thomas, Iris and I sat around the breakfast table listening to her story. 'It was for the fun, the thrills. I tried to keep them as exclusive as I could ...'

It had begun innocently when she'd been part of a somewhat decadent group of revellers at university and one thing had led to another.

'We were doing no harm,' she continued. 'Nothing was strictly illegal. I felt like there should be a place for people like us. I still do.'

Free of make-up, lines under her eyes, wearing one of Thomas's shirts, her endless legs folded under her on the wooden bench, she now looked so much younger and more vulnerable without the protection of her war paint and customary wardrobe. I pitied her.

'What do you want me to say?' Thomas asked.

'I don't know,' Tilly replied. 'You were always the brains, brother ...'

'And you ever the chief risk taker, dear Tilly ...'

Iris and I looked on silently, feeling excluded and disenfranchised from the family reunion and dilemma we were witnessing.

'I'll be blackballed from society circles if it all comes out,' Matilda stated, as if that was the worse thing that could have happened. 'Probably lose my job.'

I wasn't even aware that she worked. She was a stylist for a leading women's fashion magazine, it seemed. Made sense.

Setting up and running the rather special parties had, for Matilda, been a game, an exercise in art direction, a perverse way of applying her talents to another field.

It brought a thought to my mind.

'When I attended the event at your parents' house outside London,' I said, 'I initially had the impression it was connected to the Ball.'

Iris shot me a sideways glance.

Thomas looked on blankly, but Tilly showed a flash of recognition.

'I've heard of the Ball,' Matilda revealed. 'It's something of an urban legend. Someone at university, an older man I mistakenly got involved with, hinted of its existence. Even promised he'd take me to it one day, but he fell aside as men do. In a way, the whole idea of it was a source of inspiration for the parties. Initially at any rate. But there is no such thing as the Ball. Just a myth for those gullible enough to believe there is a whole world out there for us pleasure seekers. I'm surprised you've heard of it too. Never imagined such a daft rumour might travel all the way to New Zealand.'

'It exists,' I stated.

Iris nodded, lowering her eyes. Thomas gave her a surprised look, both astonished by her tacit admission and the fact that she had not previously mentioned this to him.

Would I be betraying Joan by telling Matilda and Thomas

what we knew of the Ball and the way it had entered our lives?

Or what we had witnessed and been part of at Cape Reinga?

Iris beat me to it.

'We've actually been,' she said. 'Just the once.'

'What?'

'Where?'

We took turns telling Matilda and Thomas our story, and as the words unfolded on that cold London morning around the breakfast table, I felt the dormant fire the Ball had once lit up inside me rising to life again, bathing the room in a magic glow.

When I finally reached the revelations I had come across in Joan's diary it was already well past midday. By then, even Iris who was unaware of this part of the story sat open-mouthed listening to my voice.

Matilda's eyes were wide open in amazement and I could see how much the tale had affected her. Thomas was pensive and thoughtful.

All at once there were no more words.

Tilly sighed.

'And Gwillam still believes he can locate this ... place? Or thing? Or whatever it is?' Thomas asked.

'He hopes to,' I said. 'He managed to find out about Joan's diaries, so I'm hopeful he will discover more about the Ball. Its location maybe, how to make contact with its representatives.'

I fell silent.

As did the others who had run out of questions and were still absorbing all the information. All I'd kept back was the revelation about Iris's origins. That part of the tale was strictly for her and me to know.

'I have a suspicion,' I hastily added. 'Someone who might happen to be connected with the Ball.'

Clarissa.

I had no evidence to support this possibility but I had a hunch that she must know about the Ball.

She had mentioned it once, for a start. The fact that she thought Tilly's parties were attempts to pass off as the Ball. But it wasn't just that. Her words, her touch, her aura, the way she and Edward had played with me, enjoyed, opened me up to pleasure.

If anyone could lead us to the Ball, it would be her.

Matilda's mood had now settled down.

We cleared away the long-neglected breakfast things and Thomas and Iris went to dress. They had agreed to meet friends from work on Portobello Road. I declined to join them.

It left Matilda and me alone.

I asked her about that last occasion on which we had crossed paths and the tears in her eyes and her distraught appearance.

Spring

'A man. What else?' Tilly answered. There was a resigned look on her face. 'Another day, another story?' she suggested with a meek smile.

One I would look forward to hearing, I knew. I enjoyed listening to stories as much I liked to tell them.

London was vibrant.

There was a palpable sense of excitement in the air, as if the whole word were slowly changing and a new era was about to begin. 'The Age of Aquarius' if one was to believe in all the infectious enthusiasm rising from the ink-stained pages of *IT*, *OZ* and other 'underground' publications that Thomas was always bringing home.

The three of us had settled into some semblance of normalcy, sharing his flat, and reached a modicum of peace and compromises. Iris and Thomas were evidently a couple, and, because of my own feelings for her, I was reluctant to do anything that might disturb this fragile equilibrium. The sexual dynamics between them still puzzled me at times, and were further complicated by the regular instances when they invited me into their games and Thomas willingly offered to switch and be 'used' by me, if 'used' was the right word to describe what we got up to. I went along with the flow, always acutely aware, though, that I formed the extra wheel of the carriage, and could easily be dispensed with at any moment.

I would watch with a knot in my throat as Thomas mounted Iris in my presence and I would hold her hand as she opened up for him, listening to her soft moans as the sounds rising from her lungs conjugated with his vigorous thrusts. Later, with Thomas now an agreed voyeur, I would hold Iris in my arms and shelter her warmth and frailty and then lower my head to her delta and nibble, bite and play with her in an attempt to multiply the intensity of her reactions, extract more authentic sounds of pleasure from her soul than he had. And then there were the nights when we brought out the toys, closed the curtains tight and abandoned ourselves to a cornucopia of excess where, by morning, everyone had taken advantage of every other and back again, and we could barely look each other in the eye over the breakfast table. We knew what we were doing was far from normal and that other more conventional friends would never land on these dangerous shores, but the compulsion to experiment held us in its thrall.

I also grew closer to Matilda during those months, although not enough to find out all her own secrets, which she fed me on a drip, deliberately holding back information until she felt I was ready enough, I reckon. She appeared to have been forgotten, considered just a minor character in the small scandal that had arisen from her very particular parties, and was ignored by the press who had larger beasts to stalk. As to the shadowy authorities who had taken an unhealthy interest in her, she hinted that they had beat a retreat after a male admirer of hers in a high place had consented to speak on her behalf.

I saw little of Gwillam, though, as he was preoccupied by his final bar exams, and as for Clarissa and Edward, they were now overseas, having left the country for a lengthy break in the Indian Ocean after Clarissa had completed all her freelance assignments. She had sent me a pleasant note, apologising strenuously for her lack of availability and promising that we would spend time together when she and Edward returned, tanned from head to toe as she mischievously put it. So, our hunt for the Ball was for now on hold.

The musical *Hair* opened in a theatre at the far end of Shaftesbury Avenue and Thomas, through a client of his law chambers, was able to obtain sought-after complimentary tickets for a performance just weeks after the controversial play debuted. We all tramped along in a high sense of excitement and watched from the top tier of the balcony. You could feel a buzz in the air at the end of the first half when all the actors stripped off and were momentarily glimpsed in the buff as the lights slowly dimmed and before the curtain fell. Breath was held back in the audience, although the four of us (Tilly had joined us for the occasion) were disappointed. We had all witnessed so much more nudity and liberation and at closer quarters over the past year and wondered aloud, over the interval, what the fuss was all about. But the music was nice. The rest of the audience seemed more impressed and conversations sizzled in the bar and the lobby.

There were free concerts at Hyde Park, Crystal Palace and Primrose Hill. When the sun was out, the loose-limbed music rose through the air alongside the bubbles we blew, reaching for the heights where the multi-coloured kites flew and we all lazily sprawled out among the soft grass, munched on home-made sandwiches and often partook of marijuana cigarettes that Thomas or friends of his had brought along.

By now I had left the part-time employ of the Princess Empire and was working as a waitress in a newly opened Italian bar in Covent Garden, where I could chose my shifts to suit myself; the work was always available and the tips plentiful as long as I wore short skirts, which I didn't mind. It also meant I had a plentiful supply on coffee on hand, a newly acquired taste that made me regret all those years when I had been wary of the drink. I quickly became an addict.

At the beginning of the summer, we all took an extra few days off work and travelled down by train to the coast and caught a ferry to the Isle of Wight. A huge new rock 'n' roll festival was taking place there. Thomas had offered to get us a room in a local bed and breakfast but Iris had read about similar open air events that had taken place in America and insisted we all stay under a tent. We took a one-hour hike from the port to the actual site, following a caravan of folk moving onwards like lemmings seeking the promised land. It took us twice as long as most of the others to erect our borrowed tent, as the fragile construction kept on collapsing when one of us got the geometry wrong or failed to dig deep enough for the pegs to properly take hold, and we all burst out in hysterical laughter over and over again. It was at this point that Matilda took umbrage and left us in the field overlooking the cliff and went in search of a hotel room. I had never thought of her as suited for camping anyway. It diminished her mystique.

That first night it rained heavily and, inevitably, water seeped into the tent and we all woke up damp, the insides of our sleeping bags disagreeably clammy. We were still struggling with the pleasures of camping in adverse weather when, simultaneously, the sun finally came out and Matilda arrived with a welcome basket of croissants and minuscule jars of jam she had picked up at her hotel and unfolded a blanket for a most welcome feast. Unlike us, bleary-eyed and wet, hair lank and grumpy, Tilly appeared pristine, smartly pressed jeans, new hiking boots with nary a scuff, man's checked shirt and make-up all meticulously in place.

We somehow cleaned up as best we could. Down the hill, which overlooked the gerrymandered concert arena, sounds of laughter, guitars being strummed, wispy notes from flutes and the distant clatter of tambourines reached us.

'The first band is not on until after lunch time,' Iris said. 'Maybe we could climb down and go to the sea?'

Unlike Matilda, we had come unprepared and not brought any swimming suits but reckoned we could get away with swimming in our underwear. We struggled down the chalk face of the cliff alongside a narrow path and emerged onto a wide beach.

Everyone was naked.

And skinny dipping.

It felt like a vision of paradise. So natural. Simple. Normal.

Laughter sailed between the waves and the wall of the cliff as we all stripped and joined the clusters of other youthful groups scattered along the shore, sprawling loose-limbed on the beach or gallivanting in the water.

I felt so liberated.

If the nudity in the theatre had felt forced, contrived, here it was exhilarating, like a cartoon book vision of life at the dawn of time, free of morality and sin. I relaxed. Watched Thomas and Iris running into the water, dodging the low waves and laughing their heads off, splashing each other like unruly kids. Matilda sat by my side.

'Not swimming?' I asked her.

'Maybe later,' she said.

Around midday, the distant sounds of the first band on the festival's slate began to percolate across the hill and down towards us, and a steady migration began away from the beach and back towards the concert area. But many of us preferred to stay here. None of the main bands we had been looking forward to would be playing until the late afternoon or evening anyway. Thomas and Iris were still in the water.

A small group of other pleasure seekers, too cold to swim but not yet ready to leave the sea behind, gathered next to us. Two beautiful young men with long light brown hair that clung in damp, salty locks over their shoulders crouched down on their haunches to my left. A tall blonde woman, her toenails painted purple, a strand of multi-coloured diamante jewels hanging from her pierced belly button, sat cross legged between them. Another girl who looked younger than the first, probably in her late teens, stood behind them. She reached up and began pulling pins from the loose knot of auburn hair piled on top of her head. We were all huddled together gazing at the receding tide.

Daydreaming. Silent. Content. Statues of skin observing the horizon.

One of the brown-haired boys wandered his hand over the blonde's breast.

Her fingers moved from her own thigh to his dormant penis. Grazed it. The cock jumped, swelled, she took hold of it, gently, lovingly until it unfurled to full length, the foreskin retreating, exposing the darker shades of his glans.

His hand negligently descended towards her opening.

Both Matilda and I watched in silence.

301

'Fuck me,' the blonde whispered.

They shifted.

She lay back, sprawled, inviting him in. He now squatted over her and with deliberate slowness lowered himself and she guided his girth into her. They began making love.

More men and women walked out of the sea ahead of us and noticed what was happening in full public view.

They stood there, eyes agape. But smiling.

'Beautiful,' one of them said, a tall androgynous girl with almost no breasts.

'Yes,' one of the men said and took her by the hand, turned her around and gently positioned her on all fours and mounted her.

There was a palpable change in the air, as if our pheromones had formed into a low-hanging, invisible mist, affecting us all with the lustful energy of the group.

Faraway over the hill, I thought I could recognise a meandering, plaintive tune by the Incredible String Band rising towards the cloudless pale blue sky.

Tilly turned to me. She leaned over and placed her lips against mine. We kissed. The other brown-haired boy stroked Matilda's hair as she embraced me. She did not object to his intrusion. Her companion stood by me, her strong thighs apart, her auburn hair cascading over her shoulders. She wore glasses.

Matilda rose and went to join the man. I buried my face

in the woman's welcoming bush of thick curls. She smelled of the sea.

Within minutes, as I took a pause to catch my breath and look around, the whole beach had become a mad stage, with couples, trios and moresomes all kissing, fucking, loving.

We never saw much of the bands that week-end.

I spent a night at Tilly's after we returned from the festival. Iris and Thomas had been so close-knit during our trip away that Tilly and I had almost by default formed a pair, neither of us wanting to unduly intrude on the couple further.

She was staying, temporarily, back at her parents' house in the Chilterns, while they were away holidaying in Europe.

'Shall we come in for a drink, Till?' Thomas asked as he dropped the two of us off. He seemed to know instinctively that something was wrong with his sister, but was unsure of the problem. I was equally in the dark. She had invited me to spend the night with her just moments before, and her expression was so woebegone that I couldn't turn her down.

'Oh no, you two go on,' she said, hastily exiting Thomas's car and grabbing both of our bags from the boot. She seemed decidedly unwilling to have them join us.

Iris shrugged, and bid us goodbye, evidently not in the slightest bit bothered by Matilda's rebuttal.

I followed her across the gravel driveway, up the steps and through the corridor to the kitchen.

It was a mess.

Empty champagne and white wine bottles were strewn across the bench top, on the long white dining room table and in the sink. Dirty crystal flutes were scattered over all the flat surfaces. There was even a mug of something alcoholic but unrecognisable on the floor by the telephone. At least she had not yet resorted to drinking straight from the bottle. There were empty candy wrappers and half-eaten chocolate bars all around, empty supermarket ready-meal plastic containers and takeaway cartons bursting out of sagging rubbish sacks waiting to be taken out to the trash. A white, gilt-edged ceramic saucer was overflowing with old cigarette butts. Fruit flies gathered in a cloud over a bunch of black bananas and a shrunken apple piled in a glass bowl.

'Sorry about the mess,' she mumbled, standing in the doorway and staring at the mess of dishes as if amazed that they hadn't managed to clean themselves while she was out.

'Not to worry,' I told her. 'Have you had a party?'

Even before she shook her head I knew that the answer was 'no'. The shambles that surrounded us was reminiscent of the state of the bedsit in Hammersmith that I had shared with Iris in the days immediately following her departure. A landscape of depression rather than celebration.

'Shall I put the kettle on?' I suggested, pushing past her

and stepping over an empty crisp packet. I picked it up and tossed it into the nearest heaving rubbish sack, ruminating as I did so on the inequity of genetics that had gifted Matilda with a perfect set of pins regardless of how much junk food she ate. I'd be the size of a house if I indulged my black moods as much as she apparently had.

She slumped onto one of the high-backed chairs and began picking from a bag of jelly beans that sat open on the table.

I rummaged through the cupboards and eventually found a box of ordinary tea bags, hidden behind a container of imported specialist coffee beans and Selfridges branded premium tea leaves.

The fridge was brimming with wilted vegetables and packets wrapped in butcher's paper that I dare not touch for fear of what oozing, now-grey meat I might come across, well past freshness. I shook the tetra brick of milk, unwilling to hold the soggy, browning open corner of the box to my nostrils, and put it back into the fridge, certain that the liquid swishing inside seemed thicker than it ought to. I didn't trust milk that came in a carton, anyway. Glass bottles were far preferable. We would drink our tea black.

I placed the two steaming mugs onto the table, pushing one across to Matilda, brushed unidentifiable crumbs from a chair, and sat down opposite her. She had abandoned the jelly beans and moved onto a packet of Cadbury's Toffee

Buttons. I took one from the bag and popped it into my mouth.

'So,' I said at last, 'care to tell me what this is all about?'

'I'm just not sure who I am anymore,' she said.

Her hair had fallen over her face and she ran her fingers through it, pushing it back from her brow. Her long red-painted nails were chipped and rough at the ends.

'Everyone changes,' I told her.

'I don't.'

I took another Toffee Button, hoping that she would keep talking if I remained silent.

'I've been dating one of the gardeners.'

'Oh.' I had presumed that one of Matilda's parents had green fingers and took care of their sprawling back yard with its manicured lawns, decoratively trimmed hedges and sumptuous flower beds. I'd never come across anyone rich enough to employ a gardener before.

'Been dating?' I asked her. 'Something went wrong?'

'Well, yes. He's the head gardener.'

'Your parents won't approve?' I guessed.

'They wouldn't, but I could live with that. Thomas has always been the golden child anyway. Nothing I do makes a difference to them when he's turning into the perfect little lawyer.'

'I'm sure that's not true.'

'Oh, it is. I don't blame Tom for it, you know, but they

think what I do is just a silly hobby, playing at a career on a disposable woman's magazine. Nothing important. No matter that I work like a dog and had to beat off about a hundred other girls for the job. They don't think I should work anyway.'

'No? What would you do instead? Lounge around here? Or study something at University?'

'Just get married. Society girl to society wife. Mother is always pushing me onto the sons of father's friends ... you know the sort, all play polo and talk like they're going to be the next Prime Minister but if you took two of them and banged them together they'd echo, their heads are that empty.'

She hunched forward over the table, shoulders slumped, and cupped her mug of tea in her hands.

'Mm hmm,' I said. Truthfully, I had no way to relate to anything that she was saying. My background was almost as far from Matilda's as could be imagined. But I could empathise with the notion of finding oneself to be different from one's peers, the one spotted zebra in a herd of stripes.

I tried to be sympathetic.

She went on. 'Peter – the gardener – is different to all that. He thinks it's funny. Puts on a posh voice, makes fun of them. Makes me laugh.'

She took a swig of tea and grimaced.

'Sorry,' I said, 'milk's gone bad.'

'Oh, it's not that. I'd just rather champagne for this sort

of conversation, but I've run out, besides the bottles in Dad's cellar and I daren't touch those.'

I went back to the pantry and hunted through it again, this time returning with the sugar bowl and a bottle of red wine that I had found lurking behind an assortment of sauces and cider vinegar.

'Probably intended for making stew,' I said. 'Drinkable, I reckon.'

Tilly rummaged through her handbag and produced a bottle opener from one of the Tardis-like pockets. She took both of our mugs of tea and tipped them over the roots of the tall, wilting plant in a deep blue ceramic pot that deco-rated the corner behind her, and refilled the cups with wine. I took a sip and winced. It wasn't actually much better than vinegar.

'Does Peter know about your … er … other activities? The parties?'

'We met at one,' she said. 'Well, the morning after. About a year ago. My parents were away again and I hadn't planned on anyone else coming by. About 7 a.m. he shows up to mow the lawns and trim the hedgerows out back and the grass was covered in litter, bottles, lingerie … all the remnants of a party. Could have explained all that away but most of the guests were still here. The tents were up and a whole group of dommes I know – women with whips like you saw at the party with your cousin, William –'

'Gwillam,' I corrected her.

'Whatever – anyway, they were all at it with a bunch of subs in there. Spanking, pegging, the whole kit and caboodle.'

'You were there too?'

'No, I had passed out by the swimming pool, one of the lounge chairs. Still dressed in latex with my high heels on and with one of the dogs – my sub – the one you met last time ...'

I recalled it hadn't been much of an introduction. I recalled the way that his ball sack had felt in my hand when I squeezed it at Matilda's command, and shivered.

'... he was curled up at my feet on a towel, nude besides a pair of hot pink rubber short shorts, with the crotch cut open and his cock flopped out ...'

I tried not to imagine it, but couldn't shake the image from my mind. I took another gulp of the wine.

'... still wearing my collar and leash too, although I'd dropped the end of it during the course of the night. Pete came clunking by with all his gear, heading for the car park to high-tail it out of there, and I woke up, and had to ask him who he was of course, because some of the guests, you know, were high profile. Can't have strangers wandering in and out. Part of my job as organiser was to keep an eye on all that, keep it discreet. You and Iris weren't meant to be there, that night we met.'

'Well, I'm flattered you let us stay.'

'Don't be. Thomas was just showing off. I like to indulge him.'

'You don't think Peter might have been the one to tip-off the press?'

'Oh god no. He wouldn't tell a soul. The poor boy, I'll never forget the look on his face when I woke up that morning if I live till I'm a hundred. Until he saw me, I think he thought our parents were responsible. Can you imagine that?' she chortled.

'I'd rather not.' I hadn't met Tilly and Thomas's parents but had formed a mental picture of them. Polite, reserved, grand, but somehow I pictured them as beacons of propriety and repression, probably one of the reasons why their children had turned out as they had.

'It made Pete curious, I think, seeing me like that. People don't know what's inside them until something tips them over the edge. Did you ever feel like that? Like you were the only one in the world who thought about sex beyond the normal sort that most people have?'

'Sure, sometimes I still feel like that.'

'Even with all us freaks around?' She shook her head. She had stiffened her shoulders and was leaning back in her chair, long legs crossed, her usual imperious posture returning.

'I don't feel like I fit in anywhere,' I told her. 'I'm not

310

a sub, or a domme, or straight, or gay … I'm just …
weird.'

'Why do you need a word for it? A label? Can't you just
be yourself?'

'I don't know who I am. I don't feel as though I belong
anywhere.'

'I guess we have something in common after all then,'
she said, laughing. She leaned over the table and topped up
my wine.

'How did you and Pete end up together then?'

'We didn't speak much that morning. I felt horrid, hung-
over and still dressed in that hideous catsuit … I sent him
packing without stopping to think about it. I'm pretty
grumpy when I'm only half-awake.'

I could well imagine it.

'I kept thinking about him though. Not because I was worried about what he'd seen. It was the expression on his face.
Shocked, of course, a bit panicked. Probably he worried about
walking in on something he shouldn't have, that he'd lose his
job. But there was something else too. Curiosity. I was pretty
sure he had a bulge in his pants. And he was terribly good
looking. All that outdoor work, it makes men hulking …
office workers and artists, they're all too thin or flabby.'

I thought of Gwillam and Edward's bodies. She did have
a point.

'He came back the next day. Luckily I was still alone.

The slaves had finished cleaning up, so the place looked back to normal, you'd never have known what we'd all been up to. A good thing the birds and bees and trees can't talk, eh, or the secrets they'd be able to tell ... Anyway, Pete knocked on the door, and asked me if he could finish the work on the hedges he was supposed to be getting on with before my parents returned, and of course I said yes. Then I sat out front, by the French doors, and watched him. Muscles rippling and all that. Eventually he moved out of sight, but I couldn't get him out of my head so I went out there with a couple of cold drinks and we got talking. After a while he asked me about the 'whips and chains', he called it. Why we do it, what we get out of it, what the men get out of it. I suggested that I show him rather than tell him. I was joking, really. I never expected him to agree.'

'But he did agree?'

'Oh, he agreed alright. Took to it like a duck to water. We saw each other every night for months. Here, in the gardens, in broad daylight, so often I started getting grass rash from rolling around outdoors. Back at my flat in Belsize Park. I've got a proper dungeon there, all the kit. Used to belong to a musician. All the walls are soundproofed so I don't need to worry about the neighbours.'

She paused. Threw her head back and gulped down a large mouthful of wine as if she needed it to gather her courage.

'He asked me to switch,' she continued. 'And I did.'

'Wow,' I said, 'never saw you as a sub.'

'Oh, I'm not,' she said. 'As a general rule at least. But you know, I think everyone has it in them. Most people, aside from the switches – who are just greedy – favour one side or the other. But I think anyone can enjoy both, if they let themselves.'

I had a vision of Tilly, arse bare, long legs open wide and teetering on sky high heels, bent over a spanking bench like the one I'd seen Iris on. It was an altogether pleasant sight.

'Did you enjoy it?' I asked her. 'Subbing for him?'

'I did. We played so many games together.'

She wriggled forward, slipped her hand into the back pocket of her jeans and withdrew a small plastic bag with a few dried green buds in it. Further rummaging in her other pocket she produced a pouch of tobacco and her cigarette papers.

'Smoke?' she asked.

'Sure,' I said, swirling what remained of the red wine in my mug. 'I'm already half cut and it's barely the middle of the afternoon, so why not?'

She plucked a bud from the bag, using her long nails as pincers. Her jaw was tight with concentration. She licked her index finger and withdrew a paper, then carefully held it taut with her thumb and index fingers, spreading a pinch of tobacco along the seam with her other hand and then breaking the marijuana apart, careful to spread it in an even mix before rolling it into a tight straw.

I flushed, immediately imagining the way that her fingers would feel spreading my lips apart, playing with my clitoris. Her nails scratching my skin.

'Ran out of filters,' she said, holding the cigarette to her lips and flicking the silver wheel on her lighter, sending a flame shooting into the air. 'So it'll burn a bit, sorry.' She took a long toke and began to cough, then passed it over to me and continued talking.

'We could go days without eating,' she told me.

I remembered the old diary entry that Joan had written, about when she and her lover did nothing for three days but remain in bed together.

'Like we just fed on each other. I missed work. Called in sick. He rescheduled his bookings. We were like two vampires in the dark, all the curtains drawn, playing at bringing each other's darkest fantasies to life. Making confessions. I told him everything. All the things I've ever been afraid of, ashamed of. All of it. There's something marvellously erotic about shame, don't you think? But once you start playing those games with someone, you're lost.'

She removed the cigarette from my lips and took another drag.

'How do you mean?' I asked her.

'For someone who has experienced all that you have,' she

replied, in her usual snarky tone, 'you're sometimes remark-ably naive.'

I was suddenly tired of being talked down to, and was tempted to pick up my bags and walk out, hitchhike all the way back to London. Find Gwillam, someone who treated me like an equal. It must have shown on my face.

'I'm sorry, I shouldn't tease. You're young, and only just getting started. What I mean is to really open yourself up to someone, you have to trust them utterly. And once you do that, you're totally vulnerable, and you end up like I am now, drunk and stoned at four in the afternoon on a Sunday, blubbering into a ceramic mug full of cheap red.'

It occurred to me then that I had never fully trusted Iris with my body or my heart. I had kept a part of myself back. The part that I hadn't wanted to own or admit to anyone. Perhaps there had always been a wall of unspoken truths between us, and that was one of the reasons why she had sought solace in Thomas.

'What went wrong?' I asked her. I feared that if I con-tinued ruminating on my own situation, I would burst into tears. And I was not yet ready to confide in Tilly. I hadn't even worked out my own mess of thoughts, yet alone been able to articulate them to anyone.

'Relationships like that never last,' she said. 'You're just consuming each other. Something has to give. Either one of you wears the other out, or the shine wears off and you get bored. Or, you just carry on and carry on, I suppose, until you end up in the newspapers because something dreadful has happened in the quest for finding edges that keep retreating further and further away. Eventually, you work out that there aren't any further erotic heights to scale. Searching for the perfect orgasm – it's like looking for gold at the end of a rainbow, and the end of the rainbow always keeps moving.'

Again I thought of Joan, and what she'd written about insatiable appetites, hunger that couldn't be fed. I had a long way to go before I reached that point, I hoped.

'So what was it for you?' I asked her.

'He got scared, like men do. Pathetic, the lot of them.'

'Hmm.'

'Said I ought to forget about him, find someone born with a plum in his mouth and get married, have posh babies, live in the country. Didn't think it could last between us, it would end eventually so might as well make it sooner than later.'

'Maybe he really cares, wants the best for you? And doesn't think he's it.'

She shrugged.

'What do you think?' I continued. 'Do you want to get married to a regular guy and live in the country?' Not that I considered any of Matilda's usual sort of men to be regular.

'God no,' she said. 'Boring as hell, that life. I'd end up like my mother. Half comatose on Valium all day and nothing but bridge circles and sports cars to keep me occupied. I'd rather be a happy pauper than rich and miserable. I know you don't think that of me, but it's true.'

'I believe you,' I said. 'But it's not me you need to convince. Why don't you call him? Tell him how you feel.'

She snorted.

'Me, go begging on my hands and knees? Not likely.'

'You've got nothing to lose. Besides your dignity, and what does that really matter in the end?'

'I'll think about it,' she said. 'And what about you? Are you going to be the spare part in Thomas and Iris's relationship forever? Or the other two ... Clarissa and Edward? Or keep cruising BDSM clubs and parties until you work out what it is you're looking for? Or worse?' For a moment there, I almost believed she had somehow found out about my brief career as a whore. Which I had not whispered a word about, even to Iris.

'I have no idea.'

She pinched the tiny remaining stub of the hash cigarette between her thumb and forefinger and took one last deep in-breath before grinding it out on the ash tray.

'Fancy going out for a pizza?' she replied. 'It's a bit of a walk from here, but the Italian waiters at the local trattoria are cute, and technically, we're both single ...'

I agreed.

★

'Did you wear a swimsuit at all?' I asked Clarissa. She was sprawled out on the leather sofa in her and Edward's apartment, naked besides a grey felt trilby that I was sure I recognised from the Princess Empire prop room. She had never felt shy about helping herself to bits and pieces of the costumes she fancied.

'Not even once,' she replied, smugly.

She and Edward had returned a few days ago from their Indian Ocean jaunt, and the previous evening had made a reservation at Joe Allen's restaurant in Covent Garden where I was now waiting tables. She had taken obvious pleasure in running her hands up my stockinged legs and beneath the covering of the short black smock that constituted my uniform. After a languorous dinner, coffee and dessert, they had waited for me to finish my shift and then taken me home with them, flirting outrageously as we left together in front of the watchful and shocked eyes of my colleagues.

Now Edward had left for work, and Clarissa and I were upstairs relaxing, she with the day off and me scheduled on a later shift. She had managed to move from the bed to the couch, and was flicking through design magazines as I opened and closed cupboard doors in the kitchen, pulling out ingredients to make American-style flapjacks and fried bananas. I had never been able to pour them thin enough to pretend that they were crepes.

'You're as brown as a walnut,' I told her. 'I'm jealous.'

I set a pot of coffee down on the table in front of her and she reached for it eagerly.

'There's cream in the fridge,' she said.

I brought it over, poured it into her mug, added a spoonful of sugar and handed it to her.

'Why don't you go away somewhere?' she asked me. 'Take advantage of living in London, travel. Have you been anywhere else since you arrived from New Zealand?'

'I'm saving,' I said. 'But haven't yet decided where to go first. Paris, maybe?'

'You must go to Paris. But so many other places too.'

'Shit,' I said, and rushed back to the kitchen. I shovelled the charred remains of the burning pancake into the rubbish bin and prepared to start over.

'First one always burns,' Clarissa called out. 'It's the law of pancake making.'

I pulled back the curtain that separated the kitchenette from the living area so that we could talk without shouting at each other.

'Your arse looks great in that shirt,' she said, as I stretched up to hook the drape up over the curtain rail.

I had slipped into one of Edward's clean shirts, since I couldn't face putting on my uniform this early in the day, particularly since it most likely smelled of a work shift – the accumulation of sweat, cooking and kitchen odours – and still lay crumpled on the floor where Clarissa had undressed

319

me. I hadn't showered, and was still wet from last night's play. Edward had just been an onlooker, as Clarissa fucked me in both holes with a harness that held two dildos at once. She still hadn't allowed me to pleasure her, and I hadn't seen Edward bring her to climax either. She seemed to take great enjoyment from holding herself back, ever remaining in charge off all situations. I wondered if she let her guard down when they were alone. She was strongly into control.

'Thanks,' I said to her. 'Hope he won't mind that I've stolen his shirt.'

'I'm sure he'd love to see you in it.'

She was lying on her side, with one leg stretched out and the other lifted up to a right angle, displaying the largest and most luxurious bush I had even seen. It was dyed purple. Her clitoris was pierced, and curiously extended. It peeped out from between her folds, a tiny glint of alluring silver.

I forced my attention back to the frying pan.

I located the plates, and piled two high with golden-brown pancakes, covered generously with butter and maple syrup. The bananas had caramelised with cinnamon and honey and the bacon had turned to a perfect crisp under the grill. I poured orange juice into a jug, arranged everything on a tray and carried it carefully into the living room.

'My, my,' Clarissa said, 'at this rate we'll need another round to burn off the energy.'

She sat up and took one of the plates into her lap, piling a large chunk of pancake, banana and bacon onto her fork.

For a few moments the flat was silent besides the sound of chewing.

'About Europe,' Clarissa remarked, speaking with her mouth full.

'Yes?'

'Do you think you could get a week off work?'

'Probably. I've been there a few months now and at the rate they churn through wait staff, I'm practically one of the most senior ... I think they'll let me take a holiday.'

'Your cousin too?'

'Gwillam? I guess so. I could ask him. Why? Do you think I'll need a chaperone?'

She laughed.

'Undoubtedly ... But that's all the fun of it.'

I waited for her to get to the point.

She picked up her glass of orange juice and took a large gulp, then set her plate down on the coffee table and leaned back against the sofa, her small breasts jutting upwards as she shifted

'You've heard of the Ball, haven't you?' she asked. 'I remember your friend Thomas's sister – Matilda, was it? – talking about her erotic parties, and wondered ...'

'Yes, I know about the Ball.'

I nearly choked on a chunk of banana that was still making its way down my throat. Clarissa patted me on the back.

'No need to get to carried away,' she said, 'though it is exciting. You're going to love it.'

'The Ball is back? Somewhere in Europe?'

'Yes, soon. The precise location hasn't yet been announced. Just the date. And since I have attended several now, I have permission to invite others, so long as I am prepared to vouch for them all. So, would you like to come to the Ball, Moana?'

'Yes, yes of course!' I told her.

'Thomas and Iris too, if you want them. All of us. One big sexy celebration.'

I leaned over and kissed her. She tasted of maple syrup and bacon.

9

Caravan of Fools

Edward made all the arrangements.

We knew the Ball was taking place abroad as he'd asked us to bring our passports along, but that was all he let us know in advance of the departure date. Both Iris and I were lucky enough that we were allowed to take a week's vacation for the occasion from our respective jobs. The three weeks that followed the news that we were going to meet up with the Ball again had us in a state of febrile excitement and apprehension too.

I lobbied Clarissa intensely to ascertain where exactly the event would be unfolding and whether it would be under the sign of a particular theme, so we could plan our outfits and be at our best, but she remained the soul of discretion.

'It must come as a surprise,' she said. 'And as for what you will dress in, I know your respective sizes, and rest assured that a form of correct attire will be provided when we reach our destination.' She always spoke in an odd, formal tone when she was discussing the Ball, as if she were reading aloud from an instruction manual.

We were to travel light, carrying just the bare essentials, necessary toiletries and little else, Edward advised.

Gwillam had also been invited to join us and gleefully accepted, but Matilda had decided to remain in London, still in the throes of her on-again, off-again relationship with Peter. I was briefly saddened by the prospect of her absence as I had grown inordinately fond of her in the past months, but the buzz of the forthcoming journey and what might lie at the end of it soon tempered my mood. My dreams were aglow with imagined possibilities, coloured by the glimpses of what we had witnessed at Cape Reinga and the further details I had gleaned from Joan's diaries.

We met up on a sunny May afternoon at Victoria coach station. The first clue to our destination was when Clarissa led our small, excitable group to a line of passengers queuing for the bus to Amsterdam. To my surprise, Patch was waiting for us there, standing out in the crowd like a creature from outer space, her head fully shaved, a carousel of thin gold-plated hoop earrings dangling from each ear and dressed in an outfit of man's three-piece pinstripe suit and two-tone brogues, the combination of which made her look quite androgynous. Clarissa and she warmly embraced, while

Edward observed their reunion without saying a word. We joined the queue and Patch introduced herself to the rest of our group. Her lipstick was a dark shade of purple. I noticed, with fascination, that she'd also fully shaven her eyebrows. She would not go unnoticed, even more so as Thomas, Iris, Gwillam and I were all in our leisure uniform of jeans and sweatshirts, while Clarissa and Edward were also understated in neo hippy loose shirts, baggy trousers that flared at the ankle and matching linen jackets in washed-out pastel shades.

As instructed, none of us had much in the way of luggage to cart along and we soon crowded into the back of the coach.

My imagination was already running wild, remembering all the tales of Amsterdam's enticing turpitude I'd heard from Gwillam and occasional acquaintances who'd actually travelled there. The love-ins in Vondelpark, the live sex shows in the Red Light district. Already in my mind I was trying to bring to life the imagined smell of the canals.

I was shaken from my daydreaming by Clarissa's voice, as if she had been reading my thoughts. 'We won't have much time to spare in Amsterdam,' she said. 'We have a train to catch there.' I looked out of the window as a panorama of green fields still layered in places with a coat of moisture from an earlier rainfall rushed by. The coach was heading for the ferry port where we'd cross the Channel to the continent. A thought struck me. I looked over to Iris, but her eyes were closed, her head buried in Thomas's shoulder. I'd never been on a boat before.

Clarissa was true to her word. We had slept overnight on the ferry and roused in the early hours of the morning, and did not even have time for a coffee on board before hurrying to meet another coach that awaited us at the port and took us down the lowlands motorway towards Amsterdam's Central Station. Within ten minutes, we hopped on a train destined for Germany. All we saw of the fabled canals was a disappointing faint glimpse in the distance before the carriage shook into motion and began its journey through industrial wasteland, anonymous suburbs and the unending, flat low-lying fields of the Dutch countryside.

During the course of our hasty passage through Amsterdam's train station, Edward had managed to gather a bundle of sandwiches, fruit and mineral water bottles before we boarded the train and divided the spoils between us, a makeshift breakfast. The whole carriage was full apart from our compartment; eager faces, travellers from other parts; it seemed as if the whole world was congregating here for the remainder of the journey. Somehow none of us was in the mood for conversation, our minds focused on the Ball, its wonders, its secrets and our own fears about what we would encounter at the end of the journey. I quickly dozed off, still tired from our early start that morning and lulled to sleep by the increasingly monotonous landscape unfurling outside the windows.

I woke as we pulled into the steel jaws of an immense station. I rubbed my eyes clean. 'Koln Hauptbahnhof'. Clarissa had risen from her seat and was smoothing out her linen jacket.

'Where are we?'

'Germany. This is Cologne.'

The others began to jostle in the aisle, pulling their bags from the overhead racks. I joined them. Somehow since London our group had trebled in size.

'Is this it?'

'Not quite,' Clarissa declared. 'We have some way to go yet, and another boat to catch.'

There was a small dark-blue van waiting for our party below the station steps, its engine already running. Beyond it the city thrummed, industrial smells lingering unpleasantly in the air from distant factories or foundries. We all climbed in. A matching-coloured van was initially parked alongside it; peering at us through its windows were another bunch of seemingly weary passengers, who had likely travelled there from different origins. As our vehicle drove off, the other followed us.

Through narrow streets buried in shadows we moved east, weaving in and out of traffic, traversing what felt like a ghost town, until the buildings appeared to part before our wake and the sky appeared, bright blue and vast. And below it the river, wide, calm, majestic.

We arrived where our boat was moored. Squat and low in the water, one extended deck interrupted by a platform, open to the elements, with a flat roof. Painted white, with a band of red circling its prow. We alighted from the van, which had parked by the quay and walked up the gangplank to the boat's bridge where a couple of dozen strangers were already parked, their faces in turn joyous, apprehensive, expectant. Further guests for the Ball. I wondered briefly where they had come from. How long they had travelled. I hoped this was to be the final leg of our journey.

The river narrowed as we entered the Rhine Gorge, the shores growing closer on both decks of the embarkation as it deceptively appeared to drift down the heavy stream. We'd waited patiently back at the Cologne dock for a score of further vehicles to arrive, and the cruise boat was now packed with Ball guests from all corners of the globe, a melting pot of different accents, languages and attire. There was little conversation or bonding between us as each successive group of arrivals stuck to their own. Like us, they carried little luggage. To any onlooker, it would have seemed like just another cruise boat ferrying tourists, but the buzz of anticipation that ran through the passengers was unmistakable. And the fact that none of us happened to wield cameras as one would expect of the average river tourist. We were no ordinary travellers.

Clarissa and Edward appeared familiar with some of the other passengers on board and flitted amiably from group to group shaking hands or pecking people on the cheek, but failed to introduce the rest of our party to the assembled strangers.

The shores of the river imperceptibly grew into hills, at first gentle in their inclination and then fiercer until we suddenly found ourselves as if at the bottom of a deep reservoir with steep cliffs on either side looking down at us, peaks distant and high in the clouds, dominating us.

We drifted slowly for what seemed like hours. I felt as though time had become irrelevant, powerless against the current of the river. Iris shook my shoulder and pulled me over to the other side of the boat and pointed at an uncommon collection of rock formations on the nearer shores, overlooking our boat as if blessing us as we continued our steady passage downstream. Light was beginning to fail, so I couldn't get a clear view of them.

'I think it's the famous Rhine maidens,' she said. 'Wasn't one of them called Lorelei?'

'Wagner?' I vaguely recalled some of the legends we had been taught back home. And how I hated Wagner's music.

Thomas joined us, and wrapped his arms around us. We both dozed off briefly, lullabied by his warmth.

When we awoke, the boat was threading its way through a wider stretch of the river bordered by eternal dark forests that seemed to reach for the sky and loomed ominously over our fragile cargo of sleepy, weary wanderers.

Dawn was breaking, tentative shards of light winding their way through thick, low-flung clouds.

Mist was rising from the river, evanescent, shape-shifting with all the fluidity of ghosts. I peered out through the gloom. On the shore to our right, a jagged tower emerged from the treetops, stark orange, much like an ancient fortress rising from primeval depths. The turret of a castle, like a blot on the landscape of tall trees, breaking through the canopy.

Clarissa had stepped over to our huddled group.

'Is that where we're headed?' I asked her. 'The castle?'

'We are headed to a castle, but not that one. We're off to one of the Mad King's palaces,' she said. 'King Ludwig of Bavaria built all these crazy retreats in the wilderness of the hills and forests. They're actually quite beautiful.'

My throat went dry.

A premonition.

Edward, who'd by now reached her side, continued the conversation.

'Ludwig created three extravagant as well as elaborate constructions, romanesque and rococo in style. But only Neuschwanstein is truly suitable for the Ball, it was felt. It translates as the Swan on the Rock. Apparently it took the

Ball organisers months of negotiating to lease it. It's all terribly hush-hush and everyone is sworn to secrecy; the Germans would be shocked to learn that some sinister organisation had managed to hire the place for a week or so, and forbidden its access to the general public for the duration.'

'I hear the place is divine,' Patch interjected. 'Crazy but unique. Like a fairy tale streaked with madness. Quite bizarre. I read somewhere that Visconti is planning a movie about the king and its construction.'

'Who's Visconti?' I had to ask.

'An Italian film director,' Thomas answered.

'Are we close?' Iris asked.

'Patience, little one,' Clarissa said.

'We have another stage of the journey yet, from Frankfurt,' Edward added. 'We'll veer off the Rhine soon, and continue up the Main. I know it seems roundabout. But the Ball organisers prefer that guests travel indirectly. All part of the secrecy, you know, and it adds to the romance of the whole thing, doesn't it? And others will be joining us there.'

It was quiet up on the top deck, besides our small group, gathered close together and chatting under the stars. Most of the other guests had repaired to their cabins to sleep, or were freshening up in the cruise ship's luxurious bathrooms.

Clarissa wandered away again and returned with a bundle of blankets and pillows.

'You'll need your sleep,' she said, laying a soft coverlet over me and placing a cushion beneath my neck. I curled up on my seat and drifted off, taking advantage of the few remaining hours of darkness.

By the time I stirred, we had nearly reached Frankfurt. Dawn was breaking, tentative shards of light winding their way through thick, low-flung clouds. The mist over the waters of the Main had cleared.

Boat staff were distributing small hampers to the passengers. The wicker baskets were light, and once the knotted cloth holding them sealed had been untied we had access to a selection of sandwiches, cheese, ham, egg mayonnaise, evenly sliced portions of dry sausage, and pine and cashew nuts to nibble on. Under the boat's central canopy, hot tea was being served from a line of towering wood-burning copper samovars set up on a wooden table, alongside squat glasses with metal handles.

I looked around but there was no coffee available. I would have to do without.

We collected a further contingent of Ball guests in Frankfurt, all of them fresh-faced and visibly excited by our arrival. By now, we were a crowd, and a whole series of coaches and liveried drivers awaited us at the dock to transport us and our luggage to the Mad King's castle.

Spring

It was dusk when we arrived at the sleepy town of Hohenschwangau and pulled into a parking lot at the base of what seemed to me like an insurmountably craggy mountain, on which the palace balanced precariously.

'There's no road to the castle?' I asked Edward, as we filed off the coaches and lined up to collect our bags.

'Not for us,' he said, laughing at my reluctance to embark on the short climb that constituted the final part of our journey. 'The walk will do us good, after so long sitting down.'

For reasons of discretion we wouldn't be reaching the famed castle by the track normally used by the thousands of tourists who visited the place.

We began our slow trek up the steep hill, threading our way through a labyrinth of tall trees that obscured the sky.

Edward, Clarissa, Patch, Iris, Thomas and I all stuck closely together as we advanced. There was a characteristic freshness about the evening air in these hills that struck me as singularly unpolluted, lusty even. It felt as if London had been left far behind and, step by cautious step through the forest's cushioned undergrowth, I was entering a whole new world.

Ahead of me, the other guests had come to a halt, standing, leaning against tree trunks or just sitting on the ledge, all eyes on the vision that lay ahead.

We reached their level. Patch was panting, unsuited to any form of exercise it appeared.

Separated from us by a shallow man-made ditch stood Neuschwanstein Castle, a totally mad edifice of towers, turrets and ochre stones, exploding outwards from the fabric of the rugged hills, like a vision out of a twisted semi-medieval legend. It looked so solid that I disbelieved it was only just over a century old – Edward had told me a little of its story during our walk.

'Onwards,' someone said, and we moved forward towards the madness of King Ludwig's folly.

There was a flutter of velvet darkness, as if I was treading among ghosts.

I was wandering the corridors of the castle, having been separated from my travelling companions shortly after our arrival. I felt lost in a maze, unsettled by the inner geography of the place which appeared to follow no ordinary logic.

I had expected to be offered an outlandish if elegant costume for the festivities once we had all gathered, but instead, after first bathing in the elaborate washing facilities set-up just for the Ball's guests, Iris and I were handed simple, near-transparent, white cotton nightdresses bordering on the utilitarian. Clarissa and Patch had moved on to other quarters and more sophisticated attire, I guessed, as anything but newcomers to the event, and the men, Edward and Thomas, had been separated from us. We had stepped out of the large hall where the nightshirts were being dispensed to some of us to go and seek out the others and travelled down a long corridor whose walls were festooned by a series of small, rectangular framed paintings of hunt scenes, but when I turned round, Iris was gone.

I ventured on.

This was so unlike the Ball I was expecting from our experience at Cape Reinga and the tales in Joan's diaries.

Maybe I had built things up too much in my imagination.

The narrow corridor opened up and a vast banqueting hall came into focus ahead of me. A mass of people were dancing slowly to a Viennese waltz, all clad – men as well as women – in the desultory old-fashioned nightshirts that had been dispensed to us. I peered at the crowd, but recognised none of my acquaintances. There was no jewellery or make-up anywhere to be seen. It felt as if I were intruding into an austerity version of the Ball, a budget-sized one where simplicity took on the mantle of poverty. Edward had told us that the interior of the palace had been totally transformed from its usual décor for the purpose of the event, so I could not be sure whether the now stark white walls of the hall hid a far more elaborate backdrop that would be reinstated when the Ball departed. I recognised the music – it was something well-known and classical whose name escaped me, even though it had once been used as a background to the finale of a play at the Princess

Empire. A tall man whose nightshirt only reached down to his knees and displayed particularly skinny, bony ankles nodded at me, inviting me to join the dance on his arm, but I shook my head. I was in no mood for dancing, not that I had ever been much of a dancer. Even less so in this formal style with male partners.

I stepped back into the corridor and retraced my path, hoping to find the changing area where we had all parted.

But this time, everything seemed different and I was soon dizzy with anxiety and disappointment. And stranded.

I discovered a half-opened door, with further echoes of music coming from its direction.

I gave it a nudge with my unshod foot and the door swung wide open to reveal a deep low-ceilinged room, its walls festooned with hundreds of sets of antlers. I shuddered at the mere thought of the herds of animals slaughtered to achieve this dubiously decorated jungle. The trophies hung among dark-coloured drapes in shades of fuchsia and purple, the effect suffocating.

I couldn't see where the music was coming from. It was ethereal, blending the sheer delicacy of an army of violins in flight and the sounds of distant wind, washing over me like an eerie wave of sound.

I was still getting my bearings when I heard a voice behind me, someone standing on the threshold of the hunting trophy room, who must have approached silently and surprised me as I stood there still absorbing the rather sinister spectacle.

'Welcome to our Ball,' she said.

With a knot forming in the pit of my stomach, I slowly turned round to face the visitor.

She was the most beautiful woman I had ever seen.

She was of medium height, her hair a sombre honey shade of auburn, her eyes a vibrant dark green that caught the reflections of the simmering fires of the candelabras I had just noticed casting a hint of light throughout the oppressive, windowless room. Her posture was straight and regal, although nothing like the imperious style of Clarissa; humble but supremely self-assured as she looked down at me, her lips forming the delicate arch of a half smile.

I couldn't help staring at her, no doubt wide-eyed.

She was naked.

From her silky hair down to her bare feet.

But that wasn't what made her so spectacular and forced me to hold my breath as I gazed at her on and on.

By now in my accumulation of adventures I had come across a score of naked women.

But none like her.

As if the mathematical equation of the balance of her features, sharp cheekbones conjugating with the downwards curve of her impish nose, and the plump thickness of her lips were not all in perfect unison and striking enough, there was something else that made her wonderfully, hypnotically unique.

Where her long neck ended, a distinctive junction, borderline, began an unmistakable pattern of interlocked tattoos that covered her whole body. Strong shoulders, delicate chest, long arms, thighs, similarly long legs. The illustrated map covered her body from neck to ankles.

I held my breath.

My gaze was captured by a plethora of details: flowers knitted in embrace, dragon heads with delving tongues – one extending all the way down from navel to cunt, another circling one breast and seemingly biting its hard pink nipple, exotic fauna and flora racing across her parchment skin, words in a variety of languages and scripts.

She was an illustrated woman come to life.

She broke the silence.

'Hello, Moana.'

'You know my name?'

'I know everyone who attends the Ball.'

'Who are you?' I asked her.

'I am the Mistress,' she replied. 'They call me the Mistress of the Ball.'

I stood riveted to the spot. I suddenly remembered her from Cape Reinga, at the climax of the Ball, in her costume of wings as she had impaled herself against the muscular, erect stranger who'd ceremoniously walked out of the crowd. Had she been covered with tattoos back then? I had been standing too far away to see clearly, or my memories were confused. But her pale face was unmistakable. She hadn't aged a day

Her scent, a complex but exhilarating, invisible broth of musk, sharp green notes and subtle threads of danger, reached out in my direction.

She beckoned to me.

'Come.'

She took hold of my hand and this fleeting contact with her was electric, shocking me to the depths of my perception, teasing every nerve-ending in my body and forcibly drawing me towards a new, febrile state of skin-surfing emotions.

Already I knew I would willingly be a slave to her will, her commands and desires as she led me along whatever path she chose to. I no longer had any awareness of my environment, of the oppressive weight of the castle's maze of corridors and elaborate architecture.

We climbed a warren of circular staircases until we reached what I guessed must be the final dimension of living space at the top of one of fairy-tale turrets which from a distance made the Mad King's castle so distinctive. Walls of ochre bricks, sturdy wooden beams criss-crossing the angular ceiling, a small window, a forest lawn of rich, thick, colourful Persian rugs, no other furniture, a brief glimpse of a profound night outside.

The night? Had we not reached the castle barely an hour or so ago, the sun only beginning to set?

I had lost all perception of time. As if I had arrived (or been lured?) into a new dimension.

The Mistress pulled my cotton shift above my head and laid me bare.

I shivered.

Her kiss warmed me.

She tasted of cinnamon, and roses and flavours that had been hitherto beyond my ken. Her lips were silken pillows of delight. I abandoned myself to the sensation.

Her eyes, wide open, just an inch away from mine, deeper than the Sargasso sea, reaching for my soul and the birthing centre of my lust, our cheeks touching, her breath an evanescent gossamer breeze, the warmth rising from her naked body shrouding me in a cloud of intoxication, triggering rapid, frantic movement between all my synapses and every square inch of my skin burning bright, coming alive.

Her tongue caressing the barrier of my teeth, parting them, fucking my mouth, hungry, generous, invasive.

I felt as if I was floating in mid-air.

The Mistress's hands, firm, tender, demanding, gripped my arsecheeks, testing my flesh's resilience, then roved across my body, wandering over me like a divining rod, exploring, unearthing every knot of desire buried beneath the surface of my skin.

I grew dizzy as the heavenly kiss persisted, my mind now suspended in the upper reaches of the atmosphere, starved of oxygen, no longer anchored to the castle, the planet.

I almost fell. Disengaged our hot lips.

The Mistress held on to me.

Then lowered me tenderly to the ground.

I was a puppet, aimless, directionless, broken, totally in her thrall.

Right then I would have done anything she could have asked me, however fatal the consequences.

Her lips moved lower.

Lighting my nipples like a match until their hardness grew so painful I wanted to scream. The silk cloth of her mouth roaming across my breasts, licking, swimming my tide, biting in small increments of torture, like a conductor orchestrating the inexorable rise and rise of my pleasure. A warm breath brushing my earlobe.

She began to speak. Her voice deep, full, as if she was addressing a vast audience, as if I was not even there. 'Pleasure is everything. Sex, life, the Ball. It's what makes life worth living, even when it is just a fleeting thing, a brief moment, it's what we aim for . . . Nothing else matters.'

Her gospel.

The true meaning of the Ball.

Why it existed and had done so from ancient times to the present. And I had now been allowed into the holy of holies, for real, and unlike Cape Reinga, when I had been cast in just a menial, minor role, I was now being finally welcomed into its wonderful harbour.

Yes, nothing else counted.

Teasing my pussy, studiously grazing my cunt lips, the sharp edge of her teeth lingering invitingly above and around my nub, her fingers penetrating me, digging, drilling, exploring my inner walls, burying themselves in my primordial heat, riding the waves of my lust unleashed.

Briefly my eyes opened halfway on the landscape of her square shoulders and her back, and it appeared as if the whole world of images decorating her was actually in movement, miraculously brought to life, morphing into continuous new shapes and colours, symbols and words as her hair shifted softly from side to side, parting like a sea to expose the delicacy of her neck and the line that separated the milky whiteness of her skin from the canvas of her illustrations.

She turned me over.

Kissed me all over.

Entered me again.

Fucked me in so many beautiful ways.

Loved me.

The world surrounding me disappeared and, untethered,

Spring

I flew on the wings of desire like a bird freed from the burden of gravity, my only connection to the days I had known and lived held through the velvet lilt of her breath as she ruined me forever, her touch a magic instrument bent on changing me from chrysalis to butterfly, coaxing the phoenix from the embers of my past and breathing on the glorious flames.

I came.

And came again. Uninterrupted cascades of pleasure falling over each other like a parade of avalanches.

Unbridled.

I was wet.

I was curled up inside the shelter of her arms, a child again. A whole new woman too.

A hostage to her warmth.

I descended the platform steps of my receding orgasm.

Opened my eyes.

The expression on her face was both tender and melancholy.

'Okay?' she asked me.

I nodded.

I felt both bone tired and exhilarated. A nonsensical combination of emotions.

She rose, her expansive wilderness of tattoos, tendrils and impossible images in full flight, colours bright in the morning light now invading the room where we had sated our lust.

The Mistress held out her hand.

'Time to join the rest of the Ball, Moana,' she said and pulled me up.

The cotton nightshirt I had been wearing lay crumpled on the rug on which we had fucked. I shook it out and lifted it over my head, although doing so seemed futile.

I followed the Mistress back to the Ball.

We travelled across rooms and down staircases and down more staircases, journeying through a horizontal maze, until we reached the base of the castle. I was thankful that the simplistic outfits provided had not included a pair of towering high heels, though I would have been even more thankful for an elevator.

I realised I was still unaware of the Mistress's name and felt I had to ask her, but it was too late. When we reached the area where most of the party guests seemed to have congregated, she darted away. I caught a final glimpse of images flittering across her back like a projector screen and a swish of auburn hair and she was gone, disappeared into the throng.

She had led me down to the dungeon. If the BDSM party that I had attended with Gwillam, where I first came across Iris submitting to Thomas's whip, had been the antithesis of everything that I had expected from such an event, what I saw in front of me was like a scene from an S&M picture postcard come to life.

Spring

The walls appeared to be made of stone. Sconces jutted out at regular right angles, devoid of any decorative features. Plain white candles affixed to them gave off a dull, flickering light and dripped fingers of wax, like creeping mould, below. It was the sort of lighting you might expect to see in a medieval prison.

I crept inside, casting my gaze around the room in search of Iris, who should have been easy to spot in her white frock, since all the guests in this room were dressed in dark grey. The men wore three-piece suits and blood-red cravats; trousers and matching waistcoats with crisp shirts beneath in a paler shade of grey. Their black leather shoes were pointed and shined mirror-sharp. The women were attired in charcoal-coloured cotton dresses that nipped in at the waist and reached all the way to the floor. Beneath their wide skirts, voluminous petticoats rustled, in the same shade as the men's pale shirts. Their hair was pulled into high knots on the tops of their heads and tied with white ribbons. Grey ballet slippers covered their feet. It was like a congregation gathered at a funeral parlour from another decade.

They broke apart for me, creating a clear path and revealing a raised stone platform at the front of the room. On it was a large X-shaped contraption, and affixed to that, back facing the audience, was a naked woman. Iris. Her wrists and ankles were strapped onto each of the four corners of the cross with leather buckles. Her hair was scooped over her right shoulder, revealing her slim, bare neck, its curved lines to me the most sensual part of her, perhaps because of the vulnerability apparent there. I moved in a daze through the crowd towards her, my eyes all the time fixed on the spot where her nape met her spine.

Thomas was dressed in the same formal attire as the men who stood around us. He was seated on a high-backed, armless wooden chair, positioned to Iris's left, legs crossed. I approached, and as I grew nearer, he met my eyes. A sense of stillness loomed over the whole scene, and I had the impression that everyone was waiting for something to happen. Iris had not so much as twitched. She was so motionless that I wanted to move around to the front of the cross to check that she was still breathing.

To the right of the cross stood a polished metal trolley on wheels, like the sort that adorned dental clinics the world over. Arranged upon it lay a variety of implements for inflicting sensations. Some I recognised: a paddle designed for beating flesh rather than sending ping pong balls flying over a net, a dark-handled flogger with long strands of heavy animal hide, a deep purple dildo and matching leather harness, a slim, tapered glass butt plug. Some I hadn't seen before; a slim silver tool with a round, coin-sized, pronged dial at the end of it, a series of vicious looking whips, one with threads of barbed wire and another made from just a single tail, thick at one end and growing steadily thinner to

346

the other, where it finished with a knot of multi-coloured strands that appeared soft, but I guessed were anything but.

'What are you waiting for?' I whispered to Thomas, feeling very self-conscious in the silent room. My words came out in a breathy hiss.

'You,' he replied.

'Me?'

'Yes.' He shrugged his shoulders and uncrossed his legs, re-crossing them again in the other direction. 'I offered, of course.' He grinned, and glanced at the selection of implements on the metal tray and then at Iris. 'But she wanted you.'

'Oh,' I said. I felt a mild thrill of pride and power. I was flattered, but still unsure of demonstrating my unskilled techniques in front of so many people who I imagined were probably experts in the sexual arts. 'How did you know I would be back?' I asked. 'I've been gone hours. You've been waiting all that time?'

He looked confused. 'The tattooed woman ... the Mistress ...' He stalled, kept searching for words. Shook his head a little as if doing so would shake what he meant to say to the surface of his brain. 'Sorry,' he stuttered, 'I'm sure she told us her name, but I've forgotten it, and she was just here ... Anyway. She told us that you would come. We've only been here a few minutes.'

There was no sign of a clock on the walls, and no windows to indicate the time of day by the light outside. Perhaps time had another meaning here, expanding and constricting according to individual experience of pleasure rather than counting down by the minute and hour.

'I don't know what to do with any of those things,' I told him, 'besides maybe the flogger. And even that, I'm not very good at.'

'You know what to do,' he responded. 'Just go with your gut. Don't think about it. Feel the thread that ties you together.' He pointed to his heart and then slowly drew his finger away into the air in the direction that I was standing, as if indicating the presence of an invisible length of spider's web that joined us.

Iris remained immobile. I mentally blocked out the presence of the grey-clad army of onlookers, pretending that no one else was present but she and I. I imagined that we were back at the Ball by the sea in Cape Reinga again, but older and wiser, and the murmur of the crowd's breaths and other inevitable sounds – bodies jostling, shoes tapping against the floor, skirts rustling – became wind against the shore, or the beating wings of sea birds.

I turned my back on Thomas and moved around to the front of the cross. Iris's eyes were closed and the ghost of a smile lingered on her lips, as if she had fallen asleep in the middle of a very pleasant dream. I stretched up onto the tips of my toes to reach her mouth and kissed her gently. She opened her eyes.

'You came,' she said.

'I came. For you.'

'Beat me.'

I nodded my assent.

She closed her eyes again.

I walked over to the trolley and examined its contents. Picked up the flogger by its wooden handle. It was slim in the middle and wider at either end, shaped like a women's body. The hide strands were slim and cool to the touch. I placed it back down again and moved through the other items, running the tips of my fingers over each one and considering Thomas's words and the response of my body to each one, the instinctive knowing that told me whether each instrument was right or wrong on this particular occasion. The silver spiked wheel; too cold, too sharp. The single tail, too fierce. The paddle, too hard, and conjuring something of the ridiculous in my mind; images of young women, skirts pulled up to their waist and laying over men's knees, more comical than arousing. That, and it would surely cause far more pain than I desired to inflict.

None of them was right.

I turned back to Iris's body on the cross. Just watching her strapped there, unmoving, made me melancholy. I was aroused by the thought of touching her, but not by the thought of hurting her. Not in the same way that I knew Thomas was, and Matilda had once been with her subs. And yet I wanted to please her also. I wished there was a juke box and I could play music. Something to fall into, to distract myself from the pain and confusion of my own thoughts.

Instead I stood behind Iris and conjured the image that Thomas had suggested. An invisible cord, joining her to me. I pictured it travelling from my palm through her back to her heart, and with that in mind, I raised my hand and swung. I imagined that the cord binding us together was elasticated, so that when I moved my hand up into the air and then brought it down again onto her buttocks, it stretched taut and then pulled me back again. She jumped in response to the impact and cried, 'Oh!' Her whole body tensed, and then relaxed again.

I hit her again, and again, each time easing the sting of my slaps by holding my palm firmly against the point of impact after each strike. Her skin had turned red, layers of handprints overlapping each other in radiating shades of pinkness. Her thighs had begun to twitch. Her spine began to move; a caterpillar-like grinding motion travelling outwards from her hips, driving her groin against the padded cross. She was moaning.

I paused momentarily, cupping her buttocks, and turned my head towards Thomas. He had pulled his chair closer but appeared to be glued to it, his torso and legs stretched forward as though he was ready to jump to his feet and run to us. His eyes were glazed, his lips parted. I raised one hand into the air and he followed its trajectory as though hypnotised.

Iris arched her spine, pushing her arse into the air as much as she could in her bound position. She was wriggling, but not in a way that suggested she wanted to escape her bonds but rather, as if she wanted me to hit her harder, taunt her more. Her parted legs were wet. My fingers found the valley of her buttocks, travelled down to her entrance. She was dripping. As wet as I had known her to ever become, even wetter than she was when I licked her and my saliva mingled with her juices to create a torrent, the essence of our fucks. I wanted to stop the spanking, fall to my knees and catch the fluid that leaked from her, fuck her with my tongue. But I knew that was not what she wanted.

I willed the voice of the Ball's Mistress to speak in my head. I wanted to know why she had brought me here, forced me to explore this part of myself. Why, for all the things that Iris and I had shared, we did not have this one crucial element of our desires in common.

There was no answer.

I thought of Iris, and all that we had shared. Memories of our childhood and coming of age spent together. Discovering the power and pleasure of our bodies and each other. The landscape at that place that felt like the end of the world, the edge of everything, where I had first buried my mouth between her legs. The crashing waves, the Ball's guests, painted like animals, seals and sea birds, freewheeling on currents of air, amid the crashing waves, against each other. I wondered where we would be now if we had never left.

The rhythm of my palm rising and falling against her flesh began to follow the pattern of the waves that moved in my mind, steadily growing in strength and height until the sea was in a frenzy and Iris's moans had become louder than the imaginary cries of the gulls soaring above the rocks. I was no longer controlling my hand as it pulled back and fell down against her, one almighty slap after another. The invisible thread that still joined us together seemed to be pulling me towards her, as though it were Iris who was orchestrating her own beating rather than me dishing it out. Or perhaps, in some mysterious corner of our souls, the Mistress of the Ball lurked, urging us to reach new heights of pleasure and exploration.

The ocean's roar gradually quieted, reducing to just the steady laps of gentle waves on the shore.

Iris's limbs shuddered and twitched. Her hands tucked into fists and then relaxed. Her breathing was shallow. She licked her lips. She turned her face to one side, eyes closed. She was still smiling, the same goofy, benevolent, deeply satisfied smile, like that of a contented cat.

'Oh, Iris,' I said.

I pulled my smock over my head and dropped it to the

floor, bent down and unbuckled her ankle straps, then reached up and loosened the bonds on her wrists. She still clung to the cross, her arms and legs tensed, each muscle taut as a whip in flight. I pressed my body against hers, our glistening dampnesses merging. The front of my legs tight against the back of hers, my breasts squashed flat to her shoulder blades, my fingers threaded through her fingers, my face buried against her neck, her dark hair mingling with mine.

Thomas had moved from his chair and was standing in front of Iris. He wrapped his hands around the cross's beams and pulled himself up to join us, kissing first Iris on the mouth, and then me. His lips brought me abruptly back to the present; he tasted of coffee and sugar. Physical sensations returned to my body. I was thirsty, my arm was tired, the flat of my palm was sore and red. Sounds began to filter into my perception. Iris was laughing and between giggles, kissing Thomas passionately. I remembered the crowd behind us and turned. They still stood passively, a silent Greek choir, bar the rasp of their breaths and the creak of stiff limbs moving.

I stepped down from the cross and Iris stepped down after me. She caught my shoulder as I turned away and placed her fingers under my chin so that our eyes met.

'Thank you,' she said, and planted a brief kiss on my lips.

'That's okay,' I said weakly. It felt like one of those

occasions where words could never be enough to express the truth of everything that I felt. My emotions were too messy, too confused.

I pulled her into an embrace and we held each other. I wished that the embrace symbolised a joining together. A strengthening of our union. But instead, it seemed to me like the beginnings of a letting go. The rope that bound us together was loosening, and I feared that it might soon fall away altogether. We would always be close. But Iris was no longer my Iris. We had grown away from each other.

'I need to sit down,' she murmured. Her face had turned even paler than usual and her legs buckled beneath her.

Thomas scooped her up into his arms as if she were a child and carried her over to the chair. He sat down and cradled her on his lap. They sat with their cheeks touching as if they were propping each other up.

The crowd gathered in the room began to disperse to other corners of the party.

'I'm going to find something to drink,' I told Thomas. 'You two will be okay here?'

He nodded. Iris looked up at me and smiled. Her eyes were glazed and unfocused.

'We're okay,' he said. 'I asked one of the Ball staff to bring us some water and something sugary.'

I wasn't hungry in the slightest.

'For Iris,' he added, 'she likes chocolate, afterwards.

Or cookies. Or hot cocoa, with honey. For the comedown ...'

'Oh ...' I still had so much to learn. I had not yet experienced that state of elation that came with the sudden drop following a BDSM induced emotional and physical high. Did I want to? I still wasn't sure. I would let the Mistress of the Ball beat me, if she wished to, but perhaps no one else.

The waiter arrived. A young man sporting a thin moustache and dressed in black and white like a formal English butler, bearing a silver tray on which three glasses rested, a pitcher of iced water flavoured with lemon and mint, and an assortment of pastel coloured macaroons and cream-filled miniature sponges, their tops cut into halves and decorated to imitate butterfly wings.

I remembered with a surge of self-consciousness that I, too, was quite naked, but neither the suited waiter nor the remaining assembled and clothed celebrants nor Thomas seemed overly shocked or titillated by the fact.

I fancied something alcoholic, so made my goodbyes and departed, this time choosing the door opposite the one that I had entered by. It linked to another long corridor and further unexplored rooms. Each one contained a different party. In one, ballet dancers pirouetted, nude besides their pale pink slippers. They were an assortment of shapes, sizes and ages, none of them matching the tall, slender physique that I associated with the ballet classes I had endeavoured to avoid during high school. There was no audience, nor any music. The dancers were apparently moving each to their own tune.

In another room, a man hung from the ceiling as a woman trussed him in a complex network of thick red rope. He had long blond hair that hung down past his shoulders and hoops through each of his nipples. She was dark haired and dressed in cream-coloured latex jodhpurs and a cream corset, so tightly cinched around her waist that her bosoms spilled over the top each time she bent down.

I saw Gwillam in the next room. The expression on his face was beatific, unsurprisingly, as he was lying on top of an enormous bed and surrounded by a bevy of men, all of them slim, clean-shaven and appearing to be aged from eighteen to thirty. They were not having sex, but caressing each other in a daisy-chain of multi-handed massages.

I continued down the corridor, moving past a veritable chorus of pleasure, isolated moans, cries, the crack of a whip, lips touching, limbs on limbs, fucking, dancing, each Ball guest exploring their own personal road to Nirvana. In an alcove adjacent to one of the larger rooms I passed Clarissa and Edward with a woman between them, and Patch standing to one side and overlooking the threesome. The woman between them was red-haired with a round body, her hills of flesh in sharp contrast to Clarissa's bony frame. Her ginger locks draped over Edward's thighs as she went down on him, her head jolted back and forth by the impact of Clarissa's thrusts as she rode her with a strap-on.

Edward called to me as I walked by, encouraging me to join them, but I pretexted a prior engagement and continued on, content to merely observe and soak in all of the games around me.

Finally I discovered several trolleys piled high with wine resting in buckets of ice, fruit juice, sandwiches, patisseries and cut fruit. They were unattended, and everything looked too perfect to consume but I tucked in nonetheless.

'Are you enjoying your evening?' said a voice behind me.

I recognised her sultry lilt immediately. The Mistress.

I turned quickly, hurriedly gulping down a piece of cherry-glazed chocolate mud cake that I had taken a small slice of.

'Sorry,' I said to her, my mouth still full.

'Don't apologise. Take as much as you want to. There are no rules here, besides those that each individual creates for themselves. Do what you want to, nothing more, nothing less.'

'Thank you,' I said, 'and yes, I am having a wonderful time. Everything is ... beautiful.' I struggled to find a word that would convey all that I intended, because no such word existed.

'How do you feel?' she asked me.

'I feel ... home.' I said. 'I feel like I've come home.'

'Good,' she replied, and continued on up the corridor. Was it my imagination, or had one of the creatures etched onto her back unfurled a wing and winked at me?

I blinked, poured a large serving of sweet white wine into a glass and sipped it.

Again I thought of Cape Reinga, and how different that experience of the Ball had been. Joan's diaries, her confessions and the apparent differences and similarities of each event. I had a sudden longing to know and understand more about it. How such a thing had been created, how it was organised, and why? I hurried back to find Gwillam. Of all those in attendance, he would be the most likely, I felt, to help me answer all of my questions. And he might know when and where we would see the ceremony that I realised concluded every Ball, the Mistress rising at dawn.

I did not come across him immediately but waltzed between a whole series of galleries of love, of bliss amplified and released and unforgettable images and movements, dances and fucks, games of celebration and ecstasy and pain, until my mind became saturated by the extreme nature of what I was witnessing throughout the endless rooms of Mad King Ludwig's castle and I somehow disconnected, wandering like a phantom along corridors, cellars and impossibly dimensioned rooms and caves and wells full of sorcerers, imps, penitents, lovers, torturers and angels.

Then morning came. And the Mistress appeared in all her

358

splendour as the Ball finally climaxed and we were released from our earthly shells. Became pure and innocent, bathed in the water of our juices and the most beautiful feeling of joy.

All of us were mostly silent throughout the journey home. Quiet and ever so tired.

'I'm spent,' Thomas said, before falling asleep in Iris's lap on the boat.

We all were. Elated, exhausted.

'I feel a bit high,' Clarissa told me.

Even the usual hustle, bustle, and inevitable delays and queues involved in exiting Victoria coach station did not snap us out of our pleasure-induced torpor.

The low came later, after we had returned to normal life.

Matilda dropped into the restaurant one night while I was working. She had made a dramatic return to the image of the woman that I had first met, all eyes opening a touch wider and turning to watch her stride through the tables towards me, clad in skin-tight jeans and a low-cut, fire-engine-red cashmere jumper, her long black hair pulled into a high pony tail that swished as she walked. She wore flat shoes and had lost some of her signature haughtiness. When she smiled, her teeth parted and her eyes crinkled up in a wide picture of happiness.

'You look great,' I told her.

'I'm in love,' she said. 'It'll do that to you.'

I raised an eyebrow. 'Oh,' I said. I glanced at the big, round, black-and-white clock that decorated the wall behind the counter. 'I still have a few hours here, but if you can wait, I'd love to have a drink and hear all about it.'

'Just dropping in,' she said. 'Peter's taking me out.' She grinned again, and inclined her head towards the window. I looked out and saw a man standing under a street light, waiting. He was tall and broad-shouldered with dark hair and even in the half-light and beneath the outer shell of his suit, I could see that his body was fit and muscled.

'Nice,' I told her.

'How are your two love birds?'

'Same as ever.'

Iris and Thomas always welcomed me to join them, both in their sexual and social activities. I was deeply fond of them both and liked to watch them together. The way the rise and fall of Iris's desire played out on her face, and how expertly Thomas orchestrated her lust. I admired, and envied, the level of trust that the intensity of their encounters had created, and the bond that they shared. But though they did not once block me out – quite the reverse – I still felt that I could never fully join them, or at least, not as anything more than an occasional passenger, like someone watching a film play out in front of them but never totally engaged in the action.

Spring

Things were similar with Clarissa and Edward, though of course we didn't share the same affection. I had spent the night of our return with them and Patch, all four of us cuddled together on the expansive futon in the top of their studio. In the morning, Clarissa and Patch had shared a double-ended dildo on one side of the bed, as Edward and I sipped our coffees nearby and watched them indulgently. But I had no wish to join their twosome and occasional triads as a third or fourth member on a permanent basis.

Even Gwillam had paired off at the Ball, having become enamoured with a young German artist, Stefan, who despite barely speaking a word of English, had returned to London with us and was now camped out in Gwillam's flat with no plans to return home any time soon.

'But he's only nineteen,' I said to Gwillam.

'Exactly,' Gwillam had replied.

I was happy that he was happy, although I knew it meant that I was unlikely to see him much socially, at least until the initial throes of their new-relationship passion wore off and they managed to get up out of bed.

Matilda invited me to stay with her and Peter in the Chilterns mansion for a few days. Her parents were away again, and had asked Peter to re-landscape and modernise part of the grounds so she was taking every advantage of the opportunity to take him in new and unusual positions, including against all of the trees in their backyard.

'Pegging,' she told me, 'he loves it.' I had never heard the word before and asked her to explain it. She gladly obliged.

'Does he like men?' I asked her.

'I don't think so,' she told me.

I added this knowledge to my growing pool of wisdom on the apparently boundless variety of ways to experience pleasure.

Weeks passed and began to blur. I was made supervisor at the restaurant and my hours and pool of savings increased. Iris and Thomas moved into a larger flat, one with a basement which they converted into a permanent dungeon. Stefan remained in London and improved his English much more quickly than Gwillam learned to speak any German. The walls of the apartment they now shared were soon dotted with charcoal sketches depicting Gwillam, nude and reclining legs akimbo over the furniture. I could not bring myself to look at them.

At night, when I was not sharing a bed with another twosome or threesome, I replayed all of my memories of the Ball and of the Mistress. When I wetted my finger and brought myself to climax, it was her tongue that I imagined delving inside me, her scent that I did my damnedest to conjure up. Thoughts of the Ball brought me inevitably back to thoughts of home, and I found that I missed the solitude of New Zealand landscapes almost more than I could bear. The comparative quiet of the cities and dead silence of small country towns. The blankets of stars that spread overhead on clear nights, never visible in London. The sea salt tang of an ocean breeze. The rolling hills, the mountains and the lakes.

For once in my life, I was homesick, and deeply so. My melancholy longing for the place that I had so willingly left without so much as a glance behind me, now clawed at my heart like a shadow from which I could not escape.

I was at work on a Sunday afternoon, half lost in a day-dream as I finished setting up that week's rota in the office out back, when I heard a soft rap on the door.

'Yes,' I called out, without looking up, presuming that it would be one of the waitresses come to ask to swap a shift.

'Moana.'

Her voice.

I would know it anywhere. That soft, sultry, accentless lilt, the way that she rolled the vowels in my name as if she were tasting each letter.

'Mistress,' I said.

'Please,' she replied, 'call me Kristiana. My birth name.'

'Come in,' I stammered, indicating a chair in front of my desk. 'Would you like a drink? Coffee? Something to eat?'

'Maybe another time,' she said. 'I don't have long today I'm afraid.'

'How can I help you?'

She walked in and sat down.

She was dressed in navy-blue ballet flats, loose jeans and a lemon-yellow jumper. A silver chain dangled from her neck, the pendant too small to see clearly, but it appeared to be a small coin, like a St Christopher medallion. She didn't seem to me like the kind of person who needed any luck. Her hair was loose, her auburn locks flowing in glossy waves around her shoulders. She wore lip gloss, but besides that, her face was free of make-up. She looked to be around twenty-five, possibly a little younger. None of her tattoos was visible.

'I have a proposition for you,' she said.

'Yes?'

Immediately I thought of Joan, and the red-haired woman by Piccadilly Circus who had invited her to join the Ball. My heart began to beat a fandango in my chest.

'Join us. We have a position open, with the Ball—'

'Yes,' I said, interrupting her before she had finished. 'Anything. I'll do anything. And follow you anywhere.'

She laughed.

'It's not in London,' she said. 'How would you feel about returning to New Zealand?'

'I would love to. I've thought of nothing else, these past few weeks. Well, not much else,' I added, and then blushed, for besides New Zealand, I had been thinking of her.

'Wonderful,' she said.

'There's to be another Ball in New Zealand?'

'Yes, but not for a few years yet. However, we have something magnificent in mind, and these things take a long time to plan. We're hoping to have a representative there – you, if you will agree – to assist us with the research and preparations. We'd like to invest in a small club, or maybe even a theatre. It's something you know about, don't you? You could run it. It would be a perfect excuse for hunting down performers, singers, dancers, you know … And fun, of course.'

'Yes,' I said firmly. 'I'll do it.' I had no hesitation.

'Good,' she replied. 'I had hoped you would agree. We have much more to go through, naturally, but not now. I'll let you think things over, and one of our staff will be in touch to arrange further meetings. Inevitably, there will be much paperwork … all the formalities. There's no rush, you know, if you want to spend a few more months here in London. We see this as a long-term venture.'

We both stood up as she prepared to leave, and shook hands. Just that single, brief touch nearly sent me into spasms of delight. I wanted more but knew all too well that I would only see her again on the occasions of our magic Ball and not in between. After she left, I went to the bar and poured myself an ice-cold glass of water to bring back my concentration.

Once I had made the decision, I was keen to move things along and leave London for good, though not in any particular rush to reach my destination.

Telling Iris was the hardest part.

'I'll miss you,' she said, in a small voice. We held each other for a whole night.

Gwillam was beside himself with excitement on my behalf, and offered to travel over and help me with the legalities as needed.

'I bet you'll need to find the right premises and negotiate planning permissions and all that,' he said, his eyes aglow with the prospect of a new challenge.

Clarissa gave me the grey felt trilby that she had stolen from the Princess Empire's costume store. 'A little piece of London to take home with you,' she said. Edwards stood beside her, as kind and enigmatic as ever.

All promised to visit me one day when the time was right. Some knew that I would be working for the Ball, but not all of them. I had preferred to keep Iris and Thomas in the dark.

They all came to see me off, our group's over-affectionate departing embraces causing quite a stir in the departure lounge at Southampton. I had decided to travel back the slow way, by boat. The journey would take around six weeks, with a stop in Egypt before we crossed the Suez Canal to continue through the Indian Ocean with further stops in Ceylon and Australia. I hoped that it would be an adventure, and also I looked forward to spending so long so close to the sea.

I was not even able to watch them disappear as I departed,

since the ship was so large and the passenger gate some distance from the visitors' lounge. I did not fix my eyes on the landmass of England shrinking behind us as we drew away, but instead kept my eyes fixed on the horizon, and the great blue expanse ahead.

There was a strong breeze, a chill wind, and a gentle sprinkling of rain. Initially I was the only passenger to brave the hard white seats that adorned the viewing platform on the outer deck at the prow of the ship. I sat alone, thinking of nothing in particular, and staring at the ocean.

My mind wandered back, missing London already but also coming to the realisation that I was now making the same journey that my own parents, or at any rate my mother, had completed but also Joan when she had travelled to New Zealand, in the early weeks of her pregnancy with Iris.

Were we all part of a book of coincidences penned by the spirit of the Ball?

'May I join you?'

A soft voice, belonging to a woman.

'Of course,' I said, before I had even looked around, instinctively polite.

She was Maori, with brown skin and sleek black hair that whipped around her face in the blowing wind. She stepped in front of me and took hold of the rail, her green cotton dress dancing around her calves with each gust. A blue jacket was clutched in her right hand. Her shift was loosely cut and low at the back, partially revealing a tattoo that covered her neck, shoulders, and beyond, the bottom half concealed from my gaze. It was the shape of a bird, and made up of intricate hatching lines and spiral patterns. I watched carefully to check if it moved, as the Mistress's tattoos had, but it remained perfectly still.

My instinct told me she would have wonderful stories to tell, about her inking and her own life.

She shrugged into the jacket.

'Brr ...' she said. 'It's freezing, I know, but I love the wind on the sea.'

'Me too,' I told her.

She extended her hand to me.

'Aroha,' she introduced herself.

'Moana,' I replied.

'I bet you had as much trouble as I did with your name in England.'

'Yes,' I laughed, 'drove me crazy, but you get used to it, I suppose.'

Her lips were full and her smile was wide.

We sat on the deck and talked until the rain began to beat down more heavily than we could bear. She half shrouded me in her jacket as we ran for the safety of the ship's cabin.

The stairs down to the lower decks were slippery, and I took her hand.

Soon, we would be home.

Acknowledgements

Huge thanks go to the team at Simon & Schuster and The Hot Bed – Clare Hey, Emma Capron, Ally Grant, Rumana Haider and Hayley McMullen, who have been a pleasure to work with.

We would also like to thank our publisher in Germany and the USA, respectively Christian Rohr at carl's books, and Jane Friedman and Tina Pohlman at Open Road Integrated Media, along with Stephane Marsan, Alain Nevant, Isabelle Varange and Leslie Palant at Bragelonne/Milady, and the team at Amber in Warsaw for their ongoing support of the worlds of Eighty Days and The Pleasure Quartet, and their trust in us. We wouldn't be where we are now without the network of international publishers who have joyfully welcomed us into their teams.

A sincere and fervent thank you to Sarah Such, our

Acknowledgements

wonderful literary agent who has been behind us from the beginning and works tirelessly on our behalf. Thank you for your faith in us as we try out new material, and manage somehow to keep on top of deadlines, and your unceasing efforts to promote us far and wide, with an eagle eye for all things contractual.

Thanks also go to our foreign rights supporters, Rosie and Jessica Buckman and to Carrie Kania. As well as to Wendy Toole, our ever sharp copy-editor who is deft in correcting all of our infelicities.

Thank you to all our fans and readers who have stuck with us for what was intended to be a trilogy and has now expanded to a whole universe and book number nine. Your comments and encouragement are always appreciated and we could not do this without you.

One half of Vina, who has been in debt to her employer from the beginning would this time like to issue a particularly fervent thank you to her boss and colleagues – RM, you are amazing, and ZA, thank you so much, I really don't know how I could have done this without you. Thank you, a million times over, for covering for me as I battled to the end of this one to get the last chapter over on time. AB, DG, and my extended family of colleagues, thank you for fielding my phone calls, sorting my masses of parcels and always keeping me cheerful.

Thank you to my friends who keep me sane and

persevere although I am such a hermit behind my keyboard – B, A and K, I'd be lost without you. Thanks to Tony and Julian who keep me in one piece despite the endless typing. Kit Laughlin's work has also been vital in keeping RSI at bay.

Finally, thank you to Terence, who puts up with my 'last weeks to deadline' madness, keeps me company at the screen and never leaves me short of inspiration. You're the best.

And the other half of Vina profusely thanks DJ, a partner in love and life through thick and thin of many years for impossible support in the face of similar deadline absence, our growing family big and small for their patience and so many other reasons. You all know who you are!

About the Author

Vina Jackson is the pseudonym for two established writers working together. One is a successful author; the other a published writer who is also a financial professional in London.

THE PLEASURE QUARTET

FROM OPEN ROAD MEDIA

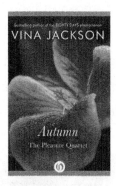
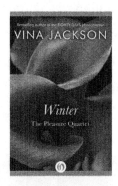

Available wherever ebooks are sold

OPEN ROAD
INTEGRATED MEDIA

Open Road Integrated Media is a digital publisher and multimedia content company. Open Road creates connections between authors and their audiences by marketing its ebooks through a new proprietary online platform, which uses premium video content and social media.

31192020921977

04 016865